I0627187

A CROWN OF SECRETS AND LIES

THE HALFLING PRINCESS CHRONICLES

BOOK ONE

K. D. EAGAN

Copyright © 2025 by K. D. Eagan

All rights reserved.

The characters and events portrayed in this book are fictitious. Any similarity to real persons, living or dead, is coincidental and not intended by the author.

No part of this book may be reproduced in any form or by any electronic or mechanical means, including information storage and retrieval systems, without written permission from the author, except for the use of brief quotations in a book review.

Cover design by Henar Lopez.

For my daughter,
You are the first story I ever wrote with my whole heart, and the one
who taught me that even in shadow, we can be luminous.

CHAPTER
ONE

They're coming for us.

The old king, my grandfather, lies dying. It's only a matter of time now. I squeeze my eyes shut. The pounding of my heart sounds like thousands of hoofbeats in my ears. It is as if they are already here. I force myself to look around at my beloved forest, at my best friend, Charaide, in hopes of becoming centered and remaining in the present.

Charaide moves before me, careful and stealthy, like the predators we're pretending to be. His long blond hair catches the sunlight glinting through the canopy overhead. It's difficult to keep our movements quiet with the early-autumn leaves crunching underfoot. Getting lost amongst the trees is usually comforting, but my mind is elsewhere today. It's back at the castle, in my grandfather's bedchamber with its suffocating tapestries of gold and red, symbols of his elemental firepower.

We find a bush wide enough to cover us, and we crouch behind it, listening for the familiar sound of animals moving through the brush. But it's quiet in the forest today. *Too quiet. Where are all the animals?* I sneak a glance at Charaide, and he meets my gaze with a shrug, the same question reflected in his blue eyes.

"Perhaps we should move deeper into the trees." He peers over the top of the bush as if checking for any sign of life.

I shake my head. "I have already risked too much by coming out with you. If my family were to learn of our unsanctioned excursion, I would never hear the end of it."

His lips twist, and I frown. I know that look. Growing up with someone grants us a deeper understanding of their various mannerisms, though I suspect it doesn't hurt that I also tend to study Charaide's face when he's not looking.

"Don't start," I warn.

He smirks, displaying a small dimple on his left cheek. "For someone who lacks the magic for telepathy, you sure seem to read my mind often enough."

My fingers immediately twist one of the bracelets on my right wrist. While the iron doesn't hurt, it does suppress my magical abilities, not that I would know how to use my magic even if I had access to it. The bracelets were placed on my wrists when I was born, spelled to grow with me.

"Maybe we should go back," Charaide whispers when I don't respond. "It's not safe for you to be exposed like this."

"Uncle Brutach has taken great pains to ensure my grandfather's illness remains a secret." I wave toward the path we just traversed. "He's even locked down the castle. There is no way the rebels already know."

"We got out," Charaide mutters.

I glare at him. "Because we've lived there all our lives and could find the secret passageways in our sleep." I turn my attention back to the forest beyond, straining to see any movement. "The rebels don't have our expertise."

Though I speak with confidence, a nagging sensation roils my stomach. Something doesn't feel right. The forest is too quiet, as if all manner of living things has collectively held its breath. As if it senses a danger I cannot see.

Dense fog snakes through the trees, adding to the ominous feel. The scent of burning wood catches me off guard, then I hear it. Not far from our hiding place, hushed voices carry on the wind.

Instinctively, I lift my head, straining to hear the words. Charaide grabs my arm and pulls me down, the fear in his eyes surprising me.

"Not long now," a harsh voice says.

"Pity. I did like the king. Well, at least until he tolerated his daughter's awful choice in a mate." The last words are stated with a sneer.

I cringe. They speak of my parents. My heartbeat quickens once more. These rebels know more than they should.

"We shall rectify that mistake soon enough," the first voice says. "No halfling scum will ever sit on the throne."

"Nor their human-loving harlot of a mother," the other agrees.

Charaide tightens his grip on my arm. I glance at him, and his lips are pressed into a thin line, his body rigid with anger. I want to tell him that I am fine, that their words mean nothing, but doing so risks our discovery. Who knows what these men would do with me if they found me out here, unprotected and my magic bound?

"Come on, you two," a new voice calls. "We need to return to camp. The castle is on high alert, and they may send out patrols."

The two men grumble their assent. I hold my breath for what feels like hours as I listen to their footsteps crunch through the leaves, slowly fading into the distance. When the forest is silent again, I take a full breath of air into my lungs, but it does nothing to calm my nerves.

"Astreilles," Charaide whispers, "we must hurry."

I nod and stand on shaky legs. We abort our hunting trip and race over the forest floor. When we reach the edge of the trees, Charaide whips around and stops me.

"Your cloak." He points at the hood of my green cloak, and I quickly pull it over my head, though avoiding discovery seems a moot point. I don't know how we will warn my family without admitting we were in the forest.

Once we're safely inside the castle, I leave Charaide in the garden and slowly make my way to my grandfather's bedchamber. My family has taken turns keeping vigil for several days, but when I enter the room, they're all there.

The gold-and-red tapestries around his bed have been drawn back. As a child, I used to love tracing the intricate designs, my fingers sliding over the smooth silk and velvet. Now they seem thick and suffocating. I close my eyes, wishing I was in my beloved forest, where the air is crisp and clean. I grit my teeth as I move closer to the bed, where my family has gathered. Their faces are pale as if my grandfather has sucked all the life from the room.

After the conversation I overheard, I fear all of our deaths may be imminent. I try to catch the eye of my brother, Laochard, but he stoically stares at my grandfather's frail form, his dark hair hanging on either side of his face.

I need to warn him about what I heard, though I have no idea what more he can do. He has already been preparing the royal army to fight against the rebels, but I doubt it will work. The rebels' words reverberate in my soul. When they come for us, they intend to kill us all.

An exhale comes from my grandfather and then silence. The silence in the room is broken only by my mother's quiet sobs. My shoulders hunch forward, not with grief but with fear of what comes next.

"God rest his soul," my father whispers, bowing his head and crossing himself in the way he always does.

He tells me it's a symbol of faith. His God is not one of ours. I wonder if his God can even hear him in this realm.

He stands, pushing his graying hair from his eyes, and goes to my mother before pulling her into his arms. We join them, all seven of us children, in the embrace. I can't help thinking it would have been better for all of us if we were never born. But instead, the rebels will slaughter us like livestock, all because my human father dared to fall in love with a princess of the fae.

"We must plan your coronation." My uncle leans against the doorframe, his blue-gray eyes sorrowful and his broad frame taking up the entire doorway. "I'm doing my part to keep our father's death a secret, but I fear word of his illness has already spread. Even now, my sources say the rebels are raising their armies and planning their attack. If we have any hope of containing this, we must move quickly. Those who are loyal to you will attend the ceremony. The show of support might be enough to delay their attack, if nothing else."

My mother gives a quick nod of assent as she wipes the tears from her eyes. She has no time for mourning her beloved father. It would be so much easier if she abdicated and passed the torch to Uncle Brutach. Then there would be no war, and we would have the time to grieve.

Uncle Brutach has said as much, but she refuses. Is it pride? I wonder. Maybe, but if I were a betting lass, I would place my coin on her blind optimism, her belief in the good of the people. The rebels, she says, are a small, vocal minority. Were they raising only their voices and not their swords, I might agree with her.

Sparing a glance at my grandfather, his white hair stark against the red pillow, I follow my mother and uncle. My father is shut out. A human cannot be involved in matters of state. He won't even receive the title of king. Instead, he will be deemed queen's consort, which has quickly become an expletive instead of a title among our enemies.

As third in line to the throne, I must attend these meetings. I hate them. The target on my head is already too heavy to bear. The crown is as much a shackle to me as the bracelets that bind my magic. This is not the life I hoped to lead. Had my mother's older brother lived or at the very least sired an heir, we would not find ourselves in this situation. Alas, wishing for a different future is childish fancy.

The council chambers are much more open than my grandfather's bedchamber, and I breathe deeply, sucking fresh air into my lungs. Windows overlook the gardens, and the pop of color from the autumn roses against the gray sky gives me the tiniest bit of hope.

"We'll limit the parade to within the castle grounds," Uncle Brutach says once we're all assembled. He takes a seat on one side of the circular wooden table and tightens the ribbon around his reddish-brown hair. Laochard sits beside him, but my mother remains standing.

"No." My mother is emphatic. "The people need to see me. They need to believe I'm not afraid." She turns away from him and walks to the window. I wonder whether the roses give her a sense of hope as well.

"But my lady, I cannot guarantee your safety outside of the castle." Uncle Brutach crosses and stands beside her before taking her hand in his and bowing his head.

"Then that is a risk we must take," my mother retorts, yanking her hand away. "I will not give the rebels the satisfaction of hiding behind stone."

I stifle a sigh and stand. My uncle has had this argument with my mother before, and it always ends the same way. But perhaps the intelligence I gathered during my ill-fated hunting expedition will lead to a different outcome. It may be the only way to make my mother see reason.

"There's something you should know," I say. Immediately, all eyes are on me, and I shift uncomfortably under the weight of so many stares. "Charaide and I were hunting in the forest, and—"

"You left the castle grounds?" Brutach shoves his chair back and rushes over to me before I can even draw breath.

I stagger away from him. "Y-Yes, but you'll be glad I disobeyed your orders when you hear what I've learned."

For a moment, I'm not sure my uncle will let me speak. His face is so red, it's almost purple. I have never seen him this angry before.

"Oh, let her speak, Brutach." Laochard leans back in his chair as if unperturbed by either my confession or Brutach's outburst. "She's still just a child, after all."

Though I appreciate my brother intervening on my behalf, I bristle at his characterizing me as a child. My eighteenth birthday is only a few months away.

Brutach glares at me but shifts to the side and waves his hand for me to proceed. I take a deep breath before focusing on my mother. I relay what the rebels said and how much better informed they were than I suspected.

"They intend to kill all of the halfling 'scum.'" I stumble over that last word and avoid looking at Laochard. At least none of our other siblings are here. This news would surely terrify them.

Once I've finished my tale, I sink into my seat. The room is quiet. As the silence drags on, I risk a glance at my family. Laochard and Brutach stare at each other and appear to be having an intense discussion with their eyes. Then it dawns on me that they're speaking telepathically. I frown, wishing for once my mind wasn't so well shielded by my bracelets. They act as both punisher and protector, though sometimes it's hard to tell which is which.

My mother's emerald eyes fill with tears. Her normally vibrant auburn hair, so much like mine, hangs limply around her shoulders. Her sadness breaks my heart, and I wish I had better news.

But no one else in the room seems the least bit surprised by my revelation.

Finally, Uncle Brutach focuses on Mother. "Well, my queen? Is this enough to convince you to scale things back? Or at the very least, add a military escort to your coronation?" She opens her mouth, a flash of defiance in her eyes, but Brutach doesn't give her a chance to respond. "If you won't protect yourself, surely you will not allow your own stubbornness to risk the well-being of your offspring." He gestures to me, and a shiver runs down my spine.

She rubs her temples and stares at the table. "I suppose I do not have a choice. It is unfortunate that news of the king's illness leaked, but I suppose, given how long he has been bedridden, it shouldn't be a surprise."

I purse my lips as I consider my mother's words. *Is it possible there is a spy among us?* I push the thought away. It will not do to further burden Mother with errant speculation when I have no proof of my suspicion.

"Thank you." Brutach bows. "Laochard and I will speak with our top generals and make the changes at once." He faces me, his eyebrows furrowing. "Astreilles, you are not to stray outside of the castle again."

"Yes, Uncle." I lower my gaze to the floor. Part of me can't wait until the coronation is over so life can return to normal. Well, a new normal, though I wonder if things will ever be normal again.

"But in light of this, I wonder if we might alter our plans for Father's funeral." A new light shines in Mother's eyes. How she maintains her optimism and hope despite the grave news, I may never know. It's not a part of her I inherited.

"I don't believe that will be wise." Uncle Brutach's mouth sets in a grim line.

"Why not? The rebels clearly knew he was dying. I doubt we

can keep news of his death from the kingdom for long. What difference will it make now?"

He shakes his head. "Whisperings in the woods by unseen fae do not mean the rebel armies are aware. It could be completely unrelated."

My stomach drops. *Is it possible there is more than one group plotting our demise?* I glance behind me, half expecting to find a cloaked assassin. Of course, no one is there. My wild fantasies do not come to fruition. *Yet.*

"H-How many people want to see us dead?" I ask, unable to keep the tremor from my tone.

Brutach looks at me, his eyes betraying the barest hint of sympathy. "I fear I do not know. But it should hardly be surprising, given the circumstances of your birth."

I wince. His words are like a knife to the gut, even though I've known this all along. It's more hurtful, in some ways, coming from him. But I know he doesn't mean it to sound so cold and heartless. He's preparing me for the world I must face.

"Brutach," Mother scolds. She looks at me, her expression softening. "You shouldn't be so cavalier with her. She is too young."

"She's old enough to know what we're up against," he counters. "And the consequences of what she is."

Again, I cringe, not at who I am but *what* I am—a loathsome hybrid monster. Or at least, that's what the rebels think. Were it something I could control, I would, but it wasn't my choice to be born this way. Anger wells up inside me, but as quickly as it crescendos, it recedes. It won't serve me to be angry at the rebels for their prejudices. Were I in their shoes, I'm not sure I would feel different.

"I still think we should alter our plans and bury the king appropriately," Mother says, bringing us back to the subject at hand. "The clandestine way we're going about this doesn't sit right with me. It's like the rebels have already won as we live our lives in fear."

"Not in fear, my dear sister. With caution." Brutach steps over to her and places his hand on her arm. "We're trying to avoid causing the spark that will ignite the war." He turns to me. "Besides, if it will protect your children from potential harm, I expect you'd welcome any precautions."

With a defeated nod, she agrees. "Fine. But promise me, once this is all over, we *will* give Father a proper farewell."

"His spirit will be long departed by then."

"Promise me," she commands, her green eyes flashing.

He closes his fist and presses it to his heart while bowing his head. "You have my word. When this is over, Father will receive a proper farewell befitting his station."

"Thank you," my mother says.

"Come now." Uncle Brutach waves us out of the room. "There's much to be done before the coronation, and we haven't a moment to waste."

I follow without hesitation. After my earlier dalliance in the woods, it's best that I keep my head down and play the part of the dutiful daughter, even if my heart isn't in it. I'll do everything in my power to protect my family from the rebels.

CHAPTER
TWO

THE DAY of my grandfather's funeral is a somber though subdued affair. Few people have been invited to the proceedings, but my heavy heart lifts a little when I see Charaide amongst the gathered. We haven't seen each other since our ill-fated trip to the forest, and I miss him.

I follow my parents and Laochard, signaling the line of succession. Somehow, this seems a moronic idea, showcasing exactly who is next in line as if we're literally telling the rebels how to pick us off one by one. But when I raised my concerns, they fell on deaf ears. *This is how we've always done it, after all.* Even though nothing else about this funeral mirrors those of the past.

As I pass a row of onlookers, a figure in a dark cloak catches my eye. There's something off about the person's stature. Their body leans to the left side as if their legs were different heights, but I assume it's either poor posture or uneven terrain. Their face is obscured by their hood and the way they've bowed their head. Unlike everyone else around them, they do not look up to see the procession.

Are they overly pious or hiding something? My pulse quickens, and I swallow the lump of fear that forms. Surely the rebels wouldn't show up here. After all, the king was a pure-blooded fae and well loved by his people. Still, after the whispers I overheard in the woods and the conversation with my uncle, I don't know that I can put anything past our enemies.

My calf tenses, reminding me of the blade I have hidden in my boot. It wouldn't be much against an army, but as I stare around the room, I don't see others who match this person in stance or appearance. Perhaps the individual is working alone. I bite back a snort. *Not very wise.* A flick of Laochard's wrist would bring the royal guard down before he or she could so much as unsheathe their sword—assuming I didn't get to them first.

I take a deep breath. My imagination is running away with me again. I continue down the aisle, and the person in question doesn't move. If they were going to attack, surely they would have done so by now. Shaking my head, I push such foolish notions from my mind. My brother and uncle vetted every guest here. It's unlikely a rebel would have gotten past them.

When we reach the front of the chapel, I avert my eyes from the open casket. Lifeless bodies fill me with unease. People never quite look the same in death, as if the whole of their person was made up of their soul and the empty body left behind is simply a vessel they inhabited for a time.

My mother drops into a reverent bow in front of the casket, and I imitate her, grateful to have a reason to stare at the floor. We move to the side, though I keep my head lowered, hopeful I look like a grieving granddaughter or at least respectful and not like someone unsettled by the dead. If any rebel spies are among us, I cannot risk displaying weakness.

Seats are set out for us behind the casket and facing the mourners. On the one hand, I prefer to keep an eye out for enemies. I would rather fight head-on than be stabbed in the back. But it's uncomfortable to have so many eyes staring at me. I pick a spot on the stone wall at the back of the room where a torch is lit, watching the fire lick the air and the smoke billow to the tall ceiling.

Uncle Brutach stands over the coffin. "Today, we lay to rest King Ríchíos, a kind and benevolent king." He raises his eyes and looks over the congregation. "Our realm is the lesser for his loss. For the last century, we have had perfect peace in our kingdom, and it was achieved and maintained by his guiding hand." Folding his arms on the podium, he gazes at my grandfather. "But I fear it dies with him."

Whispered voices fill the room as the meaning behind his words sinks in. I allow myself a glance at the gathered faeries to see their reaction. Most appear grim, with their lips pressed into thin lines. Others nod as if they were expecting this, while still others lean toward their neighbors, their eyes filled with fear and their iridescent wings trembling.

My gaze wanders, seeking the stranger in the dark cloak. He or she is still standing with head bowed, the cloak obscuring their face. I can't detect a reaction at this distance, though I'm starting to suspect they've fallen asleep. It's the only explanation for how still and silent they appear.

"There are those who would rather tear our kingdom apart than see a half-breed on the throne." My uncle sighs, and his pain reverberates off his body. "As we bury my father, I beseech the rebels to bury their old grudges and prejudices with him." He leans forward, giving more passion to his speech. "Consider how great our realm will be when we are able to let go of preconceived notions about what makes a ruler and embrace the future my sister, the queen, and her children will provide."

A small amount of grumbling follows, but no one objects outright. Clearly, my uncle has chosen his crowd of mourners wisely. There are no true dissenters here. Though initially, I wasn't sure how I would feel about people accepting my family begrudgingly, I suppose this is better than having them actively wishing us dead.

With a decisive nod, my uncle straightens as if he believes he has said his piece. He gestures to my brother. "And now, Prince Laochard will lead us in the prayer for the dead."

The rest of the funeral continues without incident. When it is time to process to the catacombs where my grandfather will be laid to rest, the tension in my shoulders dissipates. If the coronation also moves forward without incident, perhaps we can maintain my grandfather's hard-won peace after all.

As I pass the cloaked figure again, they move, faster than any creature I've ever seen, and lunge toward me. The silver knife they've pulled from beneath the folds of their cloak aims for my throat. I gasp, stumbling back into Laochard. His arms are around me in an instant, and he pulls me from harm's way but not before the tip of the knife pricks my skin.

A cry escapes my lips, and in the blink of an eye, two royal guards have my would-be assassin cornered, or so it seems. His hood slips just the slightest bit, and his teeth flash in a most grotesque smile. He lifts his hand, and a blinding spray of light erupts into the air, causing everyone in the hall to cover their faces against the sudden brightness. When it stops, the hooded figure is gone.

"Search the castle!" Laochard orders the two guards. "There's no way any of the rebels would be stupid enough to attack us alone."

My heart is in my throat as I struggle to process what just happened. One of the rebels was *here*. Laochard grabs my hand and tries to lead me out of the room, but I'm frozen to the spot. He wraps an arm around me and half carries me out of the chapel and into the catacombs, where the rest of our family is waiting.

"Laochard, Astreilles, what took you so long?" Mother's eyes are filled with concern.

"It appears a rebel assassin has penetrated our defenses," Laochard says, and I'm grateful that I'm not forced to speak.

I can't stop thinking about what would have happened if Laochard hadn't been there. The strike had been so fast I almost doubted it happened. No one I'd ever seen could move like that. It was as if he had been made for it—made for killing. But for my brother's quick actions, my body would be the next laid to rest in this tomb.

"Astreilles was nicked with the knife but is otherwise unharmed."

His words remind me of the pinprick of the knife against my throat, and my hand rises of its own accord. When I pull it away, it is covered in blood.

"Here." My mother unwraps a shawl from her shoulders and presses it against my wound. "This will staunch the bleeding."

"Thank you," I croak, shifting away from her, desperate to get some distance, as I'm on the verge of falling apart. But as I move, the world begins to spin before my eyes.

"I've got her." Father wraps his arms around me and gently sets me down on the cold stone floor, whispering to me in the strange language of his people. Though he's tried to teach it to me in the past, nothing has ever stuck. But it's comforting all the same, and I lean into his embrace.

Laochard and Brutach have a brief exchange, but I don't quite catch all that's said. Now that the danger has passed, Brutach suggests we continue on with the funeral as planned. Father helps me to my feet, and he and Mother each take one of my hands.

We pray over my grandfather as his coffin is settled into its final resting place. I try to concentrate on the prayer, but my mind keeps drifting back to the moment the assassin moved, to the quickness and surety of his attack, as if he knew the perfect moment to strike. As if he could tell the minute I let my guard down.

No one speaks as we ascend the stairs into the castle. Part of me wonders if this will cause further restrictions on my mother's coronation. It's already been difficult for me, basically being under house arrest since the revelations I overheard in the woods. I can't imagine being further confined. My heart longs to walk through the forest with Charaide again and enjoy the freedoms that I did while my grandfather was alive.

Perhaps I'm being selfish. After all, the precautions are for my protection. But it doesn't feel like much of a life to be cooped up behind these stone walls. My grandfather relished visiting with the villagers, always keeping a finger on the pulse of his kingdom. *Will my mother ever be safe to do the same?*

When we reach the ground floor, Charaide is waiting for me. He rushes over, his blue eyes full of concern, and pulls me into his arms. Warmth spreads over my cheeks as I feel the weight of many stares witnessing our embrace. I stiffen, and Charaide releases me then steps back to check me over for wounds.

"Are you hurt badly?" His hand brushes the wound on my neck.

My heart flutters from the intimacy of his touch, and my response sounds more breathless than I intend. "It was just a scratch. The bleeding has stopped."

"Thank the goddesses for that." He moves to embrace me again, but I retreat from him and hold up my hand.

"Meet me in the library later," I whisper before returning to my family.

We head into the queen's council chambers. A large oak table sits at the center of the room, ornately carved wooden chairs surrounding it. We each take a seat, and I prepare for whatever new requirements will be placed on us following this latest incident.

"The situation is much more dire than I realized," my uncle begins. He stands and paces the length of the room while we follow his movements with our eyes. "An attack during the king's funeral." He shakes his head, his gray-blue eyes flashing to black. "What an affront to our customs, our most cherished practices." Suddenly, he stops abruptly and whips around. "We must scale back the coronation and move up the date."

"But we've already done so much work," Father says, surprising me. Throughout this whole process, he's kept silent. Although he's lived here all his life, this is not his world, and these are not his traditions.

Uncle Brutach glares at him, but Mother holds up a hand, likely stopping another argument. My father and uncle tolerate each other, at best, for my mother's sake, if not to keep up appearances among our people.

"Shortening the time frame will only increase the strain on us all. I agree to scale back some of the plans. However, the date has been set and is not up for discussion." Mother fixes my uncle with a gaze that dares him to challenge her.

His mouth opens as if he intends to do just that, then he snaps it shut and inclines his head. "Very well, my lady. We will move forward as planned." His gaze alights on Laochard. "But we will need to increase security even more than we have already. And we need better intelligence. What happened today cannot be allowed to happen again during the coronation."

Laochard bows, his arm bent with his fist to his heart. "As you will it."

"We will lock down the castle until after the coronation," Uncle Brutach continues. "No one is to get in... or out."

I don't miss the sharp look he sends me. With a suppressed sigh, I nod. The coronation is only a few weeks away. I can last until then.

Once we finish discussing the changes being made to prevent another incident like today's, I slip out of the room and head to the library. Charaide is already waiting for me. We steal through the towering stacks of books on dusty old shelves to our favorite little nook in the back. I settle against the cushions I've stowed on a small stone bench built into the wall and breathe in the musty smell.

"How are you, really?" Charaide settles into a chair and props his feet on a little table.

"Shaken," I reply, closing my eyes and resting my head against a pillow. "I don't think I've ever seen someone move so fast. If Laochard hadn't been there—"

"Don't talk like that, Ast. I couldn't bear it if something happened to you."

"It's okay. I'm not so easily dispatched," I say with a teasing grin. When he doesn't return it, I take a deep breath. "Why don't we talk of something else? How fares your family?"

"Well," he says, "we're looking forward to the coronation. My mother is excited to have a queen again. It's been so long since your grandmother left us."

Not long enough. There's a bitter edge to my thoughts. While my grandfather had been willing to overlook the defect of my birth, my grandmother never forgave my mother for her so-called *transgression* of marrying a human. Grandmama clearly thought humans were the scum of the earth and that we, as halflings, were even worse. As if the intermingling of the species were an abomination, an affront to her perfect worldview. Needless to say, I hadn't shed so much as a single tear when she died.

"Of course, I expect your mother will make a much better queen," he hurries on as if he could read my thoughts.

Sometimes, I wonder if my feelings for him allow us to connect despite the bracelet suppressing my magic, but I suspect it's just that he knows me so well.

"Assuming she makes it to that title." I rest my chin on my knee and stare out the window behind him. Darkness grows as we near sunset, and it fits my ominous mood.

"She'll make it." Charaide sits up straighter. "I've, uh, joined your brother's army."

I blink, refocusing on him. "You what?"

"Don't act so surprised," he rebukes me, but the hand he runs through his hair is a little shaky. "I'm of age, and I want to defend the queen a-and her family against the rebels."

"But Charaide, it's too dangerous." I lay my hand over his, ignoring the spark that ignites within me. I've gotten used to hiding my true feelings around him.

"Perhaps, but it's the right thing to do."

"You're my best friend." When he doesn't respond, I repeat his words back to him. "I couldn't bear it if something happened to you."

His expression softens. "I'll be okay, Ast. I'm stronger than I look."

Before I can respond, my father's voice carries through the library, calling for me. I close my eyes again, willing him to go away, but Charaide releases my hand.

"You should go. We can meet again later when you aren't up to your pointed ears in coronation business."

With a sigh, I climb out of my nook, and we walk back through the library. I truly cannot wait until the coronation is over, even if it means bringing the war to our doorstep that much sooner. This between period is causing everyone to be on edge. In some ways, it feels like we are already ghosts haunting our former lives.

"Have you written your speech?" Charaide asks as we reach the entrance to the library.

I turn toward him with a frown. "What speech?"

His eyes widen. "The third in line usually gives a speech or toast at the coronation dinner. It's tradition."

"It would have been nice if someone had told me," I grumble. *On top of everything else, I'm supposed to write and give a speech?* My stomach roils at the thought of speaking in front of all of those people. So many of them look at me with quiet disdain whenever I appear with my mother. As if they expect that my human side causes me to be more ignorant. What better way to prove them correct than to blubber my way through some nonsensical speech. I groan.

This is one of the many reasons I wish my mother would abdicate. I can only hope Laochard will marry and bear many children to further the royal bloodline. The last thing I want is to be queen, something I imagine the rebels would be all too happy to hear.

"I can help you write it if you want," Charaide offers.

"Will you give it for me too?" I quip then sigh. "Thank you. I appreciate your help."

"Meet me in the library tomorrow afternoon, and we can begin."

CHAPTER

THREE

CORONATION DAY ARRIVES. Thanks to Charaide's help, I have written a halfway-decent speech. But I'm still dreading the actual delivery. Public speaking is not my strong suit. I may wear a crown and carry a title, but I've never felt comfortable under their weight.

Adding to my anxiety is the gown my mother has chosen for me to wear for the event. It is a deep emerald, which she claims will bring out the green in my eyes and contrast well with my auburn hair. I stare at my reflection in the mirror and think I look like a sickly pine tree. Perhaps it would look better if I was taller or less pale or even a tad plumper. As it is, the gown hangs off my thin frame. All the tailoring in the world won't make me beautiful, not that this is necessarily a goal.

Then again, it wouldn't hurt if Charaide found me at least marginally attractive. We've been friends since birth, but lately... I close my eyes, willing the thoughts away. I've got more important things to worry about than a silly crush. When I open my eyes, I focus on the silver frame of the mirror instead of my image. The room is draped with various fabrics, all destined to become gowns. After all, the coronation is only the beginning of my future hell.

My mother comes out looking as radiant as ever. Her dress is white with gold embellishments. Her auburn hair cascades down her back in soft waves, and her iridescent blue wings flutter as she turns from side to side, examining her reflection. I try to ignore how dull and brown my wings look in comparison.

"You have truly outdone yourself, Mauve," my mother says.

The royal seamstress bows then steps forward and makes some final adjustments.

Her assistant, Feiste, does the same to my gown, but her irritation is palpable. Every time she tries to pin the dress to hug my nonexistent curves, it falls flat. I suppress a groan. *How am I supposed to play the part of the regal faery princess when I can't even get my clothing to behave?*

"Goodness, girl. You need to eat more!"

I force a laugh, trying to hide my feelings of inadequacy. Eating more isn't the problem—it's the human side of me. It impacts each of my siblings differently. Laochard has the strength of the fae but not the cunning. Though he oversees the military, it is due to his reliance on brute force, not strategic maneuvering. That falls to one of my younger brothers, Cliste, who shares the same thin physique as me but is a certifiable genius. Together, they are a force to be reckoned with. Or they would be if they got along.

After several more attempts to get the dress to fit properly, Feiste gives up. Instead, she alters it to flow down my thin frame in an elegant way, which is a vast improvement. Still, I cannot help casting a wistful glance at my jeans folded on a chair in the corner of the room. One of the few perks of being a halfling is the ability to easily travel between the worlds. My father has taken my siblings and me to the mortal realm several times, and I definitely prefer their modern clothing to the antiquated styles of the fae. Jeans are so much more comfortable.

Once we are properly attired, Mother and I make our way through the castle to the stables. It seems somewhat ludicrous to ride out of the castle and into the village before parading back in for the coronation, but Mother has insisted we keep as many of the traditions as we can. However, even with Laochard's precautions, I still feel anxious as I ride out to the edge of the village to line up with the rest of the procession.

My mare seems to sense my anxiety as she paws the ground and flicks her white ears back and forth as if searching for danger. It seems she and I are alone in our fears, as the road through the village is lined with fae eager to see their new queen.

Behind me, my mother and father climb into the carriage together, which was another point of contention between Mother and Uncle Brutach. He believed advertising their unorthodox relationship wouldn't help win the hearts of the rebels. I hate to admit that I agree with him, but Mother's stubbornness won in the end.

A chilly breeze ruffles my hair, and a shiver runs down my spine. I glance behind me into my beloved forest, but today, it appears ominous, devoid of all its usual comfort. The trees whisper like they remember old terror, creatures that stir only when moonlight brushes the moss. I keep my cloak wrapped tight, knowing some shadows hunt not just body but spirit.

"Laochard, mount up!" Uncle Brutach commands, breaking my reverie.

It's time to start the procession, and I shake my head, clearing my mind of my imaginings. My brother has split his faction into two. Some will ride ahead of the procession and others behind. I feel safer being surrounded by my brother's men and glance over my shoulder to give him a grateful smile. He waves before flipping down the visor of his helmet and signaling to Brutach to begin.

As we ride through the streets, I'm pleased to see so many happy, smiling faces among the faeries. No one sneers at me for being a half-breed or spits at the ground as I pass. Showers of flowers mix with the leaves on the wind as the faeries use their magic to brighten our procession. I wave, my bracelets catching the sunlight, and plaster a smile on my face even as I scan the horizon for danger. Despite Laochard's reassurance, I can't seem to calm my fears.

The procession is mercifully short, and as we near the castle gates, the tension in my shoulders eases. Perhaps the rebels decided to let us have this day.

I stop my horse as I wait for my parents' carriage to cross the drawbridge. A sigh of relief escapes my lips once they are safely through. As I kick my heels to urge my horse forward, she rears up, and I throw my arms around her neck to maintain my balance.

Then I see what spooked her—a creature rising from the moat, a bow in its hand. As it moves closer, it nocks an arrow and points it at me. I scream, pulling the reins to the side.

Suddenly, my brother appears. "Go, Astreilles. Ride into the castle. Now!"

More creatures rise from the water, though at closer look, I can make out their wings and tattered clothing. The blue-black of their uniforms betrays their loyalties. *The rebels are here.*

I yank the reins and steer my horse directly at them, kicking my heels and urging her forward. She rears again, nailing one of the rebels in the head with her hoof before she canters around them. The drawbridge shakes under us as we gain momentum while the sounds of battle rage behind me. Once I'm through the gate, I pull my horse around, and my mouth falls open. So many faeries have risen from the moat that they outnumber the half of the army faction bringing up the rear of our processional.

I direct my horse to the stables, riding as fast as we can. When we reach them, I clamber off as quickly as my gown will allow and toss my reins to a stable boy before gathering my skirts and tearing across the courtyard. I must warn the others and call on every soldier to join the fray, or my brother and our castle will be overrun.

My feet pound up the stone stairs to the room where my parents and uncle are waiting to start the coronation. They turn at the sound of my approach, and I can only guess at how wild I must look, my hair spilling out of the clasps that had been so painstakingly set this morning.

"Rebels!" I cry, though I'm out of breath, and it's not quite as forceful as I intended. "The rebels are attacking Laochard's guards!"

Uncle Brutach spins on his heel and shouts orders to the guards in the room while my parents cling to one another, their eyes searching behind me. I reach them, panting, and relay what I saw.

"Is Laochard alive?" Mother demands even as her hands move over me and check for injuries.

"Last I saw, yes." I wave her off. "But they're outnumbered."

"*Dios Santo*," Father mutters, crossing himself in that awkward way he always does. He turns to Mother. "I'll go and help as best I can."

"No, Sebastián." She grabs his arm. "It's too dangerous for a mortal. They'll kill you on sight."

"I cannot let our son fight my battle," he says. When she shakes her head, he catches her face in his hands. "*Mi amor*, trust in us, trust in our love. I will return to you, I promise." Still holding her face in his palms, he looks at me. "Astreilles, fetch your bow and arrow and call on any archer you can find. We'll need to defend the castle from within as well as without."

I nod, sparing one last glance at my parents before spinning on my heel and racing to my bedroom. As I reach the hall, I begin the painstaking task of untying my skirts. By the time I enter my room, I've left a trail of fine cloth. I'm in only my corset and bloomers, but there's no time to change. My bow and quiver are right next to the door.

As I'm about to grab them, a heavy arm catches me across the chest and hurls me into the wall. The breath leaves me, and pain shoots down my back. I stare through watery eyes, trying to make out my assailant. But they are wearing a cloak that obscures their face. I reach for my blade in my boot, but they are quicker, seizing my arm in one hand and my neck in the other before slamming me against the wall again. My head spins with pain, but I thrash against the hold, trying to break free.

"Please," I whisper, tears streaming down my cheeks as I try to make out the face of my attacker, but it's covered by the hood of its cloak.

Their grip tightens around my neck, cutting off my air. I claw at their hand with my nails, but their skin is rough, almost reptilian. As I fight to free myself, I catch glimpses of their hand, and my eyes bulge in horror at the strange patchwork of their skin. It's like nothing I've seen before.

"Why?" I choke out, using the last of my breath. My vision blurs, black spots filling it as I struggle to get air.

"It must be done," a harsh voice rasps.

This is it, then. I close my eyes, preparing for death. Still, my nails claw at the hand around my throat, feebly attempting to break free. My efforts become more pathetic as my body shuts down.

"Get your hands off her!"

I open my eyes wide, struggling to see around the black spots that cloud my vision. But I would know that voice anywhere.

My assailant is ripped from me with a growl, and I crumple to the floor, clutching my neck and coughing. I lift my head as I struggle to breathe, my throat aching and swelling. Charaide isn't much of a warrior, but he is holding his own against this... creature. I can't think what else to call it. It's not faery or at least not entirely. But there's something strangely familiar about the way it moves and the coloring of its cloak. I push to my feet, hoping to get another glimpse of its strange patchwork of skin.

"Foolish boy," the creature rasps. It lunges at Charaide, but he ducks, his feet nimble and quick.

He turns to me. "Run, Astreilles. Get help!"

Still coughing, I nod and scramble to my feet, pushing aside my strange fascination with the assailant. I race out of the room and down the corridor, sliding across the floor, my feet feeling as if I'm running across a bed of nails.

"Help!" I cry, though my voice is raspy and hoarse from being strangled half to death. It chills my bones how much it sounds like the creature who attacked me. I rush into the great room, where my uncle and mother are in a heated argument. "Please, help!"

"Astreilles?" Mother runs over to me and pulls me into her arms. "What happened to you?"

"Attacked," I wheeze. "In my room. Charaide... fighting..."

Uncle Brutach signals to the guards, and they rush out. I turn to follow, but my mother grabs my arm, her eyes beseeching me to stay. I shake my head and pull away from her as I rush after the guards, hoping my friend has managed to outwit the brutal creature.

When we arrive in the room, Charaide is bleeding but alive and alone with my bow and an arrow in his hands. I tear a strip of cloth from one of the many skirts I left haphazardly on the floor and rush to his side then press the cloth against his wound. He gives me a weak smile.

"Where is the rebel?" one guard demands while the other two search the room.

"H-He flew out the window." Charaide struggles to sit up, but I press him back to the floor.

"Did you see his face?" I ask. "Can you tell us what he looks like so we can find him?"

"I'm not sure I believe what I saw," he says with a harsh laugh before grimacing with pain.

"You need to see the healer." I signal to a guard to fetch her.

"No, I want to help the fight," he protests and attempts to stand again. This leads to a coughing fit, and I hold him down.

"You have helped." I lean forward, pressing my lips lightly to his forehead. "You saved my life."

His deep-blue eyes meet mine, and he opens his mouth as if to speak, but the healer arrives and pushes me aside.

"I need room to work," she says.

I stand, my eyes never leaving Charaide's face. "I must go to the allure with the other archers, but I will come back to check on you." I take my bow from him and grab my quiver of arrows before heading to the stairs that lead to the top of the castle wall.

When I reach the top, it's pandemonium everywhere I look. Archers are firing on the rebels. They appear to be contained at the gate, and only my strange assailant has breached our defenses. That's small comfort considering how close it came to killing me, but I push the thoughts from my mind. I need to focus.

I search the battle below for my brother and father. Laochard is defending the drawbridge as more and more faeries rise from the depths of the moat. It's a wonder how they stayed hidden for so long. No doubt they were assisted by the Merrow and Selkies. These battle lines were drawn the day my parents wed.

My father is harder to locate. I'm not even sure how our archers know where to aim. The fighting makes it difficult to discern friend from foe, although my suspicions about the Selkies and Merrow are proven correct. The moat is filled with seals and fish tails as the creatures that live below the surface rise to attack our soldiers. That's where I decide to aim my bow.

A beautiful mermaid jumps out of the sea beside the drawbridge before grabbing a soldier and making to pull him under. She's quick, but I'm faster, acting on instinct alone as I pull back the arrow and let it fly, hitting her cleanly in the back. She screams, and her arms frantically flail as she tries to dislodge the arrow before she falls into the murky depths.

I stare at the spot where she fell, struggling to reconcile the fact that I just shot and likely killed one of my own people. I have killed before—rabbits, deer, the occasional fox. But this is no hunt.

If I hadn't done it, she would have killed that soldier. I had to... to save his life. But even that justification isn't enough to quell the growing nausea in my stomach.

Off in the distance, an eerie sound wails over the land. I turn wide eyes to the archer beside me.

"It's the wail of the banshee," he says, his eyes solemn.

In our world, the banshee screams like that only when someone is about to die. As I return my gaze to the battle waging below, I would wager there are multiple someones for whom the banshee cries. A chill slithers down my spine.

Then I finally locate my father. He's surrounded by three faeries and is fighting for his life. My mouth drops open as one of the faeries lifts their sword to deliver the final blow. Again, my hunter's instinct takes over as I grab an arrow with an iron point, take aim, and fire. The faery falls while its companions raise their eyes to me. Wicked smiles gleam on their faces as they grab my father and shove him to the ground. One faery climbs onto his back as the other wraps her arms around his head.

With my heart pounding in my ears, I yank another iron arrow from my quiver, and when the faery looks up to taunt me before snapping my father's neck, I let it fly. The faery dodges my arrow but releases my father in the process. I stare, willing Father to move, and take a breath only when he does.

The third faery doesn't hesitate. She grabs my father and

throws him over her shoulder like he is a mere sack of flour. I climb onto the allure, using the notches in the battlements to follow the trajectory of the faery's path. Rage fills me, and I try to quell the desire to leap down after the faery and rip her to pieces, but by the time I reached my father, it would be too late. I keep an eye out for Laochard in hopes he might be able to reach our father sooner, but for now, my best option is to fire an iron arrow into that blackened faery heart.

My father must be unconscious, as he makes no move to fight his way off the faery's back. Not that he could. His human strength is no match for those powerful arms. I pause at a break in the battlement, trying to discern where the faery is going and when I'll have a clean shot. But she seems to know I'm onto her, as she weaves through the battle on nimble feet, ducking and flying in equal measure.

I take off running again, dodging archers and keeping one eye on my target. As I reach the corner wall, a commotion sounds behind me, and I turn. The rebels have breached the gate. My heart leaps in my throat as I scan the soldiers for Laochard. He's still alive and has joined forces with my uncle and a new faction of soldiers. I hope this is enough to hold the rebels back.

When I return to my pursuit, the faery and my father are gone. I whip my head around, searching for any sign of them. I run down the next length of the allure, frantically scanning below. They can't have gone far. Perhaps the faery doubled back when she saw I was distracted. I retrace my steps, keeping my eyes on the ground.

As I reach the edge of the moat where I first fired on the mermaid, I catch a glimpse of the faery's fiery hair and orange wings. I remove an arrow from my quiver, put it in my bow, and take aim. But I hesitate. *Where is my father?*

The faery turns as if sensing me. A cruel smile tugs at her lips as she lifts an object high in her hands. My mouth falls open in horror, and it's all I can do not to drop the bow. Blank brown eyes stare back at me from my father's severed head. My father's human face, once mocked as weakness, now mocked in death. The rebels would call us monsters, but who is the monster now?

My stomach roils, but I swallow the bile rising in my throat. With a cry of rage, I pull back my bow and release the arrow, right into the faery's heart. I watch helplessly as she and my father's head fall into the moat and sink below the murky surface.

FOUR

"Princess," a voice calls, and I lift my head toward the sound. A male fae with black hair, pale-white skin, and dark, almost black eyes stares down at me. I frown as I survey my surroundings. I'm lying on the ground of the allure with the battle still raging below.

"What happened?" I try to stand, but my legs refuse to cooperate.

"You fainted, my lady. After you shot your... your father's..."

It all comes back to me then—the sight of my father's head, the cruel smile, my scream of rage. Tears spring to my eyes as the truth sinks in. My father is dead.

"Your mother requests your presence in the great room," the archer continues. "There's been some... news."

"Does she know about my father?"

He shifts uncomfortably, clearing his throat. "She does."

He offers me his hand, and I accept, standing with difficulty. My legs are numb, and I wonder how long I was out. I glance at the battle. Fewer rebels are in the courtyard, and I take that as a positive sign. Maybe this will all be over soon.

But it's a small comfort. I collect my bow and quiver before climbing down from the allure and heading into the castle. My poor mother must be beside herself with grief. For a moment, rage flashes through me. Not at the faery who murdered him but at my father. He should have heeded Mother. If he had stayed in the castle with her, he might still be alive.

When I reach the great room, the doors are closed. I take a moment, breathing in deeply, before I push them open and enter. My uncle stands on one side of the table, my younger siblings as well, and Mother...

The breath catches in my throat at the sight of her. She is pale, paler than I've ever seen her. It is as if Father's death has sucked the life out of her as well. She sits on the throne, her crown askew. I frown. *Did they go through with the coronation while the battle raged outside?*

"Astreilles," she whispers. "Come here."

I obey, going to her side and kneeling before her. "I am so sorry, Mama." My voice sounds like a child's. "I tried to save him."

Her eyes widen. "Who?"

My throat tightens. "Father." *Oh no.* The archer said she knew, but perhaps he was mistaken.

A strangled sob escapes her, though she tries to regain her composure. "I know you did, sweetheart." Her lips press into a thin line. "Your father knew the risk." She takes a deep breath. "That's not why I called you here, though. There's something else you need to know."

I look up at her. "What happened?"

Her composure falters again. "It's your brother... L-Laochard."

I stare at her, my heart pounding in my ears. She's struggling to tell me, but somehow, I already know. I close my eyes as a single tear rolls down my cheek. "He's dead," I say.

"Yes. Not long after your father was killed, he was as well."

I sink to the floor, pulling my knees into my chest. My beloved father, my precious brother, both killed, and for what? Emotions rip through me like a hurricane. I want to lash out, to hit something or someone. At least I took out the faeries who murdered my father, and yes, I count them all. Even the ones that I killed before the act was committed.

"That makes you second in line to the throne," my uncle says, coming up behind me and placing a hand on my shoulder. "And the new commander of our armies."

"W-What?" I stand and spin around. "But shouldn't Cliste take over that role? He's the next male heir."

My uncle shakes his head, his expression grave. "The law doesn't take into account gender, only the line of succession. Whoever is next in line automatically becomes the new commander." His gray-blue eyes are filled with pity. "That task now falls to you."

"B-But I don't know the first thing about leading an army," I sputter. I can hunt and fish, and I'm skilled with a bow and arrow, but *leading* anyone, especially into battle, is well beyond my skill set.

"You'll have me and Cliste as advisors, of course," my uncle continues as if I haven't spoken. "But the men will look to you for guidance." He crosses his arms. "I'm afraid your days of firing arrows from the allure are over."

"But she's just a child!" Mother comes over to me and places trembling hands on my shoulders, pulling me back. "Surely, given the circumstances, someone else can take over until Astreilles is ready." I can hear in her voice that she hopes the war will be over by that time.

I resist the urge to shake her off and shove down the annoyance at being referred to as a child. In this particular instance, it's warranted. Unlike my brother, I was not raised to lead an army or a kingdom.

"It is what the law requires," my uncle says.

My legs give out, and I fall to my knees. He might as well have signed my death sentence. It would be better for the rebels to take me out now. Then Cliste can take over the armies, and my family might stand a fighting chance. Under my leadership, we're surely doomed.

"Fetch the royal sorceress," Brutach continues, seemingly oblivious to my mental breakdown. "We will need to remove her cuffs."

I stare blankly at my uncle, then his words sink in. As second in line to the throne, I'm permitted access to my magic. I'll need it to lead our soldiers in battle. My mouth goes dry. *Why bother? I haven't the first idea how to* access *my magic, let alone wield it.* I shake my head. There is no way the royal guard will listen to me.

"The battle is drawing to a close," Uncle Brutach continues as if reading my mind. Not that he would need to, as I'm sure my panic is clear on my face. "We have driven the rebels across the bridge and into the village. But I do not expect to have long to regroup. We'll need to lead our armies to meet them head-on and squash this rebellion entirely."

I try to swallow, but a lump has formed in my throat. At least the battle that claimed the lives of my brother and father is almost over, small comfort though it is. I close my eyes, and the memory of my father's head flashes through my mind. I shudder as I force myself to stand and push the image away. It is too late for him and Laochard. All I can hope to do now is protect the ones they left behind.

Footsteps sound in the hallway, and I yank an arrow from my quiver, spinning toward the sound on instinct. The sorceress lifts her hands, and my arms seem to freeze in place. I can't even lower my bow.

"Your reliance on weapons betrays your weakness," the sorceress says as she moves toward me. "Once your shackles are removed, you'll have less need of such primitive defenses."

I wait for her to release the spell that holds me in place, but she doesn't. Instead, she gestures to a young page who has followed her in. He brings a small black cauldron, which she lifts and tips over each of my wrists, pouring a golden liquid onto the iron bracelets.

My bracelets dissolve with a slight hiss, but I don't feel any pain. The magic hums low under my skin, wild and unfamiliar, without a clear center. Whatever element I've inherited refuses to reveal itself. Instead, the energy feels chaotic and untethered, flickering in ways I can't yet understand. *What a shock. Even my magic refuses to fit into a well-defined box. Fitting for a half-breed.*

I glance at my mother. *Will I inherit her gift of water? Soft and yielding yet strong enough to shape stone?* She and Brutach share the same element, but while hers flows like a river, his holds like ice. Not unfeeling but tight-lidded. He's the kind of man who turns his grief into frost rather than release it and reveal a perceived weakness.

Then I think of Charaide and his steady calm, the way he listens before he speaks. Earth lives in him, solid and certain. It lived in Laochard too. But unlike Charaide, my brother bore it like a foundation. Immovable. Unshakable. Strength in its most relentless form. I close my eyes against the ache that rises in my chest. I still can't believe he's gone. And now I'm left to lead an army in his place.

"Someone will need to teach her to use her magic," the sorceress says with a raised eyebrow. She tucks a lock of dark hair behind her ear as she assesses me. "I suspect there's great power in this one."

A roar of thundering footsteps approaches, and I raise my bow again then aim behind the sorceress and her page. Multiple soldiers enter bearing the royal colors of crimson and gold. I put the arrow back in the quiver.

"The rebels have fled the castle," one of the soldiers tells Brutach. "The battle is over, and we are victorious."

"Thank you, Sir Raist. Recall the men and close the gates then attend the wounded."

The soldier pounds his fist over his heart, affirming the order, and bows before leaving the room. As he passes, I catch him looking me over with a wary eye, but he wisely says nothing.

"Come, Astreilles," Uncle Brutach calls. "We have much to discuss."

I turn to my mother, but she has focused on my younger siblings, sharing in their grief. My heart aches as well, but there's no time for me to mourn with her. The safety of our kingdom, of my family, weighs heavy on my shoulders.

⸻

It's been a week since my mother's coronation celebration was interrupted, and I've spent every waking moment discussing strategy with my uncle and Cliste. The rebels have mercifully not returned to continue their assault on the castle and my family, but I know they are simply regrouping. Our intelligence, while limited, has found that the troops that attacked us before were just a small subset of their amassed army. And we've been scrambling to build up our defenses ever since.

Uncle Brutach and Cliste have agreed that we must go on the offensive and attempt to catch them unawares. They tell me it is cowardice to remain within the castle's walls and seek to defend rather than strike down the rebellion and bring them to heel. Part of me questions this strategy, but as I have no prior experience, I don't argue. Instead, I trust in their guidance. Besides, if the rebels return, there may not be much of a castle to defend once the dust settles.

Charaide stands beside me as we review the map, Cliste pointing out where we should send our troops. I've appointed Charaide and Cliste generals of their own factions, and they will join me in attacking the rebels. Brutach will, of course, lead his troops as he has done throughout my grandfather's reign.

"We need more information," Charaide says, his eyes narrowing as he looks over the map. "Otherwise, we're going in blind."

"This is as much as we've been able to discover." Uncle Brutach presses his lips into a thin line. He was not pleased when I told him of my decision to make Charaide a general, and I understand his concern. Charaide knows as much about war as I do, but he insisted on joining the war effort, and I am comforted to have him by my side.

Charaide crosses his arms, glaring at my uncle. "We should do a scouting expedition."

"We've already done several." Cliste sighs. "This is all the information we have discovered."

"But you've sent knights and soldiers, who are trained for fighting, not spying." Charaide glances at me. "Astreilles and I can go, alone or with a small group. We're used to sneaking up on our prey."

I keep my face neutral, but I can see Charaide's point. We've hunted together so often in the forest, we know how to hide and wait. Still, this isn't hunting, this is war. So I turn my gaze to my uncle and make no move to dismiss or defend Charaide's suggestion.

My uncle points at me. "She's second in line to the throne. Do you really think I'd risk her for what may amount to a trap?" He shakes his head. "If you want to go on a fool's errand, be my guest."

The idea of sending Charaide off on his own twists my stomach. "No, Charaide is right." I gesture to the map my uncle and brother have been arguing over. "We have been weighing options for days now, and we're no closer to deciding which direction to choose. If we had better intelligence, it might help us decide." I glance at Charaide. "While it was pure chance that we stumbled upon the rebels plotting before the king died, we were careful and were not caught."

"A lucky break is hardly a reason to send you into the lion's den," Brutach says dismissively.

All week, I've kept my mouth shut or swallowed my ideas when Brutach and Cliste told me they wouldn't work, but no more. Charaide's idea may seem crazy to others, but they haven't hunted with us.

"Look," I begin, my voice more forceful than it has been in a while. "My military strategy is clearly lacking, and my magical ability is in its infancy. But the forest is my second home. Charaide and I practically grew up there, hunting and camping." I stare at Cliste, willing my brother to take my side against our uncle. "I know the risks, but I think they are worth it if it means we can finally act instead of just debate."

Cliste chews on his lower lip as he appears to consider my plea. His dark eyebrows, so like our father's, pull over his hazel eyes, and I begin to understand his hesitation. If something happens to me, that makes him next in line. Cliste is not quite sixteen. He's too young to be a general, but he volunteered for that position to support me.

"Astreilles has a point," Cliste says, though I can hear the reluctance in his voice. "We have focused so much on trying to overcompensate for her weaknesses by debating the best strategy for the army, we haven't considered her strengths."

My uncle glares at my brother. "I hardly think catching rabbits is much of a strength, given what we are facing." Then he sighs. "But it is clear I am outnumbered." He turns to me. "Go if you must, but take a few men with you. Neither of you can evanesce, and you may need someone who can get you out of a tight spot."

Relief and triumph flood through me. It's a small victory, but I will take it. Charaide and I head out of the room, barely able to contain our excitement. We shall be able to see our beloved forest once more after all.

I stop short, chastising myself for such thoughts. They won't do, not if I have any hope of saving my family from the rebels. That is my only goal. I have already accepted that I will likely not survive this war, but I will be damned if my family won't make it.

"I can practically hear the sound of your brain working," Charaide says, breaking me of my morbidity. "What are you over-thinking this time?"

A smile pulls at my lips, the first I've had since the deaths of my father and brother. This is why I chose Charaide to be a general—and my right hand. He can see through me in a way no one else can.

"I was thinking how this may be the last time I see the forest." I trust that Charaide will understand my feelings and not berate me for them.

"You will see it many more times, Astreilles." He stops suddenly and pulls me into his arms. "I will make sure of it."

"We're not guaranteed anything," I mumble into his chest, but I make no move to pull away. After my uncle's declaration and the removal of my bracelets, his arms feel safe... like home.

If things were different, if we weren't about to face certain death, maybe he would hold me like this not for comfort but for love. My heart thumps unevenly at the thought. If only...

"No, we're not, and yet I believe we will triumph." He leans back to look at me and taps my nose with his finger. "You're a lot tougher than you look."

I want to believe him, but I don't. Not with the way my stomach roils every time I try to picture myself on a battlefield. Shooting arrows far away from the fight is one thing, but hand-to-hand combat? I shudder, and Charaide pulls me closer.

"Have faith, Astreilles." He steps away, but I keep my gaze on the ground. His fingers slide under my chin, forcing me to look into those deep-blue eyes. "You are amazingly quick with a blade and deadly with an arrow. Add your brother's keen military sense and your uncle's experience, and I think we stand a fighting chance."

My heart pounds as I stare at him, and the determined set in his jaw softens. He releases my chin before sliding his hand along my cheek, and I close my eyes, leaning into his touch.

A sound comes from the end of the hall, and he abruptly drops his hands. My eyes fly open, and I peer around him just in time to see Cliste and my uncle departing the great room. Neither of them pays any attention to us, but their presence is enough to break the spell.

Charaide clears his throat. "We should prepare for our excursion." He doesn't meet my gaze. "I'll, uh, meet you in the gardens in an hour?"

I nod mutely, and he's gone. My lungs ache, and I realize I stopped breathing the moment he held my face in his hands. I take a ragged breath, bracing against the stone wall of the castle. I shouldn't give in to my feelings. With everything we are facing, the last thing I need is to set myself up for heartbreak as well.

An hour later, I slip into the garden, a pack of supplies on my back, my quiver over one shoulder, and my bow in hand. Charaide and a few royal soldiers are waiting next to the red-black roses my mother planted when I was born. They're my favorite, as their scent is a pleasant mixture of sweetness and decay.

The soldiers shift uncomfortably in their village attire. Wearing this clothing was one of the requests I had asked Charaide to make of them. Our goal is to get as close to the rebel camp as we can to gather intelligence and get out without being seen. The royal uniform would call unwanted attention to our expedition.

"Ready to go?" Charaide gestures toward the gate.

I swallow and nod. I haven't been outside of the castle walls since the coronation parade, and I'm not sure what I'll find there. *What if someone is waiting for us in an ambush? Will I even live to see a real battle, or will they assassinate me on the spot?* Maybe once all of her children are dead, my mother will be allowed to reign in peace.

I shake my head, dispelling the morbid thoughts. "This is a small company."

"It seemed wiser. Bringing too many men would just slow us down." Charaide looks me over. "Of course, if you would feel safer, I'm sure we can find a few others to bring with us."

"No, you're right." I face the men. "Thank you for joining us. What are your names?"

The men glance at each other, clearly surprised.

Did I just commit another royal faux pas? But they recover quickly.

"I'm Marto," the dark-haired man closest to me says. "And this is Leiftea and Saki." The two other men look like brothers.

"Nice to meet you," I say.

They nod tersely, but neither speaks.

Before I can push for more conversation, Charaide clears his throat. "We need to go if we hope to make it to the middle of the forest by dark."

I nod, and together, the five of us leave the courtyard and head toward the drawbridge. The air is still as the gate closes behind us with a loud metallic *thud* that reverberates through my bones. But the scars of last week's battle are still visible. Scorched earth and broken arrows litter the ground.

No one attacks us as we cross through the village. The people are shut up within their homes. The already brisk air seems to turn colder as if the smoke pouring from the chimneys was dispelling all the cold from the homes onto the street. I shiver in my cloak, wishing I could have brought my furs. But Charaide feared such finery would reveal my identity and put a target on my back.

We don't speak as we move toward the forest, but my heart rate increases with each step. Part of it is fear, but mostly, it's excitement, the thrilling anticipation of returning to my favorite place. The trees wave in the wind as if beckoning us into their embrace. Their leaves cover the ground like a multicolored carpet, welcoming me home.

Breathing in the scent of damp earth and decaying leaves, I lead us into the woods. The branches appear to close around us as we cross the threshold. For the first time since the battle, I feel at peace. The forest has always welcomed me when no one else would.

Charaide steps beside me and takes my hand before giving it a gentle squeeze. For a moment, I forget what awaits us on the other side of the forest and simply relish the feel of his hand in mine. But then he pulls me forward, and I force myself to focus. The forest may feel like home, but danger lurks within its dark shadows, and I must keep my wits about me.

The memory of those whispered voices is burned into my brain as we creep over the fallen leaves, listening for any sound to indicate we are not alone. But the forest is silent save for the rustling of animals in the thicket, searching for food amid the autumn scarcity. I feel relaxed for the first time in days.

Beside me, Charaide sighs. It's no wonder we both feel more at ease here than in the castle. We spent our childhoods here, running through the thick underbrush, climbing the trees, and splashing in the stream that babbles nearby.

In contrast, the royal soldiers seem to become tenser with each step we take. Their gazes dart throughout the trees, searching for hidden dangers.

The forest is thick and wide, and the farther we traverse into its depths, the darker it becomes. Sunset is nigh, but it's hard to tell through the branches. It would be ominous if I didn't savor the protection provided by the dense canopy.

"We should make camp," Marto finally whispers. We had been walking in silence for so long, his voice makes me jump. "If we leave at first light, we should make the edge of the forest by midday."

What he doesn't say is that it would be faster if we used our magic, but my understanding of my power is still too primitive. While Marto could likely evanesce us straight to the rebel camp, Charaide and I insisted on making it there on foot. Our intelligence is so scattered, we risk landing right in the middle of their camp instead of on the outskirts.

I set down my pack. Though it's been a while, muscle memory takes over as I pitch the tent and gather wood for the fire. We've brought food with us, but I'm tempted to take advantage of the unexpected trip. Fresh meat will lift our spirits and allow me a chance to shake off the rust in my joints from castle life.

"I'm going to find us something to eat," I say, jerking my thumb over my shoulder. With limited food available, I'm sure to find a deer by the stream, enjoying the cool water before it freezes over, or foraging on bark and dying marsh grasses.

"Don't go far," Charaide cautions, his brow furrowing. I understand his concern and give a brief nod before turning to retrace our footsteps.

While I'm at the stream, I gather some water into my almost empty canteen then drink deeply of the cool, fresh liquid. I avoid too much splashing, both to keep from scaring away potential prey and to avoid becoming it. The underbrush is thin, leaving me exposed.

Once I've drunk my fill, I hook the full canteen to my belt and creep into a thick bush, ignoring the way the sharp branches scratch my skin. I pull out my bow and nock an arrow, then I wait, keeping my breath steady and silent and not moving a muscle.

I do not have to wait long. The soft sound of leaves crunching under hoof reaches my ears, and I aim my bow toward the noise. A doe slowly approaches the stream, ears twitching and nostrils flaring as she remains alert to any danger. I glance around, making sure there are no babies with her. My people believe it's a crime to take a mother from a fawn, but there's no way I can know if the doe has left a baby behind in a safe thicket. Still, there are signs of a recent birth, and I do my best to check for them.

The doe continues to drink as I slip out of the bush, keeping my body low to the ground. I see no sign of sag on the doe's belly. I scan the area around the stream, knowing that if her fawn is too young, she won't have left it far away. Satisfied that I've at least tried not to make an orphan fawn, I raise my bow. Breathing in and out slowly, I aim and release my arrow, hitting the doe in the chest. She falls over with a loud crash, and I still, listening for any sign someone else might have heard.

When I'm sure the coast is clear, I slip out of my hiding spot and crouch beside the deer. I say a quiet prayer, as my father taught me, though my heart aches to think of him. Then I lift the deer onto my shoulders and carry her to camp.

Marto's eyes widen on my approach. "I thought you were just going to catch a couple of rabbits."

I shrug as I heave the doe off my shoulders and onto the ground. "I shot the first animal I saw."

"But what will we do with all this meat?" Leiftea asks. "We can't eat it all in one night."

"We'll string it up and smoke it then take it with us," I say. It would take time, probably all night, to do this, but I expect we'll take turns sleeping anyway to keep watch.

"That'll take all night!" Charaide says.

I raise an eyebrow. "And? Do you have something better to do?"

He glowers at me. "I suppose sleeping is beneath you?"

My gaze wanders over the camp and the woods beyond. "I'm not sure I'd sleep much anyway."

This sobers him, and he reaches for me. "Astreilles."

"Don't." I hold up my hand. "I'm fine." My gaze meets Marto's, and I gesture to him. "Help me butcher the deer. We can enjoy some venison for supper."

Marto is all too willing to assist and draws a hunting knife from his boot. The other two soldiers follow suit, and soon, Marto hands Charaide a few fillets to get started over the fire.

It's risky, but Marto and I set up another pile of wood to smoke the remaining meat. With a flick of his wrist, Marto shoots sparks into the wood, and the fire lights almost instantly. I envy him the ease with which his magic responds to him. Part of me wonders if I'll ever have the time to discern my element, let alone learn how to wield it so effectively.

The soldiers and I string up the rest of the meat around this second fire. My clothes are soaked in blood by the time I'm done, and I drag the carcass far away from our camp, hoping it will be enough to entice any predators away from us. It hurts my soul to leave the hide, but I have no way to cart it around with us, and tanning it will take more time than we have.

The soldiers move to their tent, leaving Charaide and me alone. We eat in companionable silence. For a moment, it feels like old times, and I can almost pretend that the last week never happened. But then a twig snaps nearby, and we lift our heads, straining our ears for an attack that never comes. It's going to be a long night.

CHAPTER
FIVE

WE SLEEP IN SHIFTS, and I take the first one, one eye on the forest, alert to the slightest crackle of leaves underfoot or the snapping of a twig. All the while, I monitor the meat smoking over the fire.

Charaide snores softly within the tent, his deep breathing a comfort amongst the bitter bite of the first frost. Winter is coming. I can feel it in my bones. *Will I live to see the first snowfall?* I shake my head, once again trying to disperse such morbid thoughts. But they hound my mind, their frequency increasing since Laochard was killed. *Will I be next? What will happen to my family once I'm gone?*

I shiver, as much from the thoughts as from the frigid air. After tossing another log onto the fire, I rub my hands together. It's somewhat foolish, keeping the fire going when any manner of beast or enemy may be prowling the forest. But I worry my limbs will be too frozen to fight should any threat manifest. Besides, Marto made it clear that my only job for the first watch is to alert everyone else to the danger then barricade myself inside the tent as best I am able.

Your uncle will have our heads if anything were to happen to you.

His words echo in my brain, but part of me questions their validity. While I don't doubt that my uncle—and Cliste for that matter—would be angry at my demise, I suspect Brutach would take a small pleasure in me proving him right, proving that this trip was indeed a fool's errand and I acted the part of that fool.

The forest is quiet save for the crackle of the fire and Charaide's snores. With the breath of winter at their doorstep, many animals are seeking shelter where they can wait until spring. I envy them the luxury of being able to hide, to burrow in a warm den, safe from the elements and predators lurking about. If I thought I could hide myself and my family, I would. But nowhere seems safe. The rebels' reach is far and wide, and the tremors of discontent are spreading.

From the corner of my eye, I glimpse something tall and unnaturally bent slip through the trees. It moves with impossible grace. I snatch up my bow and crawl to the perimeter of our camp before taking careful aim. I nearly fire, thinking it one of the night beasts. But it vanishes before I can even pull the trigger. Its appearance feels like an omen, and I stare into the dark abyss, wondering what else slithers and haunts beyond the firelight.

When nothing else appears, I return to my post, leaning against a log and staring up at the canopy. The moon is close to full, but I cannot see it beyond the crowded branches. My thoughts return to brooding. It's a wonder, how much I can be hated for something beyond my control. I didn't ask to be born, to be a halfling. In the back of my mind, I can't help seeing the prejudices against me as overly ridiculous. Fae stole my father from his human parents, brought him to this world, raised him as one of their own, then had the audacity to act shocked and surprised when he fell in love with a faery.

Granted, had he fallen for a lesser fae, someone not of royal blood, perhaps his actions would have been overlooked. Fae had stolen human children for centuries, and several halflings were spread throughout not only our world but the human one as well. The changelings the fae left in a human baby's place often did not survive, but some who did procreated with the humans, though their offspring possessed no powers of their own. Changelings were strange, sickly beings. Born without magic, they were rejected by their fae parents and left to die in the human realm. For the most part, the humans were no kinder to these poor creatures. Often, they tried to give the changelings back in hopes their own babies would be returned. Only the rarest of humans accepted the changeling and raised it as their own.

What was done was done, and there's no help for it now. I scan the forest again, seeking the strange tall creature from before. Soon it will be time to wake Marto for his shift, though I'm in no hurry. After all of the hustle and bustle preparing for the coronation and then the devastation from the battle, I haven't had a moment alone with my thoughts. I relish the solitude. I never craved the attention of others, preferring my own company. Well, with the exception of Charaide, of course.

His breath stutters, and he shifts. A moment later, he emerges from the tent, bleary-eyed and yawning. He comes to sit by my side then pokes the fire with a stick.

"Marto hasn't relieved you yet?"

"I wasn't ready to wake him," I say, pulling my knees into my chest and gazing at the flames.

I can feel the weight of his stare as he looks me over, though I try to ignore it. There are so many things I wish I could say to him, but I do not want to risk our friendship or his dedication to the war effort. And with everything I have already lost, the thing I fear losing the most is the hope that someday, he may feel the same about me.

"You should get some rest." His voice is gruff from sleep. I envy him the ability to enjoy it.

"I'm not tired," I say, and I mean it. My senses are all on high alert, preparing for whatever we will face tomorrow when we reach the other side of the woods.

"You'll be in no shape to fight if you don't," he counters, and I look at him. The heat is gone from his gaze, replaced by a frown of concern.

"It's cold," I say, stalling. I fear what I will see when I close my eyes. Nightmares have been a constant companion since the battle at the coronation and always leave me breathless and shaking. My mind likes to replay the battle scene, when that faery took my father's head. I cringe.

"I will go wake Marto for his turn and return to the tent with you. Then we can share the blankets for warmth." His eyes soften as they meet mine. "Perhaps my presence will keep the nightmares at bay."

My eyes widen in surprise, but he just nods as if I've confirmed something. He knows me so well. I turn my head to the side so he can't see the rush of heat to my cheeks. I stand and slip into the tent then pull back the blankets, which are still warm and filled with his familiar scent of pine and smoke. I slide under them and curl on my side, facing the tent wall.

A moment later, he joins me. "Good night, Astreilles," he whispers, and it's the last thing I hear before I succumb to sleep.

"ASTREILLES, CHARAIDE," a gruff voice says as I'm roughly shaken. "Wake up."

I open my eyes. The forest is still shadowed, but a bit of the breaking dawn peeks in through the leafless trees. Marto kneels next to me, his face inches from mine.

"Is something wrong?"

His eyes flitter around us as if sensing danger. I sniff the air, but nothing smells amiss. My ears strain to hear any threat, but the trees are still and silent. Not even a breath of wind floats through them.

"We need to get a move on if we want to make it to the edge by nightfall." But his nostrils flare, causing me to roll onto my hands and knees, squinting into the grayish light of the morning. There's something… unnatural about the silence. It's not the comforting one I enjoyed last night by the crackling fire. This is otherworldly, and I suspect there's a creature nearby, watching us.

Charaide seems to sense it as well. "Stand slowly, and start packing. Don't let on that you know."

I nod, rising from the ground with as much nonchalance as I can muster. But I feel eyes taking in my every move, sizing me up. My breath is ragged, and I work to remain steady. I cannot show fear, not now, not without knowing what enemy lies within the mass of trees.

Bracing myself, I prepare to run, but Marto catches my hand and shakes his head. *Don't. Keep your movement slow and steady.*

I stare at him, still not used to having access to my magic or telepathic abilities. But I understand why he's using them. Whatever is hunting us is close, and he doesn't want it to hear.

Move like a human. Biting back a sarcastic retort, I follow his lead, allowing the human side of me to take over. It's not something I do often, since humans are considered so slow and stupid here.

I see it then, one yellow eye staring at me from a break in the trees. The rest of its form is camouflaged by the light filtering through the forest. Every muscle in my body tenses, and I struggle to maintain my composure.

We move as naturally as possible, packing up camp and putting out the fire. All the while, my ears are pricked for any sound, and my skin quivers with heightened awareness. The weight of the stare never leaves my shoulders, but I'm determined to ignore it.

Within a few minutes, we are packed and on the move. As we travel deeper into the trees, the feeling of being watched lessens as if the creature is unable to follow. I chance a glance back, but there is nothing behind us save trees and brush.

"What was that?" I whisper to Charaide.

He glances at me sideways. "A fachan. A horrible, deformed beast of a faery that covets the strength and power of other fae creatures. It was wise of you to move at a human's pace while packing. Had you tried to engage your magic or attempted to fly, it would have attacked."

"But couldn't it tell we were fae simply by our wings and features?"

His eyebrows pull together. "Probably, but halflings are less powerful and thus less attractive to such a beast." His lips lift in a grim smile. "One of the few positives of being a halfling, I suppose."

I shudder, pulling my quiver higher on my back. My beloved woods are no longer a comfort, though we have never traversed so far within them before. Marto walks ahead of us with Leiftea and Saki following. It's a comfort to know that any creature or fae wishing me harm would have to get through the four of them. Still, it's strange. If such a beast covets power, why didn't it strike? My magic may be untamed, but Charaide and the others have honed theirs for years. *Perhaps it sensed something in me it found unworthy... or something it feared. Monster recognizing monster.*

"How do you know so much?" I ask, more to break the silence than anything else.

He shrugs. "I've been fascinated by the different species of fae all my life. Where they live, how they came to be." A light flush caresses his cheeks. "I have studied the human world as well, or at least, as much as I could."

My mouth drops, and I turn to him. "Why?"

His throat bobs as he swallows. "To understand you. Or... that part of you."

I squeeze his arm, touched by his words. While a large faction of the kingdom hates me solely for my human side, here is a pure-blood who wants to understand it, to understand me. My visits to the human realm with my father were interesting, but I never felt safe there. Perhaps one day, I'll see it differently. Not as an exile but as an escape. Impulsively, I lean toward him and plant a soft kiss on his cheek. "Thank you. That means a lot."

His face breaks into a rueful grin. "I mean, I'd hoped that studying your human side would explain some of your quirks, but I'm afraid I didn't have much luck."

My lips twist in annoyance, then I can't help but laugh. We continue on our way to the forest's edge. There is no path, but between my compass and Marto's keen sense of direction, I can tell we're getting close. The trees thin out, and the scent of camp-fires fills my nostrils.

Marto slows his pace until we join him. "We should hide until dusk. That's likely when they'll change the guard. Then we can slip in quietly and see what we can discover."

I nod, my heart pounding in my chest. The men scatter amongst the trees, and Charaide and I hide behind thick brush. He slips something into my hand, a piece of bread. We've snacked on the smoked meat and other food we packed as we made our way through the trees, but we haven't had a moment to stop and eat a full meal. My stomach grumbles as I quickly gobble the bread.

Charaide's ears prick at a sound beyond the trees, and I strain to hear as well. My faery ears aren't as pointed as his, betraying my human side. But I can still make out the murmur of voices, the sound of metal clashing, and the pound of feet on earth. My breath catches in my throat. The rebel army is on the other side of these trees, at the forest's edge. If we're caught... I don't allow myself to finish that thought.

The minutes pass agonizingly slowly as the sun sets around us, turning the forest into a gray-and-blue hue. Without their leaves, the branches create skeletal shapes that appear almost menacing against the advancing twilight.

Let's go. Marto's voice sounds in my head.

Charaide grasps my hand, pulling me to my feet. Together, we slip through the trees, floating above the crackling leaves on softly beating wings. As we fly, my wings brush against the limbs hanging just above my head.

When we reach the edge of the forest, Charaide lands noiselessly on a clear spot of dirt. I join him, holding my breath as we survey the enemy camp. We have timed our approach well. No guards are in sight.

As we move closer to the camp, the hunter in me takes over, and I prowl along the ground, as silent and deadly as a jungle cat I once saw while visiting the human world with my father. Its black belly slithered soundlessly over the earth as it followed its prey, a doe, much like the one I killed last night. No noise came from its movements, not a snapping twig or brush of leaf, and the deer was unaware. When the cat pounced, it sliced through the air like it could fly and landed cleanly, snapping the doe's neck. I was both awed and repulsed by it, but it had taught me the value of staying low and quiet, of not revealing my presence until I was ready for the kill.

Split up, Marto commands in my head.

Part of me wonders if I shouldn't be the one giving the orders, but I have yet to practice my magic beyond small spells. I wouldn't have the first clue how to send thoughts to the others.

We reach a tent on the outskirts of the camp, straining to hear, but no voices or rustling of bodies reach our ears. I chance a glance at Charaide, but he shrugs. As we slip through the tents, careful to stick to the shadows, I realize why the camp isn't bustling with activity. Everyone appears to have gathered in a large tent in the middle. We creep closer, my heart racing. If we're caught now, there's no chance we'll be able to escape.

Charaide stops several feet from the main tent. Snippets of the conversation reach me, but I suspect my friend can pick up much more. The effort makes my head hurt. I sigh and debate moving closer, but Charaide puts a hand on my arm.

I can let you in my head if you want. His eyes are hesitant, and I understand his reluctance. There is no way to filter his thoughts from the thoughts of the rebels. I will hear everything.

I put a hand over his and squeeze, wanting him to know that I understand if he doesn't wish to open up to me like that. He closes his eyes, and at first, all I hear is him telling himself to focus. Then the voices become clearer.

"... forces were stronger than we anticipated, even with the surprise attack. We'll have to be better prepared and send more troops."

"We've lost enough of our soldiers as it is," replies a deep male voice tinged with rage. "If we have any hope of defeating these *veilcling* imposters, we need a better strategy."

I wince at the insult, and Charaide shoots me a sympathetic look. Such language shouldn't surprise me. I've been called similar insults before. *Veilrat. Veilcling. Shadowling.* All are meant to convey the two halves of my being and the veil between them. But the venom behind the words still stings.

"At least we killed the human," another says, the tone malicious. "No chance of that mutt being the queen's consort or, worse, getting his own throne."

Raucous laughter follows, and I fight to control the rage simmering deep in my belly. Breathing deeply in through my nose and out through my mouth, I push beyond this conversation, hoping to hear other rebels. *How many of them are in there? Could our small group take them out now, before they have a chance in hell of strategizing their next attack?*

"What does our spy say?" the first voice asks.

"Not much," the malicious voice says. "It's hard to get word in and out of the castle with it being on lockdown. But our plan to delay our next attack may assist with that. Anything to get them to let their guard down."

"We can't hold off much longer. I don't want that human's plaything sullying the throne."

The simmering rage spikes, and I move to stand, ready to rip out the throat of whoever spoke, but Charaide puts his other hand on my shoulder, pushing me back down. He shakes his head, and the message is clear: *Hold it together. Don't lose it now, here, when we're vulnerable.*

"Our reinforcements should arrive in the next few days," the malicious voice continues. "And by then, I expect to have more intel."

My eyes meet Charaide's, and he presses his lips into a thin line. They are bringing in more troops and planning another attack in mere days. At least that's something to go on.

"We should just send in the assassins to take out the half-breed swine," another voice chimes in.

"There's time for that yet," the malicious voice replies. "But it's harder for them to get in with the castle on high alert. Better to distract the royal army with chaos to allow our brethren to do what they do best."

"Some army," the deep voice sneers. "I heard it's being led by that halfling girl."

"Can she even ride in all those petticoats?"

"I'll give her something she can ride," the malicious voice taunts.

Charaide's eyes flash, and it's my turn to hold him back from storming in there.

A bright light flashes before us, and I drop his hand to shield my eyes. The voices in the tent stop, and suddenly, the camp is overrun with rebel soldiers shouting to each other. Charaide grabs my hand and pulls me to my feet, and we run.

We make it to the edge of the camp, where Marto and the other royal soldiers join us. Another blinding light strikes. I throw up my hands, trying to make out what's causing these flashes. Then a woman dressed in a white gossamer gown appears in the middle of the clearing. She looks around at the camp as the men charge straight toward her. Her gaze alights on our small group, and she smiles and beckons to me. I glance at Charaide and the others, unsure of which is worse, getting caught by the rebels or surrendering to whatever strange fae creature has appeared before us. After hearing what the men plan to do with me, I opt for the lady in white.

I release Charaide's hand and race to her side. As soon as we enter her circle of light, we vanish, flying through the night at a speed that makes my stomach turn. When we land, I somersault onto the ground, the wind knocked out of me. I lie there staring at the sky, preparing for whatever fate may befall us.

The lady peers down at me, her face still shining with the brilliant light that blinded me at the camp. Her eyes are like silver stars, and I swear they twinkle as she raises an eyebrow. "Do you plan to lie there all night?"

I shake my head and scramble to my feet. Charaide is crouched beside me, his hand on his sword. Marto and his men are in similar defensive positions behind me.

My gaze travels over the clearing where we landed. I've never been to this part of the forest. A small log cabin stands behind her, with a smoking chimney and a few lights shining from the windows. It looks ordinary, but a current of magic surrounds this place. I glance at Charaide, and his face is set in a grim line, but he doesn't acknowledge me.

"Who are you, and where have you brought us?" I hope I sound more authoritative than I feel.

"Come to the cabin and get warm, then I'll tell you all," she says as she glides up the dirt path. She has no wings, but I swear her feet do not touch the ground.

I swallow, wondering if I should have taken my chances with the rebels, but Charaide stands and offers a hand to help me up. He doesn't let go as we follow the lady along the path and into the cabin.

The outside is nondescript, but the inside may as well be a palace. Beautiful tapestries hang from the windows, which do not match the ones I saw outside. These windows flow from floor to ceiling, and I gape at the bright light of the dawn shining in. I peek over my shoulder at the door we just passed through, and sure enough, it is still pitch-black outside. Rubbing my eyes, I take a few tentative steps deeper into the palace. The floors are black and white marble tiles, and the walls are clear stone. A large fireplace sits at the bottom of a tall staircase, and I resist the urge to rush over and warm myself. The bitter cold has sunk into my bones, and the adrenaline from the chase is wearing off, though my heart still pounds in my chest as I take in the rest of the cottage and our rescuer.

"Please sit by the fire and warm yourselves. Food will be provided shortly." She gestures to the wooden chairs near the roaring fire. After sleeping on the ground last night, I find a straight-backed chair too tempting to resist. I release Charaide's hand and make my way over.

Charaide and Marto take their time following me. The men are apprehensive of this strange woman and enchanted cottage. Leiftea and Saki refuse to even leave the door.

A moment later, a small Brownie with tiny wisps for wings brings over a tray of food and warm beverages. The Brownie sets it down on the table between our chairs before giving a short curtsy and going on her way. Charaide and I stare, first at the food then at each other. Aside from the bread and bits of deer meat, we haven't eaten much today. I'm not sure if we'll be able to return to the majority of our supplies. My stomach grumbles as my mouth waters, but I hesitate. We need to know who this lady is and determine whether we can trust her before we fully embrace her hospitality.

"I understand your hesitation." The lady passes by my side and stands in front of the fire, her back to us as she rubs her hands for warmth. I see the glint in Charaide's eyes as he calculates his odds of killing her. She must be very trusting or extremely powerful, as she doesn't turn for some time. When she finally does, her face is alight with a beautiful smile.

"My name is Caillea." She bows before me. "I'm pleased to meet you, Princess Astreilles."

It's been a while since someone addressed me by my full title, and my mouth falls open. I quickly recover and stand, recalling my lessons in royal etiquette from childhood.

"The pleasure is mine," I say with a curtsy. I resume my seat, and she places an arm along the mantel as she looks at each of us.

"I'm glad I found you before the rebels did," she continues. "They likely would have torn you to shreds before you made it back to the safety of the forest."

Charaide clears his throat, and I can almost read the thought on his face. The forest, while a place we both love, isn't something either of us would ever describe as "safe." Not with all manner of creatures that inhabit its depths.

"Who are you, exactly?" he asks, his gaze boring into her as if he may be able to dig out any secrets she is keeping.

"I'm a sorceress," she replies. "I used to be at the king's command until he banished me for sharing predictions he didn't like." She shrugs, a wry smile on her face. "I guess he never heard of not shooting the messenger."

I frown as I remember the sorceress who freed me from my iron bonds just a few days before. It was not the woman standing before me. But then I vaguely recall a sorceress who used to visit with my grandfather in my youth, though it has been many years since I last saw them meet. I cock my head, studying her. *What horrors did she predict that caused my grandfather to dismiss her services?*

As if reading my mind, she continues, "I'm sorry to see that my predictions are at last coming true."

"What were they? Your predictions, I mean?" Charaide asks, drawing her attention from me.

"That the king would die and leave a country in chaos." Her eyes flick to me. "His own distaste for your parents' union did little to defuse the growing discontent at the idea of having a halfling as ruler. Or even a human lover as queen." She sighs. "I tried to warn him, to show him how to appease his people and teach them to embrace their future, but to no avail." Her eyes sweep over the room. "And so I was banished to this log cabin to live out the rest of my days."

"It hardly seems like much of a punishment," Marto grumbles, and I'm inclined to agree.

"Well, I made a few minor adjustments," she counters with a teasing grin. "He couldn't very well strip me of my magic, now could he?" Her gaze darts to my wrists. "At least, not with the primitive means that control the halflings." She waves a hand. "But I've been waiting for you, young princess."

"F-For me?" I ask, my eyes widening. "Why?"

"The rebels have been building their armies just outside of these woods for weeks, but my visions told me you would come to stop them. And here you are."

I shake my head. "We didn't come to stop them. We're on a scouting mission to gather information to take back to my mother and uncle."

Something dark crosses her eyes at the mention of my family, but it clears before I can question it. "You're lucky to have escaped, then. Fortunately, I have watched these woods, waiting for you. I hoped to catch you before you made it to the camp, but at least we were able to evanesce before they caught you."

"What do you want with me?" I glance at Charaide, but his expression is guarded as he waits for Caillea's response.

"To help you in any way I can." She moves closer to me and sinks to the ground by my chair. "I'm hoping you will be more receptive to my gifts, the messages I have to pass on, than your grandfather was."

I nod, not quite sure what to think, but it can't hurt to hear her out. "I will listen to whatever you wish to share."

She smiles. "Just as I suspected. Perhaps it is your human side that grants you an open mind and heart." Her eyes flutter closed, and she settles onto the floor before crossing her legs under her skirt. I watch as her breath evens out, her hands laid open on her knees, palms up.

We should leave while she's distracted. Marto's voice comes into my mind.

I gape at him. He can't be serious. As soon as I stand to go, she'll sense it and stop us. Besides, I want to hear her out.

I raise an eyebrow, hoping to convey that I'm curious about the future she claims to see.

She's a charlatan. Marto's eyes are cold. *The king banished her for a reason. This is a waste of our time. We need to get back, warn the others.*

"I know what you're saying to each other," she murmurs, not opening her eyes.

Marto grimaces, but I just shrug. She *is* a sorceress, after all, and clearly a powerful one at that. He should have known better than to broadcast his thoughts.

She opens her eyes and meets my gaze. "There is a dark force at work."

Charaide snorts. "We know. We just left their camp."

"Not there," she whispers, her eyes never leaving my face. "Within."

"Within... me?" I press a finger to my chest.

"No, within your castle." She closes her eyes again, and when she opens them, they seem clouded. "You will succeed in pushing the rebels back. But be careful who you trust. Someone works against you. A shadow, a spy." A moment passes, then her voice deepens. "Beware the creation. It will be your destruction."

A chill runs down my spine, but before I can ask her to explain those foreboding words, she blinks, and the strange trance she seemed to be under dissipates. A frown creases her forehead, and she rubs her temples.

"What the hell does that even mean?" Charaide demands. "'Beware the creation. It will be your destruction.'"

I lean forward, desperate to learn the answer as well. Whatever the "creation" is, it will surely kill me. *Just add it to a growing list, I guess.*

Caillea glances over at him, her brow furrowing. "Hmm?"

"That's what you said," I say. "A moment ago, you said that something was working against me."

"Ah, my gifts sometimes manifest in ways for which I am not present." She stands and steps over to a table at the back of the room then returns with a quill and parchment. "But if you please, write down what was said, and I will help to decipher it."

I do as she asks, my hand quivering as I finish the message. The rebels must be the dark force, but she had said before that someone... someone I trust is working against me. I swallow as I hand her the parchment. She reads over my scrawl, her eyes widening.

"I-I don't know what the creation is. But the rest..." She raises her eyes to mine. "Be careful who you trust, young Astreilles. Allies can turn into enemies in the blink of an eye."

Charaide scoffs and stands. "Come on, Astreilles. We're leaving." He holds out a hand for mine.

I glance between his outstretched palm and Caillea's face. We do need to return to the castle. My uncle will be waiting for our report, but I am not ready to leave just yet.

Caillea nods as if in understanding. "Do not fret, Astreilles. We will see each other again soon." Her gaze travels over Charaide then to the royal soldiers who stand just beyond the cabin door. "After all, you will need someone to teach you how to wield your magic if you hope to succeed against the rebels." She bows low. "I am at your disposal, my lady."

I bite my lip, trying to hide my discomfort. I never quite got used to the bowing and scraping throughout my life. Most people at the castle who know me don't bother anymore.

I stall at the door. "How can I reach you?"

Her lips curve in an enigmatic smile, and she crosses the room to a box on the mantel. When she returns, she holds an amulet. "Whisper my name thrice while holding this, and I will come to you."

My head is full of questions I'm not sure I should ask, and I don't even know how to do so. But before I can open my mouth, Charaide takes my arm and yanks me out into the bitter cold, where Marto and the men are waiting for us.

CHAPTER

SIX

WE WALK FOR SEVERAL HOURS, Charaide and Marto determined to put as much distance between us and the sorceress as possible. When we finally make camp, my legs are stiff and leaden, as much from the walking as the cold. Charaide starts a fire while the soldiers pitch our tents. I pass the time scrounging for food. Our supplies have dwindled since our visit to the war camp and Caillea's cabin. The deer meat remains with our packs at the forest's edge, likely discovered by the rebels by now.

I take my quiver and bow, but I don't expect to get so lucky with a deer again. Perhaps a squirrel or rabbit will slip out of its den. Late-fall berries are on a nearby bush, and I pick several, keeping a wary eye out for prey and other hunters.

Caillea's words echo in my mind. *Beware the creation. It will be your destruction.*

The creation of what? Are the rebels hiding a weapon of some kind? My heart pounds in my ears. *How will we defend ourselves if we don't know what it is?* Perhaps our little group should try to sneak back to the war camp and gather more information. But my stomach churns at the very idea of setting foot near those rebels again, especially considering what they want to do to me.

Out of the corner of my eye, I see a movement that catches my attention, and I turn slowly, threading an arrow into my bow. After one hop then two, the rabbit ventures out, sniffing the air for food or danger or both. I draw back my bow, waiting for the right moment to strike. The rabbit heads for the berries, unaware of my presence. I suppose that after I've spent the last two days out in the wild, my scent is muffled by the dirt and grime covering my skin.

I duck behind a bush, careful not to make a sound and startle my prey. When I have a clear shot, I say a quick prayer and let the arrow fly. The rabbit falls, its white fur stained dark red. For some strange reason, my mind conjures up a terrifying image of Caillea in her white gossamer gown, covered in blood. It makes me sick to my stomach, and I shake my head, dispelling the thought. I've no idea where it came from, but I force myself to gather my kill. It's hardly an adequate dinner for five people, but I have no desire to spend another moment alone.

When I return, Charaide smiles, his eyes alighting on the dead rabbit. Without a word, he takes the kill from me and skins it. The fire is warm and inviting, so I sit while he prepares the rabbit. The soldiers are not at the camp, and I presume they have gone to try their luck at hunting.

A comfortable silence settles between us, and I can't help thinking how nice it would be to stay here, just the two of us, and live off the land. No more royal duties, no armies to lead, no more death threats. Just me and my best friend, living out the rest of our days in peace with the animals in the forest.

Charaide sits beside me and hands me a stick of rabbit meat. We hold our skewers over the flames.

"What do you think she meant?" he asks, breaking the silence. "About the creation being your destruction."

"Probably just some cryptic mumbo jumbo that she hopes might mean something one day." I don't know why I'm lying to him, but I suspect it has something to do with his actions at the cottage. He clearly didn't buy a word of what Caillea said. "I suspect she's hoping either I or my mother will reestablish her standing at court."

He laughs, but there's an edge to it. "That sounds about right." His brow furrows. "Still, it's ominous, isn't it? That something is going to destroy you?"

With one hand, I wave behind us, toward the rebels' war camp. "I'd say it's pretty obvious what that something is."

"But what if the rebels are just a distraction?" He doesn't meet my gaze. "What if there's something much worse that we aren't aware of, that we haven't anticipated?"

"Like what?" My thoughts return to the potential weapon the rebels have created, but it's hard to focus on that when I'm facing an entire army.

"I don't know." He heaves a sigh. "I just can't shake this feeling that we're missing something."

"We could go back." I hope I sound more confident than I feel. "Gather more information."

"No." The forcefulness of that one word shakes me to my core. He must realize how harsh he sounds because he softens his tone. "We should return to the castle as soon as possible. The army may be on the move in the next few days, and we need to warn everyone."

"And then what?" I murmur, pulling my stick from the fire. Though I've no stomach for food, I force myself to nibble on the meat. "How am I supposed to lead our armies? What am I supposed to do with the intelligence we gathered?"

His hand covers mine, and he gives me a gentle squeeze. "We'll figure it out, Ast. I won't let you do this alone."

I wish I found his words comforting, but I don't. Charaide and

I are great at many things, but neither of us has any combat experience. And while he's had his whole life to learn how to control and wield his magic, I only recently gained access to mine. There's no way I'll be able to harness it by the time we meet the rebels again in battle.

Stifling a groan, I focus on my dinner. It would be a shame to waste such a good kill, and I'll need my energy for the long trek through the forest tomorrow.

But my anxiety grows the longer I think about what I'll face when we return. I'll have to raise our armies, ready them to fight, and lead them... *Where? To the camp itself?* The element of surprise is no longer on the table. Even if the rebels haven't figured out who we are, they will likely be on their guard after our last visit. They've probably moved on by now.

Or perhaps they won't. Maybe part of the rebels' plan is to lure us into a false sense of security, make us think we have the element of surprise on our side. Then once they've removed us from the fortifications of the castle, they'll strike and annihilate us.

Charaide tosses another log onto our fire, and I flinch as flames shoot into the sky. It's enough to pull me from my thoughts but not enough to quell the apprehension building within me.

"Is the smoke from the fire or your head? I can't tell anymore," Charaide teases as he cleans up the remnants of our meal.

I roll my eyes while fighting a smile. "I'm just... thinking."

"No, you're worrying." He takes my stick and flings it into the fire. "There's a difference."

"Can you blame me?"

His eyes meet mine, and I hate the pity I see there. I move to turn away, but his fingers catch my chin and hold firm, forcing me to look at him.

"You're stronger than you give yourself credit for."

If only I could believe him. I lift my head from his grasp and sink it into my hands.

"Besides," he says in a cheerful tone, "you have Cliste to help you strategize."

The queasiness eases but only slightly. Yes, my younger brother will take whatever information I can give him and figure out our next steps. But he can only suggest and persuade. Ultimately, the decision is mine.

Leaves crunch beneath heavy boots behind us, and I turn quickly. The soldiers have returned with several fresh fish.

"I see you have already eaten." Marto sets the fish down on the makeshift table Charaide made to skin the rabbit. "But we have plenty if you're still hungry."

I shake my head, not up for more socializing. "I'm going to get some sleep." I glance at Charaide. "Wake me when it's my turn to take watch."

WE ARRIVE at the castle in the late evening the next day. The rebels did not follow us into the woods, and as far as we can tell, they have no plans to move out in the near future. As soon as I've entered the castle gates, I'm whisked to the throne room, where my uncle and Cliste are waiting for me.

"How did it go?" Uncle Brutach asks before I've even had a chance to catch my breath.

"I'm not sure that we learned much, but we were able to get in and out of the camp mostly unscathed."

He raises an eyebrow. "What do you mean, 'mostly unscathed'?"

"There was... an incident," I begin. Charaide enters the room and gives me an encouraging nod. "We were listening to the men talking in the tent when a bright light flashed, blinding us. The rebels saw it as well and came storming through the camp to find the source. We ran, with them on our heels, when we saw another flash, and a woman appeared before us."

"A woman?" Uncle Brutach furrows his brow. "Why would a woman be out—" His hand rubs over his face. "Caillea." It's said as more of an expletive than a name.

"You know her?" I move to the table where he and my brother are still poring over a map.

"Unfortunately." He swears. "I'd hoped she'd moved on by now, or died, but I suppose we're not so lucky."

"Well, she saved us from the rebels, so you'll forgive me if I'm a little less unkind," I continue. Charaide shoots me a warning glare, but I ignore him. "She told me to be careful because there is a spy inside the castle, though she didn't tell me who it was."

Brutach snorts. "I highly doubt that. We've vetted everyone inside these walls. And they have all proven their loyalty during the last battle with the rebels."

"Someone tipped them off about the king's impending death," I retort. "And they clearly knew enough detail regarding both his funeral and Mother's coronation to attack us."

My uncle's face darkens. "We're still working to determine how that occurred." He raises an eyebrow. "Anything else?"

I bite my lip, unsure exactly how to explain the rest of Caillea's message. "She did say something that I have not been able to decipher."

"Which was?" Cliste leans away from the table, fixing me with a questioning gaze.

"She said 'Beware the creation. It will be your destruction.'" I glance at Charaide before surveying my uncle. "Does that mean anything to you?"

He waves a dismissive hand. "No, but that old witch was known for spouting nonsense. I wouldn't give her warning another thought."

"She went into a trance as she said it," Charaide counters, his lips pressing into a hard line. "I think we should at least keep it in mind as we prepare for war."

My uncle sneers. "If you want to waste time worrying about the nonsensical ramblings of a failed sorceress, be my guest." He gestures to Cliste to continue whatever they were doing when we walked in. "The rest of us have more important matters at present."

I put a cautioning hand on Charaide's arm as his face flushes with anger. He and I will look into this at our leisure. It does no one any good to argue about it now.

"We also learned that the rebels are delaying their next attack," I continue, carefully changing the subject. "They're awaiting reinforcements and hoping that the delay will be enough for us to let down our guard."

"Then we should go on the offensive." Cliste slaps the map. "They won't know we're coming, and we can gain ground. Force them back, away from the castle."

Brutach purses his lips. "It's an idea, but we can't be sure their plans won't change if they learn it was the princess who entered their camp the other night. And while I do not believe the sorceress, if there is indeed a spy in our midst, they could share our plans. We should be cautious."

"Caution is only going to leave us as sitting ducks," Cliste shot back. "We don't need to spare many men." He turns his attention to me. "How many would you say were in the camp?"

"A few hundred or so," I reply, pointing out on the map the area where we found them. "We likely could avoid hand-to-hand combat by attacking with magic when they don't expect it."

"And whose magic do you plan to wield?" Brutach asks, his voice hard. "Yours isn't a match against true fae."

I wince at the harshness of his words, but he's right. What powers I have are limited both by my human side and by their disuse. It will take a miracle for me to learn how to wield them in time for what's coming.

Charaide's eyes flash, and I quickly speak before he says something we'll both regret. "But surely our forces have enough magic between them to avoid bloodshed for as long as possible."

"They rightly do," Brutach says. "However, they will look to you as their leader, and if you cannot rise to the occasion, you will lose not only their trust but their loyalty." He shakes his head. "You need to increase your training. Have you found someone to teach you how to wield your magic?" Charaide opens his mouth, but my uncle raises a hand. "Someone who is *qualified* to teach a princess?"

My gaze drops to the floor as I wring my hands. For not the first time, I wish my eldest brother were still here. As the firstborn and next in line to the throne, Laochard possessed magic stronger than mine, as he'd had the entirety of his short lifetime to build on his powers and train his faery side. I am out of both time and options.

Caillea had as much as offered to train me, but my uncle's reaction to her appearance tells me that he wouldn't welcome that suggestion any more than he would welcome Charaide offering.

"The royal sorceress, Medea, may be able to at least teach me some basics before we leave."

"And I am happy to teach her as well," Charaide pipes up. "I've trained most of our soldiers. The only difference between them and Ast is a title."

My uncle's expression darkens, and I cringe. "Try a royal bloodline. And it's Princess Astreilles, commander of our armies." He points at Charaide. "You would do well to remember that when we face our enemies in battle."

"And *you* would do well to remember that even without training, *Princess Astreilles*"— Charaide's voice takes on a mocking tone

—"held her own when our enemies showed up on our doorstep. She defended the castle with the best of our archers."

Brutach rolls his eyes. "No one is denying that my niece is excellent with a bow and arrow. But we're not talking about her archery skills. We're discussing the responsibility of leading a magical army, and I stand by the fact that she is not ready."

"Then what about you?" I ask, growing weary of this argument. "What if we assign our strongest soldiers to your battalion? Cliste and I can be ready for a physical assault, but you lead the magical one."

Brutach strokes his chin as if considering my words, and I hold my breath. "It's not a terrible idea."

Such high praise. Irritation swells in my chest, but I keep my expression neutral because, for once, he's agreeing with me.

"But one battalion of magical fighters will not be enough to win this war. You should train as much as you can over the next couple of days. Unless you have any objection, I suggest we leave at the week's end."

Less than a week to train. Awesome. I force myself to smile. "That sounds reasonable to me."

My uncle's eyebrows pull together. "Tell no one else of our plans until the last possible moment."

Relief sweeps through me, the tension in my shoulders dissipating. I'm suddenly very aware of how tired I am. Cliste nods, rolling up the map, and I trudge out of the great room with Charaide on my heels. It occurs to me as I head to my chambers that we decided all of this without so much as consulting the queen.

I train for the next few days with the sorceress, Charaide, and Brutach, as well as anyone and everyone who will help me. Even

Mother and I go a few rounds, which lifts my spirits since it's the first she's been out of bed since I returned. My magical ability is rudimentary at best, and I still find myself preferring my arrows. I can't seem to help it. The suppression of my magic for most of my life has forced me to learn other strengths. And now I struggle with accessing and harnessing my powers. When this is all over, my mother and I are going to have a long talk about the law that restricts halflings from using magic.

"You're thinking too much," the sorceress says for the tenth time. "Your mind is getting in the way of your power. Let it flow through you. Don't hold back."

I grit my teeth, biting back all the things I want to say. It's been a tense session, since we have only one more day before we leave. They might as well leave me here for as much use as I'll be on the battlefield, magically or otherwise.

"Stop denigrating yourself." Medea's tone is sharp.

I glance up at her, vacillating between surprise and horror. *Did she read my mind again?* It has been a source of contention between us since I meekly asked-slash-begged her to teach me.

Just as I'm about to call her out on it, she holds up a hand. "It's written all over your face, Princess. I don't *need* telepathy."

My eyes close, holding in the tears that have formed behind them. I will *not* cry. But even as I tell myself that, a tear slides down my cheek. I brush it off in frustration.

"Take a deep breath," Charaide calls from the sidelines, and I look at him. "You can do this. You're the only thing standing in the way of your power." He taps his temple with his finger, a smile tugging on his lips. "You think too much for your own good."

I stick my tongue out at him, and he laughs. But he's right. I'm too much in my head, so worried that I'll fail that I'm causing the stagnation in my power.

Instead of starting again, I glance at the other fae that are training nearby. Most of them have been gifted with an elemental magic. Some spark fire from their fingertips and wield its destruction in precise attacks. Others draw air into strong gusts of wind, sending it whipping through the training field with deadly accuracy.

My heart sinks. It seems to come to them so naturally, but every time I try to access my power, it doesn't respond. Perhaps it was dormant too long. Or maybe prolonged exposure to the iron has weakened it beyond repair.

With a deep breath, I shake out my hands, my wings, my head, hoping to dispel my doubts. I breathe in through my nose and out through my mouth. Part of me wonders if allowing Charaide to watch these sessions was a bad idea. His presence seems to only increase my anxiety over my poor performance.

"That's it," Medea says. "Now, imagine your power as a light inside of you. Build that power from your core, up through your chest, moving into your shoulders, down your arms, and out through your hands."

Visualizing powers I've never used is difficult, but I try. I feel a warmth in my chest as I work to imagine the light. It's green, the light I see. Beautiful, deep forest green, swirling in my chest and moving through my body to my hands. When I open my eyes, my hands are actually glowing, and I blink in disbelief, my magic faltering.

"You're doing it, Astreilles, just don't think about it. Allow yourself to feel. Do you feel it building? Like a wave rising as it heads toward the shore?"

I nod, though it's not exactly the way I would describe it. It's more like a river, a fluid coursing through my veins. But the flow feels stuck in my hands, as if they're damming my power.

"Now you need to let it go." Medea moves back, gesturing to the target in front of me.

My heart pounds as I hold up my hands and point them where I want my power to go. But nothing happens. The flow is starting to become unbearable as it continues to build. I close my eyes, willing my hands to release the pressure.

"Focus, Astreilles," Medea whispers. "Clear your mind and imagine that light shooting out of you."

"I believe in you, Astreilles," Charaide calls, and his praise ignites something in my chest.

An explosion sounds, and my eyes fly open. The target stands before me completely unscathed. The tree behind it, on the other hand...

"Well, at least you hit... something." Charaide tries and fails to keep a straight face.

"Ugh, I'm useless!" My head dips forward, and I put my hands in my hair, debating whether to rip it out.

"You're not useless." Charaide comes up beside me and gently lifts my chin. "But you can't close your eyes and expect to hit a target." After stepping behind me, he lifts my hands in his own and holds them toward the target. "Now, build your power again. I'll help you aim."

It's hard to concentrate with him so close. The warmth coursing through me isn't the magic I felt a moment ago. His skin against mine is like lightning, and the flush of his broad chest against my back makes me too aware of him. It's all I can do not to brush my lips against his. I shake my head, trying to rid my mind of these distracting thoughts. I'll never hit the target at this rate.

"Deep breath in," he says into my ear.

I resist the shivers running down my spine as his breath tickles my skin. I obey, breathing in through my nose, both to center my power and to calm my raging hormones. If he senses the latter, he doesn't let on.

The power builds again deep within my belly, following the same pathway as before. I don't close my eyes this time, determined not to miss the target again. As my hands spark with green energy, I raise my head, focusing everything I have on the target.

Charaide pushes me forward, bringing my hands and power closer to our goal.

"Let go, Astreilles," he breathes, and I do.

Flames shoot from my hand, the green light twisting as the target catches fire. My chest tightens. *Is this truly fire... or something else wearing its shape?*

Charaide pats me on the back with a chuckle. "The rebels won't stand a chance against you if you can keep doing that."

"Does this mean my element is fire?" I take a step away from Charaide and direct my question to Medea.

She shrugs. "I'm not sure, but it's definitely possible. Regardless, it's not a bad thing."

A rueful smile tugs at Charaide's lips. "Well, as long as you don't set the whole forest on fire, I suppose."

I frown. Every faery has an elemental magic. I was hoping for water, as it's one of the easiest elements to wield. Fire is powerful but too destructive in the wrong hands. With a sigh, I shake my head. If fire is my element, I need to learn how to contain it so as not to risk the lives of the soldiers I lead. Lifting my hands, I draw on my magic once more.

CHAPTER

SEVEN

THE MORNING we are set to leave, the servants help me with my armor, if it can be called that. Most fae are susceptible only to iron, but as a halfling, I also possess all of the human frailties, which means every vulnerable inch is swaddled in plates or leather. How I'm expected to fire arrows in all of this, let alone wield my magic, is beyond me. It's a wonder the rebels have amassed such an army to take out my family and me. *Wouldn't it be simpler to use assassins who can slip in and out of the castle, slitting our throats in the night?*

We've gone over our strategy several times. My uncle's battalion will lead the fray, trying to take out the rebels with magic. Then, once my brother and I have joined him, we'll engage our archers before we move to hand-to-hand combat.

I slide my quiver over my shoulder. A belt is added to my armor, a sword sheathed on its side. I slip a blade into my boot and stand, staring at my reflection. There are bags under my green eyes, more evidence of how I've struggled to sleep the past few days. Even though each night, I climb into bed exhausted from a day of training, the nightmares continue, and I have spent many nights staring at the ceiling, wondering if I'll survive the upcoming battle.

"My lady," says Feidre, my personal attendant, "it is time."

I take a deep breath and square my shoulders, though they feel heavier. So much is riding on me, and the weight is crushing. Feidre seems to understand as she pats my back, a sympathetic smile on her lips.

"Thank you." My voice cracks with emotion.

Her eyes soften in understanding. "May your arrows be swift, your aim be true, and may the enemy fall at your feet."

"We would be so lucky," I murmur before walking out the door. I don't look back, afraid that if I do, I won't be able to take the necessary steps toward my uncle and brother, who are awaiting me in the throne room.

When I enter, I blink at finding my mother there as well. Her green eyes are filled with worry as her gaze moves over my armor and the quiver on my back. She rushes forward, arms flung open, and pulls me into a fierce embrace. I blink again if only to stop the tears that threaten to spill over my cheeks. I must be strong for her.

"We should get a move on," my uncle calls, interrupting our moment. "If we hope to reach the edge of the forest by sunset of the second day, we must make haste."

I nod, swallowing thickly as I release my mother. She touches my cheek, and I force a smile. "Do not worry, Mama. I will protect you with my life."

Her watery gaze does nothing for my resolve. "That's what I fear most." She lifts my hand and presses it to her heart. "Please be careful."

"I promise," I say, though the words feel empty.

She moves to the side as I approach my uncle and brother. Cliste goes over the plan one last time to make sure we're all in agreement, then we leave to rally our troops and begin the march.

In the courtyard of the castle, the villagers have poured in to see us off. Their faces are solemn as we form our lines, and I know they hold hope for our good fortune. It's not only my family that I fight to protect but also these innocents, who will be caught in the crossfire if the rebels bring their fight here. They've already lost so much in the last attack.

"Mount up," my uncle commands, barely giving me so much as a second glance.

I obey, climbing upon the back of my black steed. Cliste and my uncle follow suit, with Charaide mounting a mare behind me. I spare one last glance at my mother, who is surrounded by my younger siblings, four of the remaining six of us, clinging to her skirts. With a silent prayer to the deity my father believed in, I turn my horse and lead the way out of the gates.

More villagers line the streets as we parade past, just as they did during my mother's coronation procession. But no smiles or cheers erupt to send us on our way.

I keep my head high and my back straight as I ride by, hoping to instill in them some faith, some hope of our victory, even though I doubt it myself. My uncle and brother ride on my flanks with Charaide and other knights riding behind them. The rest of our army—at least, the portions we're bringing with us—march on foot. Uncle Brutach said it was meant to be a show of force and power. Personally, I find it more than a little ridiculous since we'll have to dismount when we enter the forest. The limbs and brush are too thick for both horse and rider to navigate together.

At the tree line, I chance a look back. The villagers continue to watch our solemn procession, some with their hats in their hands. Their pointed ears seem to almost droop forward, whether in sadness or reverence, I can't tell. I turn back as my horse crosses under the canopy of bare limbs, and the shadows of the forest practically swallow me whole.

The usual sense of peace and relief I feel at entering my

favorite place doesn't come. My beloved forest is more still than I've ever known it, as if even the trees are holding their breath in anticipation of the coming battle. I keep my wits about me, searching the woods with all my senses for any hint of danger. Although we kept our plans a secret for as long as we could, we had to give our men at least a day to prepare. *What if there are spies among our own soldiers? What if the rebels are lying in wait and I'm now leading our forces to almost certain death?*

But there is nary a twig snap, a leaf crunch, or a whisper of an ambush. Even with my limited fae hearing, I would expect to be able to tell if the enemy was close by. Cliste sighs beside me, and his shoulders drop from his ears as the tension in them eases.

As we move deeper into the forest, the brush thickens, and I must duck and lean around low-hanging branches to stay in my saddle. I glance at my uncle, raising an eyebrow. With a solemn nod, he dismounts, and Cliste and I follow suit.

Our plan is simple: Make it as far through the forest as possible before nightfall, set up camp overnight, leave before dawn, then attack at sunset. I'm counting on not only the element of surprise but also the blinding setting sun at our backs to disorient the rebels.

The only downside is that the men will likely be tired from moving through the forest for two days and sleeping on the hard ground. But I'm hopeful we'll be able to rely on magic more than on physical strength during the battle.

"It's too quiet," Cliste complains, interrupting my thoughts. "I've never been in the forest when neither beast nor butterfly disturbs the silence." He shudders. "It's eerie."

I mumble my agreement, though there have been times when the forest has been this still. When I overheard those whispered voices during that stolen hunting trip with Charaide, it was as if the forest was listening as well, trying to learn the rebels' secrets. The memory does nothing to staunch the fear that kindles in my belly. *Was the forest as still because something sinister lurked in its depths, or was it listening to us, learning our secrets this time?* Perhaps trees hold no loyalty.

"At least it allows us time to think," my uncle replies, gazing up at the still branches, not even a hint of wind blowing through them. "It's a welcome reprieve from the hustle and bustle of the castle."

"It's creepy." Cliste steps purposefully on a stick and snaps it in half, startling some of the soldiers nearby.

"I'm glad the villagers came out to see us off," I say, gently changing the subject as I maneuver around a bush. "I hope it lifts the men's spirits."

Uncle Brutach scoffs. "Don't expect that they came out in support of you, my dear. They simply hope that whoever returns from this battle victorious will leave their humble abodes intact."

My heart sinks. "Do even the villagers who have lived so close to us hate my family?"

"Of course not," Charaide says, coming to my side. "I'm sure they're just frightened by the attack and fear a reprisal."

"If only it were that simple," my uncle retorts, pausing to toss a large branch out of the path, if it can be called that. "I'm sure fear factors into it, but not of the rebels. More like fear of the unknown." He looks at me. "Halflings are still viewed with a lot of distrust, even with the iron bracelets that stifle their magic. The potential of one becoming our next ruler makes everyone a little uneasy."

Charaide opens his mouth as if to protest, but Cliste beats him to it. "The way you speak sometimes, Uncle, almost makes me believe you side with the rebels instead of your own kin."

I gape at my brother, but his face is set in stone. For a moment, he almost looks like Laochard, and my heart aches in my chest. Perhaps when our eldest brother died, he sent his fae gifts to each of us, and Cliste's was Laochard's inner strength.

"Nonsense." Uncle Brutach grimaces and shakes his head. "You are my flesh and blood, and I have vowed before our gods and your mother to protect you at all costs." He sighs. "I'm merely trying to explain the politics of the situation, as it is important that you understand what you're facing in this war. Your allies are few and far between." Waving a hand behind us, he continues, "Even the soldiers in this outfit only fight because of their devotion to the kingdom. Not you, not your mother. They protect their sovereign regardless of who sits on the throne."

I swallow, trying not to show how much the words sting, though I don't know why it hurts. I've known my whole life that my siblings and I have no true allies but each other. It's one reason we've remained so close.

Even Charaide is quiet in the wake of this revelation. I can't bring myself to look at him, not wanting to see if the truth of my uncle's words lies in his eyes. My heart couldn't take it if my best friend agreed with that sentiment and if the only reason he was on this mission by my side was to protect his kingdom.

We continue in silence, though the forest is now alive with the sounds of marching footsteps, the swipe of swords cutting through errant limbs, and cursing when a soldier's feet get entangled in the brush. But the sounds aren't comforting. This isn't my forest anymore, and I wonder if it ever will be again.

It's difficult to tell, as we continue marching our way through, when the darkness of the forest changes from day to night. The shadows move with the sun, but the thick branches overhead hide the sky. Only the feeling of heaviness in my limbs and the growling of my stomach provide clues to the time.

"We should stop soon," I say, my voice a bit hoarse from disuse.

Cliste clears his throat. "I think there's a clearing up ahead where we can make camp."

Sure enough, a few moments later, the thick brush and gnarly roots of the trees dissipate, revealing a wide opening. A collective sigh of relief sounds among the men behind me as we break our lines and set up camp. Fires start, and the somber mood breaks a little as ale is passed around to the bone-weary soldiers.

I choose a spot off to the side to lay my sleeping bag. I opt not to set up a tent, just to make it easier to pack up and leave in the morning. After placing my things on the ground and clearing the spot of twigs, I find Charaide behind me, watching my every move.

"What?" I tuck a stray piece of hair behind my ear.

Whatever spell has possessed him breaks at the sound of my voice, and he smiles. "Sorry, I'm not sure where I went just now." He gestures to the spot beside my bag. "May I join you?"

Warmth floods my face. During the scouting trip, it made sense for us to share a tent, as I wouldn't have felt comfortable sharing with one of the royal soldiers. But now, with my uncle and brother here, it hardly seems appropriate for us to sleep so near each other. Not to mention how distracting he was during my training with the sorceress the other day. I can't imagine I'll get much sleep if he's lying so close by me.

He arches an eyebrow at me, and I realize I still haven't responded to his request. "O-Of course." I wince at my stammer, but he doesn't seem to notice as he lays his pack beside mine. Close, so much closer than I would have expected. It would be so easy to roll over into him in my sleep, so easy to wrap myself up in his arms and blame it on my unconscious state.

I shake my head slightly, dispelling the thoughts and images that come to mind. "Come on. Let's get something to eat. I'm starved!" Before he can respond, I hurry away, desperate to put some distance between us lest I act on my thoughts and do something I'll definitely regret.

Already, the cooks among our forces have stoked the fires, and the scent of roasting meat wafts over me. My mouth waters in anticipation. We didn't stop to eat all day, though we all had rations of deer jerky and fruit to snack on as we walked. It would be nice to have a hot meal and a mug of ale with which to wash it down.

Charaide catches my hand and pulls me to a table where platters of fruit are set out. We each grab a plate and fill it with our rations before moving on to the meat. One of the soldiers cuts a serving of chicken for each of us. After grabbing our mugs of ale, we head to a log beside one of the fires. The small space forces us to sit close together, and I try to ignore the tingles of my skin wherever it touches him.

"We should practice some more while we have the time," he says before shoveling a large piece of chicken into his mouth.

I stifle a groan. "Shouldn't I conserve my magic for tomorrow?"

He raises an eyebrow at me. "You described it as a flow, not a wave, which implies that there is no end to your source."

"Even rivers dry up," I retort.

Setting aside his plate, he turns to me, his expression serious. "Is that what this is really about?"

Damn him. He knows me too well. With a sigh, I shake my head. "I suppose not." I take a long drink from my ale, hoping he'll take the hint and drop the subject, but he gazes at me expectantly. I roll my eyes. "I'm still afraid of what happened with the target. What if I miss and light the whole forest on fire?"

"All the more reason to practice." He bites into an apple and chews thoughtfully. "We can determine whether your element is truly fire later. It's more important for you to learn how to control the magic itself."

At first, I don't answer him. It feels a little too much like the "chicken and the egg" argument my father once described. *Wouldn't it be easier to harness my magic if I understood how it manifests?* I suppose I understand his point to some extent. We can learn more about my magic and how my human side may impact it, but for now, I need to learn how to control it so I don't cause massive destruction to the kingdom itself.

"What do you want me to blow up this time?" I ask sarcastically.

His face breaks into a broad grin. "Well, if it wouldn't hurt our numbers, I wouldn't mind having you take a crack at your uncle."

I shoot him a glare. "Not funny."

The smile fades, and a deep anger simmers in his eyes. "I wasn't trying to be funny."

With a sigh, I finish my food and swallow the last of my ale. "Brutach... means well."

He scoffs. "If by 'means well' you imply that he demeans you and your siblings every chance he gets, I suppose you're right."

Fixing my gaze on my empty mug, I shrug. "What has he said that's untrue?" When Charaide doesn't respond, I finally raise my eyes and meet his. "We halflings are hated, and we don't have allies."

"You have me." He says it so quietly I think I may have misheard him, then he takes the mug from my hands and, after placing it on the ground, holds them in his own. "I would never betray you, Ast."

"You wouldn't betray your sovereign," I say, trying to pull my hands free.

But his eyes, so intensely blue, bore into mine, and he clutches my fingers tighter. "I didn't join this army to fight for my sovereign or to save my kingdom. I joined it because you are my best friend. I fight for *you*."

His words mean so much more to me than he could ever know. Even if a large part of me wishes he fought for me for love instead of friendship, at least he's fighting for me. At least I have someone in my corner who cares enough about me to stand by my side. And as I stare into his eyes and bask in the intensity of his gaze, I allow myself to hope that maybe someday, there will be something more between us.

I squeeze his hands. "You have no idea how much that means to me." The words are there, the words I have wanted to say to him for well over a year, but I swallow them. If we survive this, maybe I'll finally find the courage to tell him how I feel. But I can't risk his loyalty, and I can't risk my heart. Not tonight. Not with what we're facing tomorrow.

"Are you finished?" He gestures to my plate, breaking through my reverie.

I nod, not trusting myself to speak, afraid that I'll try to call the moment back. Without a word, he takes my plate and drops it off at a table to be cleaned. Then he returns to me and holds out his hand, helping me up. We head into the forest to practice, but my steps are heavy, weighed down by what I've left unsaid.

I'M SHAKEN awake hours later, and the first thing I see when I open my eyes is his beautiful face looming over me. For a moment, I forget where we are and what we're about to do and revel in the sight of him. But as he moves back and holds out a hand, the memories of the day before come crashing in, and I groan. It's our turn to keep watch.

Soldiers are scattered around the camp, some huddled close to fires, others in small groups along the edge of the clearing, like us. We move into the inner circle of the camp, waiting for the faeries from the shift before ours to brief us on what occurred.

Cliste is there as well, arms crossed over his armor, his dark hair falling in his eyes. His expression is troubled as he surveys our troops. He barely acknowledges Charaide and me as we approach, and my dinner curdles in my stomach.

"Has there been news?" I ask, hoping to break him from his brooding.

He shakes his head. "Not yet, though I've sent a few scouts around the perimeter to check for spies." Finally, he turns toward us, though his eyes fix on me. "If you have no objection, I'd like the two of us to pair up for our shift. There are things we should discuss."

Charaide stiffens beside me, but I can't deny feeling a little relieved. When we're alone in the forest, patrolling and keeping a watchful eye out takes only so much effort. It would leave too much time for talking, and as sleep deprived as I am, I can only imagine what I might blurt out given the opportunity.

"That sounds fine with me," I say. "But who will Charaide be paired with?"

A young warrior I've seen a handful of times steps up behind my brother. "He'll be with me." The warrior holds out a hand, and I take it. "M'lady, I am Tessack, one of the soldiers in your brother's battalion."

"Pleased to make your acquaintance, Tessack," I say with a smile. He looks as if he's the same age as me, which causes an ache in my heart.

The faeries who were on watch join our small group to debrief. They report no sightings of any rebels, and the forest seems to be sleeping peacefully tonight. I'm grateful for small favors. Hopefully, our shift will be as uneventful. I need to conserve my energy for tomorrow.

"Shall we?" Tessack gestures for Charaide to lead the way to the other side of the camp.

I watch them go, my chest constricting with conflicting emotions.

Cliste offers me his arm, and we move to our guard point. Neither of us speaks as we walk, but his steps are heavy, and I can feel the weight of his mood on my shoulders. Once we're far enough away from any listening ears, I stop him. "What's wrong?"

My brother stares at the ground, and I start to wonder if he didn't hear me. Just as I'm about to ask again, he lifts his head, and the sadness in his green eyes causes me to take a step back.

"Have you ever thought of abdicating?" He asks it so fast, it takes me a moment to register the question.

I cock my head as I study him. "What's this about, Cliste?"

He scans behind me before putting a hand on the small of my back and leading me farther into the trees, away from camp. When we're completely alone, he sits on a log and picks up a stray stick then clears a mess of leaves from the forest floor.

"I'm just not sure it's worth it."

I bite my lip, considering how to approach this. Of course I've thought about abdicating. The moment I learned Laochard had fallen and I would be the new military commander, every instinct told me to refuse. But with all that's at stake, I'm not sure this is the time to admit that. We need a united front if we have any hope of defeating the rebels.

"What brought this on?" I ask gently, laying a hand on his shoulder.

Tossing the stick to one side, he stands abruptly. "What do you *think* brought this on?" He waves a hand toward the forest, and I know he's referring to the rebel camp. "We're fighting in a war for a world that doesn't want us—"

"That's not fair."

"It's the truth!" He gestures to the forest. "We don't belong here, and they don't want us. They would rather see us rotting in the ground than seated on the throne."

"Not all of them feel that way," I murmur, but even I don't sound convinced.

He paces. "Do you remember what happened at school when

we were young? How they harassed Laochard and me? How they twisted our human strengths into weaknesses?”

I nod, unable to argue.

“And now, I’m supposed to risk my life, the life of my family, the only people who have ever truly accepted me for who—what I am.” This last is said with a sneer, and I flinch. “For what? A throne I have no desire to sit on, ruling a world I’ve never fit into and a people who will never accept me?”

“It’s not that simple.”

“Isn’t it? What would happen if we all abdicated? Don’t you think they’d leave Mom alone? She could remarry. She’s young enough, especially by faery standards, to have several more children. Then this war wouldn’t even be necessary.”

I take a deep breath. “Based on what I heard those men say at the rebel camp, I’m not sure they’d allow Mama to remain queen.” The words “human lover” and “harlot” echo in my brain, but I shove the thoughts from my mind. “Besides, what would we do then? Just live at the palace in some other capacity? And what if her new husband banished us? Then where would we go?”

“I don’t know about you and the rest, but I would go to the human world.” He lifts his chin in defiance, and it’s clear he’s dead serious. “You may not know this, but Papa and I talked often about his religion and beliefs. We even visited churches when we would venture to the human world. I was always fascinated by the customs and ceremonies and the priests who carried them out.” His eyes turn wistful. “That’s the life I would like to lead.”

He’s right. I had no idea he and Father had had such talks. I stifle a sigh. He makes it sound so easy, living amongst the humans, but we’re “other” enough that they’re unlikely to accept us either, especially in a position of trust like a priest. The last time I visited the mortal realm with my father, I was spied on in a dressing room, and I truly feared the people who saw my slightly pointed ears and caught a glimpse of my wings were ready to call in the authorities to detain me for further study. I'm not sure which is worse: dying at the hands of the rebels or spending the rest of my existence as a lab rat.

"You haven't been to the human world as much as I have. We wouldn't be any more accepted there than we are here."

"It's still worth a try," Cliste insists, crossing his arms over his chest. "And as a man of faith, I expect I'd be treated with respect instead of ridicule. Besides, anything must be better than here."

But he's wrong. Yes, the rebels are a threat to all of us, but humans have done so much worse to their own kind. The books Father brought back for me to read were evidence enough of that. Forget being a halfling. If your skin had too much color to it, you were othered at best. At worst, you were sold as a slave or hung from a tree. I could only imagine what the humans would think if they saw me perform magic. They would probably burn us at the stake!

For Cliste, it would be even worse. His skin is darker than mine, more like our father than our mother. My father told me of the persecution his people faced when they migrated from their home to other countries. No, it would not be safer for us in the human world.

A lump forms in my throat. "I would caution you, brother, to reconsider this plan. Abdicating is one thing, but leaving is another thing entirely. You should read the things that the humans have done before you hold them up as better than the fae. They have a saying in the human world, 'The devil you know is better than the devil you don't.' But I can tell you that I *know* what humans are capable of. I've seen it with my own eyes, and I promise you they are no better or less prejudiced than the fae."

"I've read many of Father's books as well, and I'm willing to risk it." His jaw sets, and I glower at him. Stubbornness is a family trait, but my brothers seem to have inherited it in spades.

"Would you really abandon the rest of our family now, when our siblings are too young to fight for themselves?"

His expression falters, though it will take more than that to convince him not to run. I pray to the spirit of our father that I will find the words to reach him.

"They could come too," he hedges, but his tone is less sure.

"And you would deprive our mother of her beloved children?"

His eyes flash, and I realize a moment too late that was the wrong thing to say. "Better they are alive and safe in another realm than lying dead in a crypt beneath the castle."

A twig snaps behind him, and he whirls around. I stand and join him, both of us straining our limited fae vision to see in the dark. No hint of a faery or beast is in sight, but the feeling of being watched weighs heavy on my shoulders. I shiver at the familiarity of the weight, as if that gaze has followed me before.

"Look," I say, keeping my voice low. "Let's just get through the battle tomorrow, and then we can continue this discussion." Maybe if we are victorious, it will give my brother pause and he can be reasoned with.

He clenches his jaw but gives a stiff nod. "Just promise me this stays between us."

"Of course," I say, bowing slightly. "I would never betray your confidence."

We turn our attention to the forest beyond the clearing, searching for any threat to our camp. I suspect my brother is more concerned with the possibility of our uncle learning of his defection than Charaide, but I will keep his secret even from my best friend. The last thing we need is for discontent to spread through our ranks. *If the soldiers discover the prince doesn't believe in our cause, what hope do we have of convincing them to fight for it?*

CHAPTER

EIGHT

I WAKE the next morning bleary-eyed and bone weary. The late shift left little time for me to catch up on sleep, and the camp is alive with movement. We'll be heading out soon, marching through the remainder of the forest on our way to the rebel camp. My uncle has sent scouts ahead to ensure the element of surprise is still on our side, but my stomach is so tightly tied in knots that I barely eat a morsel at breakfast. Charaide notices but wisely chooses to do little more than give me disapproving looks.

A flurry of activity helps to keep my mind off the impending battle as I assist my battalion with breaking down our camp. Once everything is packed away and set on our horses, we begin our trek through the second half of the woods. If it's possible, the forest seems even quieter than it did the day before, as if it's waiting to see who the victor will be.

It takes the rest of the day for our large army to cut our way through the thick brush and twisted trees, but as the sun begins to set beyond the canopy overhead, the scent of woodsmoke and roasted meat wafts to our location. We slow to a crawl, careful to avoid snapping twigs or crunching leaves and announcing our arrival.

Cliste, Uncle Brutach, and I slip through to the edge of the trees to take stock of the rebel camp. They are settling down for the night, and some of the fae are setting up card tables while others are drinking their first of many pints of ale. It's the perfect time to strike, but we decide to wait until the sun has fully set. Let the ale work its magic on their bodies. Let them be lured into a sense of complacence.

We return to our troops and whisper the plan through the ranks, then they stealthily move into position. As the sun disappears behind us, my uncle's battalion steps forward, ready to wield their magic before the rest of our forces strike. I stand with my archers, where I've managed to manifest a small spark in the air using my magic. They each will light their arrows from the floating flames and, when I give the signal, release them onto our unsuspecting enemy.

My uncle's battalion begin to pick their targets. The kitchen tent goes up in flames first, which causes some alarm, but most of the rebels appear to believe it was just a consequence of cooking dinner. However, as more of their tents catch fire, panic sets in. The rebels race to form some line of defense and counter our attacks, but they can't see us. Some of Brutach's fae have put up a glamor to shield us, but the chaos occurring within the rebel camp is aiding us much more than I ever imagined.

I can just make out shouts of the generals as the rebels organize and more targeted arrows find their marks. As some of my uncle's battalion fall, the glamor around us shimmers and disappears, but we still have the cover of darkness. In the distance, Cliste shouts to his troops, though he's too far away for me to make out the command.

This is it. My hands are clammy, but I wipe them on my armor and push my shoulders back. Like it or not, I'm a leader now, and it's important that my troops see me as such. I flutter my wings to raise myself slightly above them, though not too high. The last thing I need to do is give the rebels a clear target.

"Ready, archers," I call. My spark floats down the line as my troops ready their bows. A line of lit arrows breaches the darkness. I move to the side, pulling out my own bow and nocking an arrow. "Aim." I choose my target, a general barking orders at his men who are quickly advancing on the woods. "Fire!"

A volley of arrows shoots through the air, and I feel a grim satisfaction as mine finds its mark in the neck of the general. He is still yelling as it lodges in his throat, blood choking off his words, and he falls over. One down.

"Again," I yell, quickly nocking another arrow. But the rebels are running, and I know in a moment, they'll be on top of us. I order my archers once more as they close in on us. "Swords!"

There's barely enough time for my troops to unsheathe them before the rebels are upon us. I find myself face-to-face with a particularly dark fae, his hair as black as the night and his eyes dull gray. He grins when he recognizes me and lifts his blade in the air as he gives a taunting bow.

"Princess, it will be my honor to end you," he says before slicing the air with his sword.

I block him, gritting my teeth against his strength. Shoving his sword away, I lunge toward him, but he's ready for me and parries easily.

It takes more out of me than I would like to admit, and my opponent seems to sense this. His next lunge is confident, and I feint to the right, barely avoiding the tip of his blade. I attack again, but I've put too much force behind it, and I stumble forward. His eyes gleam as he takes advantage of my poor footing and hits my back with the hilt of his sword.

My magic reacts faster than I do, providing a wall of air that keeps me from landing face-first on the ground. I spin around, blade raised to meet his blow.

But Charaide has stepped between us and is crossing blades with him instead.

"Why don't you pick on someone your own size?" Charaide hisses, shoving the brute back.

I scramble to my feet, ready to continue the fight, but Charaide blocks my path. "Go, Astreilles. Take your archers and fall back."

My first instinct is to argue, but there isn't time. Besides, I can see the logic in his words even if my blood is screaming to finish the fight. I call for my archers, and we join some of the fae from Brutach's forces where they wield magic behind the front lines. We take positions and send volley after volley of arrows through the rebel forces as they rush forward to join the hand-to-hand combat at the front lines.

It's hard to tell who is winning, if anyone ever really wins a war. My ears ring from the clashing metal, screams of the wounded, and the hiss of magic. I ready another arrow in my bow, though it's difficult to choose a target at this range. We fire blindly into the rebel forces, hoping to cut down as many of them as possible to lessen the assault on our troops.

Between shots, I search the fray for Charaide. I regret leaving him. Perhaps we would have fared better together. But he likely knew I was wearying quickly. I doubt I would have lasted much longer. Still, my stomach churns at the thought of my friend facing the rebels head-on. And so with each arrow I shoot, I hope to in some small way help Charaide from afar.

A cry rises from across the forest, but it's too dark to see what is happening. Footsteps thunder through the trees, and I realize that my brother's battalion has joined the fray. My heart jumps into my throat. I cannot risk my mother losing another child. Shaking off my fear, I call to my archers, and we run down to join them, pausing occasionally to fire on the rebels in hopes of providing whatever advantage to our troops that we can.

The rebels don't seem to bother with bows and arrows. While they wield magic when necessary, they appear to prefer hand-to-hand combat, though my perception could be colored by my lack of formal military training. Maybe magic is difficult to conjure at such close range. Or maybe the rebels just relish the chance to rip apart our soldiers with their bare hands.

I don't feel the same way. It gave me no pleasure to dispatch any of the rebels. These are, after all, my people. That they chose to revolt against my mother's rule does not change this fact. And while I will protect my family by whatever means necessary, I wish it hadn't come to this.

When my troops and I reach the spot where my brother charged, the rebels are already retreating. We join the fray, pushing them back even farther, into their camp and beyond. Their magic falters as the fae wielding it are forced to run. Cliste and Brutach are at the front of our lines, screaming orders to our soldiers to push forward. I race to join them, shouting the same to my troops.

"Retreat!" someone calls, and I risk a glance to see a general waving at the rebels. Other generals join in, and their lines fall back. Rebels not engaged in combat turn tail and run while those who are still fighting make moves to disengage. We press on in case this is a tactic meant to confuse us or lead us into a false sense of security. But they continue to flee, not even bothering to cover their backs.

I stop, breathing heavily, and put my hands on my knees as I watch them run away. All around me, I hear triumphant shouts.

My uncle claps me on the shoulder. "Well done, Astreilles. This is a promising first victory for us."

With a forced smile, I survey the damage to our forces. There are more wounded than dead and even more soldiers who are completely unscathed. Though relief floods my veins, a wave of nausea overtakes me. Something doesn't feel right.

"Was..." I consider my next words, as I don't want to come off as cruel or rude. But I'm not sure how else to ask this. "Was it too easy, do you think?"

Cliste gapes at me while my uncle presses his lips into a thin line. "Too easy?" He waves his hand over the fallen men wearing our colors. "The lives of so many lost, and you think it was an easy battle?"

I swallow, hanging my head in shame. But the feeling doesn't dissipate, even with the anger simmering in Cliste's eyes. *It isn't even midnight, and we've already won?* I expected this battle to last well into dawn, if not through the following day. But after just a few hours, it's over.

"I'm sorry, Uncle," I say. "I admit I'm not well-versed in war, but I didn't think it would be over so quickly."

"My dear girl, you have much to learn. Think of everything that was on our side and why we so carefully honed our strategy." He begins ticking things off on his fingers. "We had the element of surprise. It was dusk by the time we struck. We prioritized magic over brute force." With a shake of his head, he tells Cliste, "Clearly, our little Astreilles has much to learn."

Cliste gives me a dark look. "Enjoy this victory, dear sister. There may not be many more like it."

After giving a brief nod, I turn on my heel to hide my burning cheeks and head back to help the wounded. But before I can take so much as a step, I run smack into a broad chest. Two hands grasp my shoulders, and I panic, raising my fists to defend myself.

"Whoa! Astreilles, calm down. It's me." Charaide releases me and steps back, holding his palms out in front of him.

"S-Sorry," I stammer, struggling to calm the wild beating of my heart.

He gives me a quick once-over before jerking his chin back to my uncle and brother, who are watching us. "What happened?"

"Nothing," I say, stepping around him and walking briskly back to the battlefield.

He falls into step beside me. "Your face would suggest otherwise." I cut a look at him from the corner of my eye, and he grins. "I can't help it if you wear your heart on your sleeve."

Grumbling, I explain the brief conversation with my uncle and brother. I expect him to brush me off as they did, but instead, his brow furrows.

"I had the same feeling," he says.

My steps falter as I look at him. But perhaps he's just placating me. I stop walking and cross my arms.

"I'm serious, Ast. I don't know that I would have expected the battle to rage on as long as you did, but I definitely didn't think it would have been over so quickly and with so few lives lost." He shakes his head. "I don't know much about battles or war, but I can't help feeling that the rebels let us win. That they gave in too easily and retreated."

"But why would they do that?"

He shrugs. "It's possible they were waiting for reinforcements and they'll come back to fight us again once those arrive." His eyes darken. "Or it's possible they have something else up their sleeve."

"A trap?" My eyes widen.

"Maybe." He gives me a lopsided grin that causes my heart to skip a beat. "Care for a scouting mission, or are you too tired after going head-to-head with a brute?"

I scowl at him. "Of course not. We'll go now."

But we don't leave immediately. I insist on helping the wounded and grabbing a few hours of rest. If we meet with the rebels, I want to be as close to full strength as possible. There's no way I'm going to let Charaide fight one of my battles for me again.

A couple of hours later, we creep out of our tents and meet up on the edge of the camp. The guards pay us no mind as we travel in the direction the rebel army fled. I have my quiver strapped across my chest and my bow over my shoulder, and Charaide has several blades attached to his person. We probably look like we're going hunting.

"We need to be back here by first light," Charaide whispers as soon as we're alone. "If the enemy catches us, catches *you*, we'll be lucky to see another day dawn."

I swallow and nod, following close behind him. The darkness makes it difficult for my half-human eyes to see. Not even the moon shines to give us a helpful silver glow. It's just as well, since we don't want to be seen either.

"How far do you think they went?" I keep low to the ground and strain my ears for any sound of an army lurking nearby.

"Hard to tell." Charaide sniffs the air. "With their many wounded, I would say not far." He points at the ground, where there are gouges in the dirt from the rebels' hasty escape. "We'll follow the trail, but they may have evanesced once they realized we weren't following them."

I stifle a groan. "Which means they could be anywhere."

He grins lazily. "Think of it like an animal you're hunting and use that amazing tracker ability."

"I can't track something that disappeared into thin air," I retort with a glare.

"You don't know that. You've barely begun to tap into your magic." His expression grows serious. "There are many things you think you can't do, but you haven't allowed yourself to try, Ast."

I'm not sure if he's referring to my powers or something else, but he turns away from me before I can respond.

Even in the darkness, I feel exposed on the hilltop as we climb, following the trail the rebels left behind. *What if this is a trap and they await us on the other side of this hill? What would my death do to my mother or my brother, Cliste, who wouldn't want to lead an army, let alone a kingdom of people who hate what he is?*

When we reach the summit, the trail stops abruptly. I use my limited fae sight, but there's nothing for miles. Charaide grunts as if frustrated. The rebels must have taken to the skies or evanesced elsewhere, and it could take days to find them again.

"We'll just have to continue into rebel territory." I sink into the soft grass to rest a moment. I've barely slept in the last twenty-four hours, and it's catching up with me.

"That feels like a grave mistake," he counters, kneeling in front of me. "They could have gone anywhere at this point. We'd be walking in completely blind."

"What other choice do we have?" I fiddle with a blade of grass. "We can't very well return to the castle. We need to stave off this rebellion before it catches fire throughout the rest of the land."

"Assuming it hasn't already," he scoffs. After pushing to his feet, he walks a few yards away from me, scanning the horizon with his fae sight. The sky is turning deep violet as we near sunrise. It takes a decent amount of effort for me not to lay my head on the soft ground and rest my eyes. But we're not safe here. Well, *I'm* not safe anywhere but especially exposed on a hilltop far from my army.

With a sigh, I scramble off the ground, wiping my hands on my pants. My muscles protest, the soreness from wielding a heavy sword setting in. I walk over to Charaide and put a hand on his shoulder. "We should head back."

He nods, glancing at me before returning his gaze to the horizon. "I wish things were different."

"How do you mean?"

His hands rake through his hair as he stares into the distance. "For you, for your family." He glances at me again. "For us."

My heart skips a beat, but I keep my expression neutral. "We'll get through this. And then maybe things will be different for everyone."

His expression becomes unreadable, and I wonder if his words held a deeper meaning. I open my mouth to respond, but he just walks back the way we came.

A twig snaps behind me. That eerie feeling of being watched returns, and I slowly turn to see what has joined us on that hill.

The figure is hard to make out, his dark cloak almost blending into the shadows around us. Only the lightening sky allows me to see the silhouette. There's something familiar about that cloak. I lean forward.

"Who are you?" I whisper. And then it dawns on me where I've seen a similar cloaked figure before. "Y-You!" I stagger back, bumping into Charaide, who must have heard my fear and returned. "You were at the king's funeral. A-And you attacked me in my bedchamber."

The cloaked figure just stands there, still as death, watching us. Charaide shifts me behind him and unsheathes his sword.

"To get to her, you'll have to go through me." His voice is menacing, but I can hear the strain, the fear. We should never have come out here alone.

"That won't be necessary," a deep voice rasps from within the cloak. It's the strangest sound I've ever heard, as if several voices have been combined into one. My blood freezes in my veins at the otherworldly sound.

Charaide steps back, and I move with him, pulling an arrow from my quiver and aiming my bow over his shoulder. The ghost of a laugh floats through the air, and I tense, ready for the attack.

"Astreilles, why don't you head back to camp?" Charaide's eyes never leave our assailant. "I'll join you shortly."

"I'm not leaving you here," I hiss, stepping around him, my arrow still aimed at the cloaked figure before us.

Go! The command comes into my mind so loudly, my arm

shakes, but I recover quickly. Charaide glances at me from the corner of his eye, his lips set in a hard line. But I shake my head. We leave either together or not at all.

"Such loyalty..." the strange figure whispers. It is as if the sound comes from all around me instead of from in front of me.

I shake my head, trying to reorient myself.

"Such... love."

"Get on with it, then!" Charaide snarls, slashing his sword through the air.

Another ghostly chuckle comes. "I'm not here to fight you, boy."

"Then what do you want?" The force of my own voice surprises me. There's strength there that I don't feel.

"I had hoped to find you alone, to finish what I started in your bedchamber. But it is no matter. We will meet again, Princess." The cloaked figure begins walking backward, away from us. "When you're ready."

"I'm ready now!" I growl, moving forward and pulling my bow tight, my arm aching with the effort of holding the arrow ready.

I expect him to run, to turn tail and flee, but he doesn't break his stride as he moves farther away from us. I refuse to let him go. He's already attacked me twice. With a rageful roar, I release my arrow. I wait for the cry of pain, the gasp of a shallow breath as it pierces skin. But there's only silence and an empty hill before me. The cloaked figure is gone. But the air still vibrates with his voice, as though the shadows themselves are whispering my name.

"You went out last night without alerting anyone to your plans." Uncle Brutach paces before me and Charaide, his steps quick and loud, like his anger. "And then you almost got yourselves killed by the same assailant who attacked you before?" He whirls on me, eyes blazing. "What the hell were you thinking?"

We're all tired, especially Charaide and me after our late-night rendezvous with the cloaked figure. But my uncle has ordered us to his tent, where a large table has been set up. A map is spread over the surface with various markings of where the rebels may have evanesced to.

Charaide opens his mouth—with an equally angry retort, no doubt—but I grab his arm and speak first. "We were trying to find out where the rebels had gone so we could plan our next attack." It takes effort, but I manage to keep the tremor out of my voice. "I'm supposed to be leading this army, am I not? What kind of leader would I be if I didn't do reconnaissance and strategize our next move?"

"As a leader, you should be delegating such tasks, not risking your own life to do them." My uncle points an emphatic finger toward the opening of the tent, where no doubt hundreds of soldiers are listening to our argument. "They are here to serve *you* as much as they are here to serve the crown. Your life is far too valuable for you to be traipsing about in the night."

"She wasn't alone." Charaide steps forward, and I stifle a sigh. "I was with her. Do you really think I'd let something happen to her?"

But my uncle just chuckles darkly. "The last time you were up against this particular assailant, you were bested, so forgive me if I don't trust you with my niece's life."

Charaide bristles, and I prepare for an outburst, but Cliste holds up his hand from the other side of the table.

"We appreciate the efforts you were trying to make, but it would have been more prudent for you to have taken a few men with you." He levels me with a hard stare. "Your life is too important to take such risks."

I read between the lines of what he says. If something happened to me, that would place him second in line, a position he doesn't want. Putting him in that situation would make it harder for him to abdicate, knowing what he would be subjecting our younger siblings to, some of them not even ten years of age.

"I'm sorry." The words are simple, but I hold Cliste's gaze, and he seems to understand the sincerity in my tone. He inclines his head in a slight nod, which suggests I'm forgiven. But his expression is clear. *Don't ever do something like this again.*

Charaide shifts beside me, and I suspect he's not thrilled with my apology. We've always gone off on our own, and it was never a problem before. But I understand this is different. We're in a war where my family's very lives are at stake. I must protect myself as much as I protect them.

"Then what do you suggest we do?" It seems Charaide isn't as willing to accept Brutach's criticism with grace.

"I've already sent a small group of soldiers to try to determine where the rebels have regrouped." My brother stands, pointing at the map. "We think they'd evanesce to this area, as it's where a lot of dissenters have been located previously." His mouth sets in a grim line. "We suspect they're recruiting."

I swallow the lump in my throat. While I knew one battle wouldn't make or break this war, I'd hoped that the show of force might have given the rebels pause. Then again, I still can't shake the feeling the battle was too easy. Perhaps the rebels planned to use it to their advantage by painting our armies as ruthless. One could only imagine what sort of tales they were spinning about the halfling royals.

"How successful do you think their efforts will be?" I ask, not sure I really want to learn the answer.

"Very," my uncle replies, his blue-gray eyes boring into mine. "And if they are, yesterday's battle will be like child's play."

"Then we should recruit as well," Charaide declares, slamming a fist into the table.

My uncle snorts. "Good luck finding anyone else loyal enough to the current queen to fight for her." He waves a hand toward the tent opening again. "These soldiers dedicated their lives to the crown, regardless of who wears it." His mouth turns down as he shakes his head. "Not many fae appreciate the prospect of a halfling princess"—he glances at my brother—"or prince for that matter."

"Maybe you underestimate your own people," Charaide retorts, his hands clenching into fists at his sides.

"If you want to lead recruitment efforts, by all means, be my guest." Brutach's expression darkens. "But I wouldn't hold my breath for much success."

"I would be happy to find more soldiers to fight for my queen." Charaide bends forward in a mocking bow. "One would think you would appreciate any action that aids this effort, but perhaps your loyalties lie elsewhere."

My uncle's face turns a deep shade of red, and I step in front of my best friend before Brutach can enact his wrath. Charaide grasps my shoulders as if ready to shove me out of the way if needed, but my uncle's anger dissipates almost as quickly as it arrives.

"As I said, be my guest," Brutach sneers. Then he focuses on my brother, and they resume the conversation they were having prior to our arrival, effectively a dismissal.

"The nerve of that jerk," Charaide seethes once we're out of earshot of the soldiers. "The way he speaks and acts, I wonder if that old saying is true. With allies like him, who needs enemies?"

I choke on a laugh, half shocked by the boldness of Charaide's statement and half because I acknowledge he has a point. My uncle has always been a hard man to like. He's made no secret of his distaste for my parents' relationship, and I doubt he shed so much as a single tear over the loss of my father. Still, it's clear he cares for me in his own way. He wouldn't have bothered berating me for putting myself at risk if he didn't.

"I know he can be harsh sometimes." I take a seat in our tent, stretching out my legs and relishing the chance to rest. "But I think he just wants us to understand what we're up against."

"Do you truly hold your people in such low esteem?"

With a sigh, I lie back and stare at the fabric above me. "But they're not *my* people. Not really. They may be part of who I am but not the whole. And there are enough among them who hate the half of me that doesn't belong that I wouldn't be surprised if they were easily swayed by the rebels' cause." I close my eyes. "And I wouldn't blame them."

"How can you say that, Ast?" Charaide demands so vehemently that my eyes fly open in surprise. "You had no control over the circumstances surrounding your birth." He picks up a stick and scratches the dirt. "If anything, the fae brought this on themselves when they stole human children."

"I've thought the same myself many times, but I guess I never understood why the children were stolen." Once I roll over, I prop my head on my hand and look at him. "Was it to intimidate the humans?"

Charaide shifts beside me and clears his throat. "There are several reasons, none of them good. Sometimes fae stole a child for spite after a human slighted them. Others wanted to raise a slave for the family. But I think, at least in your father's case, his family brought him because their own changeling wasn't expected to survive and they so desperately wanted a child." His eyes meet mine. "But not all humans come here as children or infants. Sometimes, fae bring them here for love."

My eyes widen. "Really? I've never heard of that. Where are these other humans?" I'd met a few who, like my father, were stolen as infants but none that had chosen to come here.

His gaze drops to the ground. "They're outcasts." His throat bobs as he swallows. "Such relationships have always been frowned upon in our world, and many fae families would rather see their children die than marry a human. Some of the fae try to return to the mortal world with their human lover, but it never lasts." He gives me a sad smile. "We don't blend in as easily as you halflings." His smile fades. "Other fae build homes where they are less likely to be harassed. There are communities in certain areas of the kingdom where these couples and their halfling children live in peace, for the most part. But they're shunned, persecuted for their relationships." He nods at the slight scar that the iron bracelet left on my wrist. "And their children suffer the consequences."

My chest hurts for those unknown fae and humans but mostly for my parents. "That's awful."

"It is. And it's so stupid. It's not like humans are some beasts in the forest. They're not much different from us save a lack of power or the gift of flight." He lies down on his bag, facing me. "I've never been to the mortal realm. What's it like?"

"It's so much different from here." I slide my hand along the ground, and he grasps it in his. "They may not have the gift of flight, but they've found ways around it. Several humans can fly at once on things called airplanes, and much higher than fae would feel comfortable flying." I smile. "Above the clouds where the air is thin."

My body starts to succumb to sleep when I hear Charaide shift beside me and feel his hand pull mine closer. "Will you show me someday? When this is all over?"

"Of course," I whisper, though I have no idea how I would accomplish that. As Charaide acknowledged himself, the fae tend to stand out to humans. Before I can dwell on the logistics, I slip into unconsciousness.

"Welcome, Princess." The voice is familiar, raspy. I can't quite place it.

"Hello?" I say, turning to find the source. I'm in a strange room, alone. The colors here are different, more vibrant, and they blend in a unique way I've never seen before. It's disorienting, and I search the space for a chair. As if the room senses my need, one appears, though it's ethereal.

I sit, but I don't feel the relief of getting off my feet. Something doesn't feel right. My gaze falls to my hands, and I gasp, frightened. They are translucent, as if they're not fully there.

"Am I dead?" I ask, unsure to whom exactly I'm directing this question since there's no one with me.

"No, not yet," comes the reply, raspy but laced with a humor that chills more than it comforts.

"Am I dreaming?"

"Hmm. Not quite but close."

"Are you going to make me keep guessing?" I stand, my eyes seeking the source of the strange, familiar voice.

"I trust you'll figure it out eventually. Perhaps not today." It gives a ghostly chuckle. *"But soon."*

"What do you want from me?" I demand, reaching for my bow and quiver, but they're not there. I glance down, noticing for the first time that my clothes are different. A sheer white gown flows down my body, barely concealing the skin beneath and clinging to my every curve. I clutch my hands over the dress in a vain attempt to cover myself.

"It's a little late for that, don't you think?" the voice says with a bite of sarcasm, and I flinch.

"What do you want?" I ask again, trying to sound forceful, but it comes out as barely a whisper.

"So many things." The voice echoes off the walls of the room, and I struggle once more to find its source. *"You can stop looking for me. I'll reveal myself when the time is right."*

"And when will that be?" This time, I sound as angry as I feel, and there's a pause in the air, as if I've caught whoever is taunting me by surprise.

"That depends on you."

I clench my fists in frustration. *"You're wasting my time."* Closing my eyes, I will myself to wake up from this awful nightmare.

"Oh, you're not sleeping," the voice drawls, sounding almost bored by this conversation. Can it read my mind? I push my thoughts away, clearing aside anything that could be used against me.

"That sounds just like something a monster from a nightmare might say."

A whisper of a mirthless chuckle comes. "You think I'm a monster."

"You've given me no reason to think otherwise."

I cross my arms over my chest. The sheer fabric of the gown stands no chance against the icy chill in the room.

Footsteps echo behind me, and I spin around, raising my fists to *defend myself. But there's no one there. Just a shimmer of light like a mirage in the desert. The footsteps continue as the shimmer grows nearer, and my breath catches in my throat. It's both terrifying and beautiful in a way I don't understand.*

"You're right," the voice says from the shimmer, and I stagger back. "I am a monster." There's a tinge of bitterness in the tone and a touch of sadness as well.

I cock my head, not sure what to make of this change in demeanor. "Have you brought me here to kill me, then?"

"Nothing can hurt you here," it says. "Not even me."

The words lodge in my chest, inexplicably tender and cruel at once. "Then why did you bring me?"

The shimmer moves, circling me. If I squint, I can just make out the shape of a body, but doing so causes my head to ache.

"I didn't do anything. You came here on your own."

"How is that possible?" I move my hands to my hips and take a step closer to the shimmer, trying to force it to take a discernible shape.

"That's what I'd like to know." The shimmer pauses, and a heaviness settles over my skin as if the shimmer is assessing me. "It takes great skill to astral project. Near impossible for humans. Even the fae struggle with it."

A laugh bubbles out of my throat. "Astral projection is a myth, a legend among the fae."

"Is it?" The voice turns hard. "Is that what they've taught you?" The shimmer moves to one of the floor-length windows on the other side of the room, a curtain flowing around it in a nonexistent breeze. "And yet, here you stand. Interesting. I thought halflings were more breakable. You continue to surprise me."

I don't like what it's implying, that I've been lied to by my family, my friends. But I also don't see the point in arguing with it. If I have somehow projected my soul to another plane of existence, I need to get back before anyone notices anything is amiss. Were the rebels to discover my body, limp and lifeless...

"Your body is well protected," the voice says as if reading my mind. *"That... friend of yours watches your every move. Even now, though he thinks you're sleeping, he watches over you."*

Charaide. *I must get back to him. Yet I have so many questions.* "How do you know he's watching over me?"

"I'm surprised you can't feel the weight of his stare, even here. It's quite pointed and full of undeniable longing."

I turn away to hide the blush that should be staining my cheeks, but the familiar warmth is absent. "It's not like that. He's my best friend."

"If you say so."

I've had enough of this strange dance, talking in riddles. "If you didn't bring me, then I can leave of my own accord?"

"Of course. You're not my prisoner." It gives a harsh laugh. *"Not yet, anyway."*

A chill runs up my spine, but I ignore it, lifting my chin. "Then how do I go back?"

"That, I can't tell you, since I'm still trying to figure out how you arrived in the first place." There's a pregnant pause as the shimmer turns from the window, and that heavy sensation slides over my skin again. *"But since you thought this was a dream, perhaps you just need to wake yourself up, Little Star. Before I decide I don't want you to."*

The nickname rattles through me like a secret only I should hold, but I force myself to focus. Taking a deep breath, I close my eyes and will myself to wake. I imagine I'm back in my body, the shape of the tent over me, the sound of Charaide's steady breath beside me. And suddenly, it feels like I'm flying. I don't dare open my eyes for fear of what I'll see and instead focus on returning to my body, until the weightlessness I felt in that room dissipates and the gravity of the physical world presses down on me again.

Before I open my eyes, I flex my fingers, and the rough blanket scratches my skin. My back aches from sleeping on the hard ground, and I roll over. As the voice promised, Charaide is watching me, and he smiles when I meet his gaze.

"You slept like the dead," he teases as I rub my eyes.

Only I don't feel rested. My body hurts all over, and I'm so weary, it's as if I've been up half the night. *Is it possible I actually astral projected?*

I shake my head, willing the thought away. It's impossible, especially for a halfling like me. Even the most powerful fae have tried and failed to do so. I sit up, wiping a hand over my face.

"It wasn't a restful sleep," I say. "I had the strangest dream."

"Oh?" His eyes fill with concern, and the words "undeniable longing" echo in my head. It's too early, and I've had too little rest to try to piece that together. Besides, it was a dream, my subconscious projecting my feelings onto my friend.

"I was in a bright room, blindingly bright," I begin, closing my eyes to try to remember, but already, the details are escaping me. "But I wasn't alone. There was someone there with me. They seemed so familiar, but I don't know why." An icy chill runs down my spine, and I shudder.

Charaide moves to my side and gathers me into his arms then strokes my hair. "Shh, Ast. It was just a dream." He squeezes me tighter. "You're safe here. Nothing and no one will hurt you."

But he's wrong. I'm not safe here, not with the rebels preparing for our next battle gods knows where. And if the strange being was right, and somehow, I managed to astral project, then I'm not even safe in my sleep.

TEN

I PULL myself together long enough to dress and prepare for the day. My brother and uncle are waiting for me in the main tent, the same map spread out over the same table. I hope they've discovered the location of the rebels so we can plan our next attack. I need something to distract me from what happened last night.

"Ah, Astreilles," Uncle Brutach says dryly as I step up to the table. "Nice of you to join us."

I duck my head. It is much later than I usually rise, but this morning took more effort than I'm used to. Keeping my head low, I pray they won't notice the smudges under my eyes or the slight limp in my step.

"Have you made any progress in determining where the rebels are?" I ask.

"We have." Cliste points at the map. "We believe they evanesced here. It is close to villages that were very vocal about their disapproval of the queen's marriage. Now that the king is dead, the rumbles of discontent are growing."

I search the map for our location. After I do some quick calculations, my mouth falls open, and I stare at my brother. "But that would take us several days to walk."

His lips set in a grim line. "I know. But not all of our soldiers have the ability to evanesce." He gives me a hard look, and I understand what he doesn't say. He can't evanesce either. Of its own accord, my gaze strays to the iron bracelet on his wrist, and I quickly look away. I've never tried, but I suspect it would take too long for me to learn how to evanesce a short distance, let alone one of this magnitude. Even flying would take too much time, especially for Cliste and me. Unlike other faes, ours aren't strong enough to fly for long journeys.

"Then what do you propose we do?"

My uncle leans back in his chair, his hands behind his head. "We have a few ideas, but I'm curious to hear yours."

I try to swallow, but my mouth has gone dry. *This is new.* Since I've never led an army before, my uncle's counsel has been invaluable to me, even if it's often given in a rather gruff manner. I glance at Brutach, but his expression is unreadable.

Part of me wishes Cliste would take pity on me and share some of his military strategy. But I can't bring myself to look at him, so I stare at the floor, racking my brain for any idea of how to handle this latest setback.

Some fae are powerful enough to evanesce a passenger, but I'm not sure if any of our soldiers fit that requirement. So trying to have them carry my brother and me seems a fool's errand. At the same time, the longer it takes us to reach the rebels, the longer they have to recruit and build their army. Time is of the essence.

"We could fly," a familiar voice says behind me.

I whirl around to find Charaide leaning against the tent pole, clearly eavesdropping.

"Why are you here?" my uncle demands, fixing a steely gaze on my friend.

"I asked him to be," I lie, shooting a questioning look at Charaide.

His lips turn up in a half smile before he gives his attention to my uncle.

"I'm Astreilles's second in command of her battalion, so it would seem prudent that I be kept informed of the strategy."

Brutach mutters something under his breath but doesn't challenge Charaide's assertion. "Astreilles and Cliste cannot fly that far." He waves his hand as if dismissing Charaide and faces my brother.

"Wait." I hold up my hand. "Charaide has a point." I gesture to Cliste. "While my brother and I cannot fly long distances, the rest of the soldiers can."

Brutach raises his eyebrows. "Are you suggesting sending your army into battle without your leadership?"

"Of course not," I say.

"I can carry Astreilles." Charaide moves to my side.

It takes a concerted effort for me to hide the flush threatening to overtake my face. The idea of being in Charaide's arms for miles and miles of flight... I shake my head, forcing the image away.

"And what of Cliste?" Brutach's brow furrows as he glances at me before looking back at my brother.

"While it may not be as cozy as flying with Charaide," Cliste teases, his knowing smile making me hide my face behind my hair, "I'm sure I can find a strong enough fae to carry me as well."

My uncle settles back in his chair, studying the three of us. Part of me is hoping he calls this a ridiculous plan. The intimacy of flying with Charaide over such a long distance makes my heart pound. But we don't have another feasible option, and we haven't the time to brainstorm one either.

"I suppose flying would be faster than walking and less dangerous than evanescing. While we have pinpointed the village where we suspect the rebels are, we should plan to land far enough away to send scouts in before we attack so we can assess the situation." Brutach shoots a meaningful glance at me. "I will send a small group tonight so they can arrive under cover of darkness to do a scouting expedition. Then the rest of us will head out first thing tomorrow." His eyes travel from me to Cliste. "Agreed?"

Cliste nods. "I will speak to the soldiers and find someone who can carry me. Let's prepare to leave at first light."

I stand and head out, barely looking at Charaide as I pass. Between the prospect of flying with him tomorrow and the remnants of my dream still floating in my mind, it's all I can do to focus on putting one foot in front of the other. But I can feel him behind me as I head to our tent.

IN THE WEE hours of the morning, Charaide shakes me awake. It's time for us to leave. I rub my eyes, still exhausted but grateful that last night involved no strange dreams. I climb out of my bag before rolling it up and securing it to the pack I'll carry on my back. Charaide is busy packing up the rest of the tent, and I scramble to help him.

As I step out of the tent, the camp is busy with activity even though it's still dark outside. All around me, grim-faced soldiers prepare themselves for what is sure to be an even bloodier battle. If the rebels have been successful in their recruitment efforts, I fear what we may be walking—or flying—into.

I head over to the main tent, where I'm sure to find my uncle and brother. When I enter, neither of them acknowledges me as they pore over the same map again. I clear my throat to announce my presence, and Cliste looks up.

"What's the report from the scouts that evanesced last night?" I ask.

A glance passes between my uncle and my brother. My heart sinks. This can't be good news, then.

"They never returned," Cliste finally replies in a clipped tone.

I stare at one then the other. "Where are they?"

"We don't know." My uncle runs a hand over his white hair. "We've been discussing sending a search party, but we don't want to stretch our forces too thin."

"Should we postpone our flight, then?" My stomach churns, and I'm grateful I haven't attempted to eat breakfast yet.

"No." Uncle Brutach slices a decisive hand through the air. "We can't afford to stop our offensive movement."

"But we're going in blind!" I protest, crossing my arms over my chest. "We need better intelligence before we make our next move."

"That's what I said," Cliste mumbles, and my uncle shoots him a glare.

"We can fly to a clearing just outside of where we believe the rebels are and then send another group to scope out the rebels, but they'll go on foot this time. Perhaps our calculations were off and the last scout evanesced right into the rebel camp. They may have been taken prisoner..." Brutach's throat bobs. "Or worse."

A chill runs down my spine, but I stand my ground. "I'm not leading my battalion into an ambush. This is suicide."

His blue-gray eyes cut to me. "War demands sacrifice." He turns to the map in what I suspect is another dismissal.

My heart is in my throat. Everything in me is saying this is a fool's errand, but I'm no military strategist. I'm just a silly halfling who got tossed into a role in which she had no business being. Besides, my uncle has a point. If we continue to delay our next attack, we're setting ourselves up to be sitting ducks.

"There must be another way." I address my brother. "Are we able to communicate with the scouts? Send a message to them and see if we can ascertain where they are?"

"It's too dangerous," Brutach says before I've even finished speaking. "What if the rebels intercept the message? Then they'll know where *we* are or, worse, what we're planning to do."

"Then we will put together another scouting group who will fly ahead of our army." I find myself saying this before I have a chance to think it through. "And this time, I will join them."

Two pairs of incredulous eyes stare at me. They exchange another glance, but my brother is already shaking his head.

"It's too risky. If we are wrong about where the enemy is, you'll be a prime target." Cliste's green eyes bore into mine, and though I understand what he's not saying, I ignore him.

"We need intelligence." I raise my chin in defiance. Maybe it's reckless, but if I'm to lead this damned army, then I'm going to do so from the front lines. "And I'm not risking any more of my men without seeing for myself what we're up against."

Brutach crosses his arms. "You can't fly that far, and you risk the soldiers' lives if one of them can't defend himself because he's carrying you."

"The plan was always for Charaide to carry me. That won't change." My stomach drops at the thought of risking him, but I know Charaide. He wouldn't have it any other way.

"So you gamble not only with your own life but also that of your so-called best friend." My uncle shakes his head. "With friends like you..."

"That's enough," Charaide says from behind me.

I spin around, taking in his red face. *How much did he hear?*

"Astreilles is right. We agreed I would carry her. Whether I carry her with her own battalion or with a small scouting group is of no consequence." He narrows his eyes. "Wherever she goes, I follow."

My heart swells at his words, both with pride and something more. I raise an eyebrow at my uncle, daring him to continue his challenge after so declarative a statement.

Brutach throws up his hands. "Fine, but you'd better survive this. I refuse to tell your mother that she's lost another child."

My stomach twists, but I keep my expression neutral. "Do you have any suggestions for who else should go with us?"

"I would suggest you take the same men that went to the rebel camp with you," Cliste responds. His voice is strained.

Guilt needles at my belly. *Am I condemning us both by insisting on joining this risky mission?*

I nod, swallowing the lump forming in my throat. "Charaide and I will find Marto and start making preparations." It may be a mistake, and my brother may never forgive me, but in my gut, I know it's the right thing to do.

As Charaide and I leave the tent, I can feel his eyes on me, assessing me. Once we're out of earshot, or at least far enough away that no one will be paying attention to us, I stop.

"What?" I ask.

"I know this wasn't a role you ever saw for yourself, but I think you're better at it than you give yourself credit for."

His words bolster my resolve, and for the first time in days, I smile. We gaze at each other, and something sparks in his eyes. My dream comes back to me in that moment. *Undeniable longing.* My heart skips with hope.

"We should meet up with the rest of the group." Charaide turns away, and the moment ends.

Marto is sitting by the fire, roasting a skewer when we approach. He inclines his head in acknowledgment as I take a seat beside him, but his eyes never leave the flames.

"We're putting together another small scouting group, and I'd like you to join us," I say.

"Just the three of us?" He glances behind me at Charaide.

"And the other two fae who went with us to the rebel camp."

After pulling his skewer from the fire, he finally looks at me. "Because that went so well the last time."

Warmth rushes to my cheeks, and I duck. Charaide steps forward, but I hold up a hand to stop him from interfering again. I'll never win the loyalty of the army if I don't fight my own battles.

"It wasn't well thought-out," I acquiesce. "But we have a better plan now."

"And what's to say we don't get killed or captured by the rebels?"

When I don't immediately respond, Marto turns to Charaide.

"We can't guarantee we won't meet the same fate." Charaide shrugs. "However, the alternative is much worse."

"Oh?"

I press my lips into a thin line. "We lead the army to where we *think* the rebels are and hope we don't run into an ambush."

Marto glances between Charaide and me. "Those are our options?"

I nod grimly. "I'm afraid so."

Instead of responding, Marto lifts the skewer and takes a bite out of one of the pieces of meat. His expression is thoughtful as if he's mulling over what would be the best course of action.

"We're at a disadvantage," Marto says. "If we'd had more time to plan, prepare, I would have suggested we fly under cover of darkness." His eyes stray to the lightening sky. Dawn approaches. "But by the time we arrive, it'll be midday." With a furrowed brow, he assesses Charaide and me. "Are you able to cloak yourselves?"

"I can cloak her," Charaide answers before I process what Marto means.

Marto gives a terse nod. "It's not ideal, but it'll have to do under the circumstances." He tilts his head as he looks at Charaide again. "You know you'll be limited in your ability to protect yourself if you're carrying *and* cloaking her."

"I'm aware," Charaide replies with a glance at me. "But I'm betting on her arrows."

A sly smile brightens Marto's face. "Fair point. She did manage to kill that delicious doe. What she lacks in magic, she more than makes up for as an archer."

I'm not sure if this is meant as a compliment, as it feels a bit backhanded. But I smile all the same.

"All right, I'll go find Leiftea and Saki." Marto tosses the now-empty skewer into the fire. "We'll leave within the hour."

He heads off into the camp, leaving Charaide and me alone. I check my pack to ensure I have my quiver and arrows.

"You should probably leave the rest of that here." Charaide gestures to my heavy pack. "It'll just weigh us down."

I stare at him incredulously. "But what about all of my things?"

"We can leave them with your brother. I'm sure he can have one of his men carry them for you."

My teeth worry my lower lip. "Weren't you going to have to carry me and all of this anyway?"

"Yes, but we would be surrounded by other fae that could cover us in the event of an attack from the rebels. Now, there's only four of us to protect you."

"You just said you were betting on my arrows!"

"And I meant it. But I'm also realistic enough to know that you'll be a lot nimbler in firing them if you're not shifting that heavy thing around while you do it."

I sigh in defeat. "Fine. I'll let Cliste know."

An hour later, Marto returns with Leiftea and Saki. The men are all business as they begin beating their wings before shooting into the sky. Charaide scoops me up in his arms in one swift movement, then we're air bound. I keep my eyes on his face and not on the earth far below. But even that does little to quell the queasiness growing in my stomach.

"A faery afraid of heights." Charaide chuckles. "What a spectacle."

I shoot him a glare while pressing my lips tightly together. It would do neither of us any good for me to lose whatever food may remain in my stomach. I'm very glad we didn't bother with breakfast, though if our reconnaissance mission turns into a full battle, I'm going to regret not having the store of energy.

As we soar through the air, I try to ignore the feel of Charaide's arms around me, the hardness of his chest against my cheek. It's all I can do not to nuzzle against him and savor the warmth and scent. Fortunately, or perhaps unfortunately, the higher and faster we fly, the more pronounced my nausea grows, which at least keeps me from doing something I'll likely regret.

Neither of us says much on the journey. The wind whipping past us doesn't make conversation easy, and I'm too focused on trying not to vomit to come up with anything to discuss.

Just as I'm finally getting used to the rhythm of flying, Marto appears beside us. "Look sharp, Princess. There's activity on the ground."

I turn my head, sneaking a peek at the earth just in time to wish I hadn't. My head swims, and I moan, covering my face in my hands.

"She's afraid of heights," Charaide explains, and I grimace at the humor in his tone.

"I can't tell from here if it's the rebels or just a village we're crossing over."

"We couldn't have reached the rebel camp already," Charaide counters.

I open my eyes and watch his face as he scans the terrain.

"That's what I thought." Marto gestures to the ground. "But look at all the metal glinting in the sun. From here, it's hard to make out, but Leiftea flew closer and said it appears to be a series of cannons." His eyes darken. "What reason would a village have for such a large armory?"

I shake my head, concern creasing my brow. If my uncle's intelligence was this far off, no wonder our last scouting group didn't return. They were probably still searching for the rebels.

"We need to land before they catch sight of us," Marto says. "I would suggest on the other side of those trees."

Charaide nods and angles his body as if to turn. I keep my eyes closed, though it doesn't help my nausea.

Our landing isn't gentle, but I'm so grateful to be back on solid ground, I don't care. My stomach settles as I lean against a tree. Charaide keeps close to my side, his hand on the small of my back. I'm not sure if he's trying to steady me, but it's having the opposite effect.

Marto and the others land around us, their gazes darting between the forest and the open field beyond. There is no sign of the rebels, but as they're only on the other side of this grove, we don't want to take any chances.

"We need to get closer." Marto's lips press in a thin line as he assesses me. "I'd rather not bring you so near the enemy, Princess, but I suppose you won't wait here."

"Your supposition is correct." I straighten my spine and level him with a hard stare.

He sighs. "Fine. But don't do anything foolish."

CHAPTER

ELEVEN

W‌HILE M‌ARTO never specified what he would consider foolish, I decide it's best to let him lead our group. There are five of us in total. I'm once again struck by how similar in stature the other two men are to Marto: tall with dark hair and eyes, their wings translucent shades of red. *Are they brothers?* I hope not, as I would hate for this mission to deprive a mother of all her sons at once.

We creep through the grove of trees, so much different from my beloved forest. There's little brush here, as if it's well maintained instead of allowed to grow wild. As such, it doesn't take us long to reach the tree line, and Marto motions for us to duck. I crouch low, Charaide by my side, and nock an arrow into my bow.

The cannons we saw from the sky are indeed lined up around the perimeter, but otherwise, it appears to be a normal village. There are no signs of rebel soldiers either in uniform or on patrol. We glance at each other with frowns. *Why all the artillery if this is not a war camp?*

"Perhaps one of us should go and speak to the people," Leiftea says.

Marto tilts his head as if he's considering this suggestion.

"Most of us are dressed for battle and armed to the teeth. I'm afraid we'll scare them off."

"Then send her," Saki replies, pointing at me. "Have her leave her bow and quiver. Carrying a sword won't strike anyone as odd, and she's hidden her other weaponry well."

"No," Charaide says, not even allowing me the opportunity to respond. "I'll go."

"You'll just cause more trouble." Marto jerks his chin at me. "What say you, Princess?"

"I can go." I straighten my spine and hope I appear braver than I feel. I remove my quiver from my chest and set my bow on the ground.

"Astreilles, might I have a word?" Charaide spits out through clenched teeth.

I raise my eyebrows, but he spins on his heel and heads into the grove before I can reply.

I shrug at the others before stalking after him. He may be my best friend and right-hand man, but that doesn't give him the right to boss me around like this. After walking much farther than necessary, he finally halts and whips around.

I open my mouth to call him out on his behavior, but he cuts me off. "It's too dangerous."

A laugh bubbles up in my throat. "I'm literally fighting for my life here, and you think a walk through the village to talk to people is too dangerous?"

"Your face is too recognizable, Ast. What if this is a trap? What if the rebels are waiting for us here?" He waves his hand. "One look at you and they'll either kill you on sight or they'll ransom your life in exchange for your mother and siblings abdicating."

"I can handle myself," I retort, though I'm not sure either of us believes this statement. With my bow and arrows, I'm a deadly force, but hand-to-hand, I'm mediocre at best. And I haven't had time to practice my magic since we left the castle. Nonetheless, I lift my chin defiantly. "I'm not a coward."

He staggers back as if I've slapped him. "No one is calling you that."

"You may as well if you're going to suggest I hide behind a tree while someone else takes the risk. I'm supposed to be leading this army."

"You can lead the army without taking unnecessary risks with your life." He steps forward and surprises me by cupping my face with his hand.

The warmth radiates through my skin, and I close my eyes, momentarily allowing myself to forget where we are and what we're facing.

"Leaders delegate. Your uncle did that with the first scouting expedition."

"And look how that turned out!" I pull away, needing to put some distance between us. "Besides, you heard them." I point back at the soldiers waiting for us. "I'm the only one who they won't see as a threat." I take a deep breath to calm myself. "We're far enough from the castle that these people may not recognize me immediately." Bending down, I scoop some dirt into my hands and rub it on my face. Then I tangle leaves into my hair.

Charaide pinches the bridge of his nose like he's praying for patience. "That's your disguise?"

"Brilliant, isn't it?" I grin, daring him to argue.

His shoulders shake, and though he tries to smother it, a laugh slips out. "You look like a child who lost a fight with the forest."

"Perfect. That's exactly what I was going for." Satisfied with my makeshift costume, I head back to the men with Charaide trailing me.

"What's it going to be, Princess?" Marto asks once we're at the edge of the trees.

"I'm going in."

OF COURSE, even after my declarative statement, I don't leave immediately. First, the men decide I need to look the part, so we scavenge the outskirts of the camp and find some peasant clothes drying on a line. I shiver as I pull the skirt over my leather pants, the material half frozen. The top is too sheer to wear over my armor, so after finding a thick tree to provide some privacy, I change into it. When I emerge, Marto assesses me, braiding my leaf-tangled hair into a style befitting a villager. Charaide barely gives me a second glance. His anger radiates off him in waves, but he doesn't try to dissuade me again.

"Now, if you get into trouble," Marto says as we stand on the edge of the trees, surveying the hustle of the village, "just whistle three times, and we'll come."

"Got it." My voice sounds stronger than I feel. I sneak a glance at Charaide. His jaw clenches as he stares into the distance, but there's worry burning in his eyes. I swallow my fear. "Wish me luck."

The men murmur well wishes, but Charaide doesn't join them. His eyes meet mine briefly, and I read the plea there. *Come back in one piece.*

We procured a bucket as we scoured the edge of town for clothes. It's filled with water but also serves as a hiding place for a couple of arrows. My quiver remains with the men, but my bow is carefully hidden beneath my cloak. Charaide insisted I take the weapons with which I'm most familiar, and for that, I'm grateful. Without my quiver, I still feel naked and more vulnerable than I would like, but at least I have a few arrows at my disposal.

I walk into the village, head bowed, as the women here are wont to do. No one looks in my direction, and I assess the camp from my peripheral vision. There aren't any signs of the rebel soldiers, though I hardly expect them to come out and announce themselves either. I listen to the voices around me, filtering the conversations for any suggestion of where the rebels may be hiding.

But that's not what catches my attention. Laughter—real, happy laughter—surrounds me. The townsfolk greet each other merrily as they go about their business, and the smiles I catch from the corner of my eye cause me to stumble. Far from being a war-torn village, this place is the epitome of peace. *Do the rebels protect it? Are they using it as a front?*

"Excuse me, miss," a deep voice says behind me.

I spin around, my hand reaching toward my bucket to grab an arrow. The face that greets me isn't harsh or hard like so many I've seen recently. This one is weathered, but a kind smile brightens it. "That bucket seems awfully heavy. Might I carry it for you?" He tilts his head. "Where are you headed?"

"Th-Thank you, but I'll manage," I say, pulling the bucket into my chest.

"You aren't from around here," he observes, looking me over.

"No, sir, I'm here for my family." There's some truth to that. I'm protecting my family from whatever or whoever resides here. I glance behind him, searching for threats, but I mask my scrutiny by pretending to be mesmerized. "It's so peaceful."

He gives a nod of understanding. "You must be from near the castle, then." His gray eyes soften. "So tragic, what happened to the queen's consort. My heart is with the family."

Tears spring to my eyes, but I blink them back. I haven't had a moment to grieve my father, with the scouting trip to the rebel camp, the battle, and now pursuing the rebels to wherever they fled. I dash my hand across my face, forgetting that I've marred it in mud to hide my identity. My hood falls back, and my companion gasps.

"Why, what happened to you? Come, follow me. We'll get you cleaned up."

"No," I say more forcefully than intended. It's clear he hasn't recognized me. Perhaps he has never seen a portrait of me or my family to know what we look like, but that's not a chance I'm willing to take. "I-I mean, thank you, but I really should be getting this water to the house." I bend in a brief curtsy and turn away. But his willingness to help gives me pause.

"Is there something else?" he asks.

"How has this village stayed so safe from the ravages of war?" I craft my question carefully. Mentioning the rebels might show my hand.

He sighs. "It's not without difficulty, but..." He waves toward the cannons surrounding the town. "Those help. Most don't get close enough to see they're old relics, not used for many a year." With a wink, he leans closer. "Best not be telling our secret, though, mind."

I can't help smiling. Making a cross over my heart, I nod. "I promise I won't tell a soul."

"There's a good lass." His gaze falls to my hands once more. "Are you sure I can't help you with that bucket?"

"I'm sure, but thank you for the offer." His eyes have grown curious, and I expect he'll watch to see which house I turn in to. I keep my steps slow and leisurely as if I'm not in a terrible hurry. When I reach the edge of the street, I head toward the last house on the right. He nods and moves away. The moment he's no longer looking, I stash the bucket by the house, withdraw my arrows, and scurry around the perimeter of the town, using the cannons for cover.

"Well?" Marto demands when I've returned. "What did you find out?"

"The rebels aren't here," I say, breathless from running back to the trees. I point at the cannons. "They use those as a deterrent against any who might do them harm."

"Are you sure there weren't any rebels?" Marto gazes back at the village, his brow creased with suspicion.

I recall everyone I encountered during my brief walk for any sign of rebel uniform or weaponry aside from the cannons, but nothing comes to mind. With a determined nod, I say, "I'm sure."

"Then we should keep moving to the place your uncle marked on the map." Marto addresses the rest of the men. "To the sky."

They all spread their wings and take flight. Charaide gathers me in his arms and pulls me tight against him.

"I'm glad you're safe, Ast." His eyes darken. "But don't ever put me through that again." Without another word, he launches us into the air.

It's another several hours before we finally reach the place my uncle had marked. In the distance, smoke rises from multiple campfires, and Marto silently signals for us to land a mile away.

Our landing is quiet, and we move for cover behind a large rolling hill. Crawling on our bellies, we reach the summit and keep low to the ground. One bonus of our visit to the village of cannons was that it delayed our arrival here until dusk was settling across the land. The darkening sky provided cover from any watchful eyes and aids us now in blending in with our surroundings.

The others are narrowly focused on the camp before us, but I can barely make out the fires from this distance. *What must it be like to have fae sight and hearing?* From my time in the human realm, I saw many instruments used to assist them with their limited abilities. Binoculars were used to see things at slight distances, while my father told me of satellites that drifted among the stars and allowed them to take snapshots of places throughout their world. But none of their technological advances could make up for their lack of magic.

Charaide shifts beside me and grasps my hand. I'm about to pull away when he closes his eyes, and I can suddenly hear everything at the camp. When he reopens his eyes, I see what he sees: first my face then the camp in much more detail. Envy floods through me, and I shove it down, trying to concentrate on what I see.

The rebels are here all right. Soldiers are everywhere but no sign of our wayward scouting group. Marto checks the coordinates against the ones the last scouts were given and swears.

"They evanesced right into the center of the camp." His mouth sets in a grim line as he searches the camp for any sign of them. "If they're still alive, they're probably being tortured for information."

My stomach drops. "How was our intelligence so wrong?"

Marto opens his mouth as if to respond, but Leiftea shoots him a look. He rolls his eyes and glances at me. "I have theories…" He gets another warning glare from Leiftea. "But none that hold water, I'm afraid."

"Enlighten me," I say, raising an eyebrow at Leiftea, challenging him to silence a direct order from his commander. I've never been one to use my rank before. Like Cliste, I would gladly abdicate if I didn't feel a sense of duty to my family. But I suspect Marto's theories are of grave importance.

With a grimace, Marto nods. "There's a rumor that someone on the inside is working with the rebels."

"I've heard the same." All eyes are on me.

"Do you know who it is?" Saki asks.

I shake my head. "No, and until recently, I wasn't sure I

believed it." Charaide has not released my hand, and I can still see the soldiers milling about, still catch bits and pieces of conversations. "But they knew my grandfather was dying despite the castle being on lockdown, and they knew when to attack during the coronation. The battle the other day felt too easy, like they wanted us to win, to lure us into a false sense of security. And while I could blame poor intelligence on our part, it just feels too coincidental that we sent our soldiers behind enemy lines."

"More should be done to discover the traitor," Leiftea says, his eyes flashing. "The rebels at least have their convictions, but anyone who would play both sides is not worth the air he breathes."

Murmurs of agreement flow through the rest of our group. My heart swells to know that others didn't see my family the way the rebels did. My uncle said they are loyal to the crown regardless of who wears it, but I hope my actions today will prove fruitful in winning their respect.

"We should find a safe place to make camp." Marto turns to me. "I dispatched a message to your uncle relaying our coordinates, and the rest of the army should arrive overnight. We are to wait for them here."

"Shouldn't we head back to our camp?" Charaide asks, shifting beside me.

I understand the strain in his voice and his discomfort. It wouldn't take much for the rebels to realize we're here and attack. We're safer with the rest of the army.

"If we fly back, we'll be too tired to join the army in the morning." Marto begins making his way down the hill. "We won't make a fire so as not to draw attention, and we'll stick to the trees." He glances at me. "Do not worry, Princess. I will not allow anything to harm you."

We all follow suit, sliding backward on our bellies and keeping low to stay out of sight. Once we reach the bottom, we slip into the trees and keep to the shadows. My heart hammers in my chest, being so close to the enemy.

A small bend in a tree makes for a decent shelter, and we huddle underneath. It's close quarters, but without a fire, we'll need the body warmth to survive the unforgiving cold night.

TWELVE

I'm shaken awake the next morning by Charaide. When I open my eyes, ready to curse him, he holds a finger to his lips. My heart races as I strain to hear anything amiss. The tree we found barely hides us from view, and if someone looks at just the right angle, they'll have a clear shot.

But I hear nothing, and I don't think it's just my limited fae abilities. The forest is silent save for the slight rustling of what leaves remain on the trees. I frown at Charaide, and he gestures to our companions, who are still asleep. *Ah, so there's no threat.*

I stand and stretch, spreading my wings to hover over the ground. We move toward a creek not far from the rest of the men. Kneeling beside it, we fill our canteens with water, and I drink deeply, relieving the dryness in my throat. As satisfying as it is to drink, I shiver at the icy chill. What I would give for just a few moments beside the warmth of a crackling fire.

"I expect your uncle and Cliste will be arriving with the rest of our forces soon," Charaide says, wiping his mouth.

"Who do you suppose is leading my battalion, since you're my second in command?" I ask. My stomach growls, and I can't recall the last time I had more than bits of bread to eat.

"I'm sure your uncle has assigned someone to take charge until you reunite with your men." He shrugs, filling his canteen again and taking in our surroundings. "It doesn't take much to order them to follow the rest of the army, especially since they mostly consist of our archers."

"True."

"Are you ready for today?" he asks.

It's my turn to shrug. "As ready as I can be, given the circumstances." I watch the water trickle by, allowing myself to enjoy this peaceful moment, even if it's fleeting. "Besides, we won the last battle. I expect we'll succeed here as well."

"I'm not so confident." His eyes harden. "Something feels different."

"How do you mean?"

He leans back, propping up on his elbows as he surveys the trees. "You said yourself that battle felt too easy. The last time we met with the rebels, it was little more than a skirmish. Their army was small. The camp was an outlier." His lips press together in a grim line. "Even from as far away as we were, I could clearly see that they've increased their numbers." He kicks a rock free from the dirt, and it lands in the creek, making a small ripple.

I wait for him to say more. When he doesn't, I try to think of something to fill the silence. "It's true that things are different, and we may be outnumbered." With a sigh, I skip a stone off the water's surface and land it on the other side of the bed. "But I believe we will again have the element of surprise on our side."

"They've captured our soldiers," he points out with a meaningful look.

I bite my lip. "We don't know for sure what happened to the scouting group. We didn't see them in the camp or their bodies put on some grotesque display."

"That's probably because they're hidden in a tent somewhere, being tortured." The hardness in his voice catches me off guard.

"Do you really think the rebels would stoop so low?" My eyes widen. "Their quarrel is with the royal family, not the soldiers who fight under our flags."

"If it means garnering necessary information on you, your location... your weaknesses?" A grim nod. "Then yes, I think they will do whatever they feel they must."

My mouth goes dry, and I swallow more water, but it doesn't help. Footsteps sound behind us, and Charaide jumps to his feet, his hand on his sword.

"Easy there." Marto holds up his hands as he and the others approach. "We're just here for a drink, same as you."

Charaide relaxes his stance, but his hand doesn't leave his sword. "Any word from Brutach about their arrival?"

"They're on the way as we speak," Marto says, bending to fill his canteen. "Should be here within the hour."

"Then we should head to the hill to meet them." I stand, brushing off the grass and dirt from my pants.

"If we go up there now, we'll be sitting targets," Marto says with a dismissive wave of his hand. "Best to wait until the rest of the army lands before exposing ourselves to the enemy."

I hate thinking of them that way. The rebels are, after all, also my people, a part of my kingdom, though Cliste's words echo in my head. We don't really belong here.

"Shouldn't someone act as a lookout for the arriving troops?" Charaide asks.

But Marto shakes his head. "Brutach ordered us to stay out of sight until they arrive. Unless you intend to disobey an order and risk getting yourself killed, I suggest we stay here." He gestures to the trees. "There's enough cover for us to remain unseen in this scant forest." His eyes travel skyward. "And we'll be able to see the troops arrive as well."

So we wait. Charaide and I scavenge for food near the creek, not wanting to venture too far away. We eat berries and spear a few fish. In the daylight, we feel safe enough to create a small fire since the smoke would be harder to see and the scent would be masked by the rebel army's fires nearby.

About an hour later, the soft flap of hundreds of wings drifts down from overhead. We all look up to find the first line of our troops flying by. After scrambling to our feet, we head toward the hill we climbed last night. We would use the high ground to our advantage, and I pray it will be enough to earn us another victory.

My uncle and Cliste stand in the center of our army. The rebels have spotted us and are organizing for battle. Cliste's eyes travel over me, and I could swear he sighed in relief to see me alive and unharmed.

"Good work, Astreilles." Uncle Brutach claps me on the shoulder. "I don't suppose there is any sign of our other scouting troop?"

I shake my head, unable to meet his eye. "Charaide thinks they may be in the camp and the rebels may be..." The word sticks in my throat, and I have to force it out. "Torturing them for information."

Uncle Brutach is unfazed by this news. "He's probably right. Well, once we drive the rebels back, we'll search the camp and see what we find."

I nod, though I don't voice the thoughts that cross my mind. *What if we don't drive them back? What if we lose?*

"It's time," he says, unaware of the internal battle I'm fighting. He looks to Cliste then me. "We'll begin with magic, same as last time. Astreilles, ready your archers. I'm hoping to take out a good number of them while we hold the high ground. Cliste, prepare your battalion for hand-to-hand on my signal."

We split up, calling our battalions to order. I line up my archers on two sides of the hill, leaving the middle for the other battalions. Brutach's will take front center, giving them a clear shot for their magic, while Cliste will move in behind. On this tiny hill, we seem massive, but I know better. Our numbers are no match for the army that approaches from the rebel camp. Our only chance is maintaining the high ground.

The rebel army marches closer, and I swallow my growing panic at the sheer size of their forces. They seem to stretch for miles as more and more bodies pour out of the camp. Their black armor gleams in the sun. My uncle barks an order to his battalion. Fire sparks in some of his soldiers' hands while others draw water from the stream Charaide and I sat beside this morning. If only it were enough water to wash out the field below.

But the rebels are ready for us, and across the field, their powers ignite. At first, they only appear to be countering our movements. Air to whip the water into harmless droplets, water to quench the fire.

A part of me wishes we could finish this with magic alone. Whoever has the stronger power wins, but I know that's not how this is going to work. The goal of each side will be to target the magic wielders to diminish their numbers before the hand-to-hand starts.

The ground rumbles as more fae with different gifts join the fight. I hold my breath, signaling to my archers to ready their bows and arrows. Still, the rebels march ever closer, and I wonder if they plan to march right through us. But then, as if by some silent command, they stop in unison.

A fireball scorches across the field, and some of my uncle's battalion fall. He barks an order, and I shield my eyes from the blinding flashes. It's difficult from my vantage point to see who is being targeted and who is hitting their marks. But as more of our soldiers succumb to the rebels' magic, my uncle meets my eye. My turn.

"Archers ready," I call. "Aim... Fire!"

Somewhere in the distance, a scream splits the air, sharp and sudden, like a branch snapping under too much weight. I flinch. The smell of burning cloth drifts up from the field below, acrid and cloying.

The rebels fire arrows back at us, but gravity and the wind are not on their side. I order my men to fire at will. As more rebels fall under our assault, it seems that despite their numbers, the tide is turning in our favor.

Now seems like the right time for Cliste's battalion to charge, but my brother still hasn't given the order. Brutach barks more orders to his magic wielders, who conjure up more power to throw at the rebels, but it's clear that the impact is dwindling. Wielding magic takes a lot out of the fae, and our soldiers are draining fast. In contrast, the rebels seem content to use only magic to block our maneuvers, though they aren't wasting it on stopping the arrows. I face Charaide with a frown.

"They're hoping to wear us down so we'll be too tired to fight when they finally attack," he whispers in my ear.

I glance at Cliste, and his jaw clenches. I expect he's come to the same conclusion.

He signals to my uncle and me to meet in the middle of our army, and we step away from the battle to talk strategy. When I look at him, Brutach's blue-gray eyes are as hard as steel. Clearly, this is not the quick battle for which he'd hoped.

"My battalion can't hold out much longer," Brutach says, his voice steady as if he can't hear the shouting and screams around us. "Arrows aren't going to shrink their numbers enough for us to overpower them." He raises an eyebrow at Cliste. "I know you don't want to engage in hand-to-hand given the size of their army, but I don't think we have much other choice."

"We'll be decimated." My brother's hand shakes as he reaches for his sword. The earth rumbles beneath our feet as our earth magic fae send tremors through the hill and into the valley below.

I close my eyes. *How many men do we stand to lose? A hundred? A thousand?* Our army is already too small. I doubt this rebellion will end today. *Will there even be enough of them to fight the next battle?*

"Should we retreat?" I ask.

"Of course not," my uncle scoffs, but Cliste meets my gaze, his eyes pleading. It's written all over his face. Whatever we decide to do, we're doomed. We can't fly away fast enough to avoid losing many of our numbers, and not everyone can evanesce. But if we fight, we stand to lose far more.

"We still have the high ground," Cliste says, staring at the ground with a frown. "Maybe if we make *them* charge us? That might give us a fighting chance in hell."

"And how do we do that?" my uncle demands, crossing his arms.

"We drive them out." Raising my hand, I point at the camp. "There are still soldiers in that camp. We can kill two birds with one stone here. A small group of us can sneak into the camp and light it on fire. Obviously, some of the men will stay and try to put out the flames, but if they know we caused it, they'll charge us for revenge. Then, while we're in there, we can try to rescue our scouts."

"Exactly how do you propose we sneak into an enemy camp undetected?" My uncle's eyes narrow at me, the skepticism plain on his face.

"Everyone in our scouting troop except for Charaide and me can evanesce," I say.

"Don't you think they have spells and wards over their camp to prevent anyone from evanescing into it?"

"I'm sure they do." I wave his concern away. "But we don't have to evanesce directly *into* the camp, just close enough to get in without being seen." I hold up a hand as he opens his mouth to make his next protest. "The guards are of no consequence. We'll take a large enough group to incapacitate or distract them, with the element of surprise on our side. And then we can split up to search the camp, all while setting the fires."

My uncle stares at me with newfound appreciation. Perhaps I'm not as terrible at leading as I first suspected. Cliste gives me a nod of approval.

"Go give the orders to Marto, then prepare your archers for the attack," Cliste says, taking a step to return to his men.

"Oh, I'm going with the group." I cross my arms over my chest, bracing myself.

Cliste whirls around, his mouth falling open. But my uncle assesses me with those cold blue-gray eyes. If I didn't know better, I could swear there is a hint of pride sparkling in them. He inclines his head. "As you wish."

"But, Uncle—"

Uncle Brutach shakes his head. "I'm aware of your concerns, Cliste, but I think it's best to trust Astreilles on this." His eyebrows furrow. "But do be careful."

I give my word and rush off to find Charaide and the rest of our small group. We will need to add a few to our numbers for my plan to work. With each heartbeat, I pray this harebrained scheme of mine will come to fruition.

IT TAKES a while for us to get organized, and during that time, the magic wielders and archers continue to send volley after volley toward the rebels, barely making a dent in their numbers. If we don't do something soon, we'll run out of arrows and magic, with retreating or charging as our only options.

Charaide listened to my plan with a darkening frown but didn't attempt to dissuade me. Still, I'm sure that the next time we have a moment alone, I'll likely get a tongue-lashing from him like I've never heard. The others in our small group are more than eager to evanesce into the camp and wreak whatever havoc they can. And to my surprise, several additional members volunteer to join, mostly to assist in the search for our missing scouts.

We will all evanesce at the same time so no one is standing so close to the enemy alone. Charaide and I will evanesce with Marto, while the others divide themselves amongst those who have the power and those who don't.

As we line up to leave, I take one last look at our gathered troops. Cliste meets my eye across the crowd and gives a nod. I know if I don't make it back, he'll never forgive me, but I hope one day, he'll at least understand why I keep risking my life.

I put Marto in charge of this expedition, and he gives the order. A moment later, I'm swirling through the air on a cloud of mist, feeling as though I'm being torn apart from the inside. If there's one faery power I don't envy, it's this one. Evanescing is an awful experience, no matter who does it. When the spinning stops, it takes everything I have not to heave what little I've eaten today on the ground.

We've landed about a hundred yards away from the camp, near a small rock formation at the bottom of a hill. It's not much cover, but we won't need it for long. The others arrive around us, and I feel validated by the sight of other fae with the same sickly green coloring on their skin as I suspect is tingeing mine.

Once we're all gathered, Marto signals for us to move in. Charaide and several others unsheathe their swords, readying for a fight. Several groups of guards are stationed around the camp, and we split up. Charaide cloaks us as best he can, but it will dissipate the moment we engage. We'll have to work quickly and limit the attention we draw to ourselves.

Before we left, Marto insisted that I stay behind Charaide and him, avoiding as much direct contact with the rebels as possible. It was a risk, he had said, bringing me there since I was one of their prime targets. As we approach the guards, I hang back begrudgingly. While I may not be much of a fighter, I want to hold my own in this group and not be a burden.

Marto makes contact with the first guard. It's over quickly, with the guard's throat slit and bleeding. His companion opens his mouth to sound the alarm, but Charaide guts him before he can, the yell gurgling on the blood emptying from his mouth. And so we move through the remaining guards in our path, cloaking and revealing, cloaking and revealing until we're inside the camp. I have little time to spare a glance for the rest of our group, but I send up a silent prayer that they meet with success.

Though I'm still struggling with my magic, fire must be my element, as it comes easiest. As we clear each tent, searching for our comrades, I set the fires. Smoke and flame engulf the camp, adding to the confusion and chaos while allowing us a different kind of cloak. No one pays us any mind as they rush to put out the fires.

Our plan is working. Some soldiers are dispatched to search the camp for us, but many, suspecting the attack to be an air raid, rush toward the front lines with angry shouts for revenge. The empty camp makes it easier for us to search, though the smoke causes my eyes to water. Forget fae sight; I barely maintain my human vision as the smoke thickens around the camp. On the one hand, I hope for a helpful breeze to alleviate the suffocating air, but on the other, the thick smoke provides better cover.

The panic within the camp is impacting me more than I care to admit as we flit from tent to tent, searching for the other scouts. Marto communicates telepathically with the rest of our party, and the grim press of his lips tells me no one else has found our missing men either.

A coughing fit overtakes me, and I pause to catch my breath, which is impossible amidst the smoke. Charaide holds me up as I double over. He shouts something I can't make out to Marto, who glances at me with a frown. My other arm is draped around Marto's neck, and they turn me back the way we came. It takes a moment to understand they're dragging me out.

"No!" I shout, my voice hoarse from smoke inhalation. "Not until we find the scouts."

"They could be dead for all we know!" Charaide yells in my ear.

Perhaps he's right, but I'm not willing to give up just yet.

"The others aren't as affected by the smoke as you are," Marto tells me, his voice gentle. "They'll continue the search while we get you out."

With effort, I shake my head. It feels heavy, and I become disoriented as we move through the camp. My pitiful protestations fall on deaf ears.

But then I catch a glimpse of a familiar dark cloak and a strange patchwork of skin. I wrench free of their grasps. Shouts sound behind me as I half run, half stumble after my assailant.

He heads into a large tent at the center of the camp, where we haven't lit a fire yet. I take a deep breath to steel myself, which is a mistake, as smoke courses down my lungs. My throat burns as hot as the flames around me, but I refuse to allow myself to succumb. I follow him into the tent, keeping to the shadows along the canvas walls.

After dropping to my hands and knees, I crawl behind a pile of bagged flour, peering around it into the center of the tent. There, chained to a pole, are our missing scouts. Relieved to find them alive, I am surprised by how much easier it is to breathe on the floor. I glance above me at the billowing smoke. If I must crawl my way out of this place, so be it.

"Come on," the familiar, raspy voice commands as the cloaked figure bends and helps the scouts stand. "This whole place is going to burn to the ground."

I cock my head. *Is he moving them to a new location so the rebels can continue interrogations, or is he rescuing them?* Based on past experience, I assume the former, but then he cuts through their chains with some strange magic, freeing their hands and feet.

"Where are you taking us?" one of the scouts demands, his voice trembling.

"To the edge of camp. From there, you can evanesce back to your troops."

"Why are you helping us?" another asks, his eyes narrowing in suspicion.

"Would you rather I let you burn alive?" the raspy voice sneers.

They shake their heads. He gestures for them to follow him, and he sinks to his hands and knees, crawling under the smoke. I duck into my hiding place, knocking over a bag of flour in the process. His head jerks toward me, and a pair of honey-gold eyes meets mine. A grisly smile comes across his face, but he doesn't give me away. Instead, he holds a finger to his lips and points at the entrance of the tent.

The smoke is becoming unbearable, so I follow him out. When we reach the entrance of the tent, he shouts something to the scouts, and they take off running to the edge of the village. I make to join them, but he steps into my path, drawing his sword.

"Wh-What?" I move back. "But you were helping us!"

"I was helping *them*," he counters with a careless shrug. "You just happened to be in the wrong place at the wrong time."

I remove my sword, though my hand shakes. "This is ridiculous. This whole place is about to go up in smoke, and you want to fight me?" Shaking my head, I try to walk by him, but he blocks my exit again.

"It's nothing personal, I assure you." His blade meets mine, and it's all I can do to block the attack. "Not bad, though your footwork leaves a lot to be desired." While his hood hides his face, I catch the ghost of a smirk. "Don't they teach you how to fence in that castle of yours? Or are you too prim and proper, Princess?"

With my heart pounding in my ears, I force myself to focus. While fencing was never my forte, I have learned enough to hold my own. But with him, it doesn't feel like a fight, more like a dance as he dodges my attacks and I meet his blade.

"Astreilles!" a voice shouts in the distance, but I don't blink. One wrong move and I'm dead, though my assailant seems in no hurry to kill me.

"I think your boyfriend is very upset," the cloaked figure rasps out.

"He's not my boyfriend," I reply through gritted teeth, blocking another swing of his sword.

He gives a harsh chuckle. "Could have fooled me." He lunges, and I barely have time to slide to the right. "He put up quite the fight to save you."

"It's been you all along, hasn't it?" I demand, lunging toward him, but he skips away, laughing quietly. "You've been stalking me. First the funeral then my bedchamber. That night on the hill—"

"And your dreams," he whispers, spinning away from another of my failed lunges.

I start at his words. *How does he know of my dreams?*

"You clearly have unfettered access to me," I retort, trying not to show how unnerved I am by his words, but the soreness in my throat belays the harshness. "Why attack only in broad daylight?"

"Should I slit your throat while you're sleeping, Princess?" he purrs as he circles me.

"Wouldn't that be easier?"

While I can't see his face, something in his countenance shifts. He lowers his sword. "I'm no coward."

The statement has bite to it, as if he's offended by the suggestion. I don't have time to examine it as I take advantage of his lowered sword and lunge. He swipes aside my attack as if it were nothing. My jaw tightens, and we circle again.

"You are a warrior," he continues when I don't say anything. "You've led this army through two battles now, always volunteering to put yourself in harm's way. It would hardly be a victory to kill you when you're defenseless."

My throat and eyes are burning from the smoke, and it's all I can do to stay on my feet. "Why does the method matter? Isn't the goal for you rebels the slaughter of my entire family?"

I see a flash of white teeth beneath his hood.

"Who says I'm a rebel?"

"Astreilles!" The shout is closer this time. Charaide must be fighting his way through the camp to get to me. I hope he's delayed a little longer.

"If you're not a rebel, then why are you trying to kill me?"

"I have my reasons," he says, dancing away from my next swing.

"Do tell," I spit through gritted teeth, hoping he will indulge me before Charaide arrives.

"I'm afraid we're out of time, Princess." In one fluid movement, he sheathes his sword and steps right beside me, whispering in my ear. Before I can react, he disappears into chaos and smoke around us.

The sounds of battle reach my ears. It's almost as if we were in a cocoon of our own, blocked from the noise and fire and flame. But once he's gone, the smoke overtakes me, and I double over in a coughing fit.

"Astreilles." Charaide is beside me now, pulling on my arms. "We have to go."

I can't get a breath; the smoke is too thick. He doesn't hesitate, scooping me into his arms and shooting into the sky. The air is cleaner here, the smoke billowing away with the wind. I gulp down the fresh oxygen, ignoring the burning in my chest.

But even as I begin to breathe easier, I can't shake my encounter with the cloaked assassin. While I should be dwelling on the fact that he is clearly intent on killing me in a so-called *fair* fight, the one thing that stood out to me was when he said he stalked me in my dreams. *Was that meant as an unsettling joke? Or something more?*

Charaide descends just outside of the camp, to the place where we evanesced with our group. As we land, the knot in my stomach eases at the sight of the scouts, alive and well.

One of the men was badly burned, his face marred by flame-red skin. I drop to my knees beside him and rip my tunic before pressing it to his face, but something inside me surges. A jolt comes, soft and warm, like a glow. His eyes flutter open, and I stare in horror and fascination as the charred skin begins healing under my hand.

Charaide gasps behind me.

Marto moves to my side, pulling away the tunic and inspecting the injured scout. "How did you *do* that?" he asks. "I thought your gift was fire."

"I-I don't know." My breath catches. I'd wanted only to bandage the skin, to help protect the injury until we could get the scout to our healers. I hadn't summoned anything, but my magic didn't care. It responded to my concern, not my will.

Marto gazes at me for half a moment too long before turning to Charaide. "Where were you two?"

At first, Charaide doesn't answer, as he's still staring at the healed skin of the scout. Then he shakes his head and looks at Marto. "Astreilles was fighting someone."

"Did you kill him?" Marto raises an eyebrow.

I push myself off the ground. "He left when Charaide reached me."

"Who was it?" Charaide's eyes are wary. "It looked like you were having quite the conversation."

"It was the cloaked assailant," I whisper, shuddering at the memory of how the assassin had stood a hair's breadth from me and breathed the words into my ear. "He told me to tell you 'better luck next time.'"

CHAPTER

THIRTEEN

When we land at the hillside, my eyes immediately go to the battle at hand. We've held onto the high ground but just barely. Cliste spots me as I step out of Charaide's arms, and he stalks over.

"Where the hell have you been?"

I stare at him with raised eyebrows. "What do you mean? You knew we were going to the camp."

"It was supposed to be an in-and-out operation," he seethes. "You've been gone the better part of an hour. We need you here."

"I'm sorry," I say, though I'm not completely sure what I'm apologizing about. "It took longer than anticipated to find the missing scouts."

"Did you find them, then?"

I gesture behind me with a nod. "All alive and accounted for."

"Good." He rubs his eyes as he bends his head forward. "We need to call for retreat."

My gaze turns once more to the battle occurring all around me. We stand in its center, like the eye of a hurricane. Our forces

150

are fighting strong, but we're weakened, and if we keep this up, our numbers will be further reduced.

"I'll call for it," I say and am about to do so, but Brutach catches my arm.

"No." His blue-gray eyes are all fire. "We fight this to the end."

"And if we lose?" I challenge. "What then? We have no army to protect my family, *your sister*?" Before he can reply, I rip my arm from his hand and stomp over to Charaide.

"I need your help."

"Anything," he says, and in any other circumstance, the way his voice softens would likely make me weak in the knees.

"Can you channel my voice into the minds of the men?"

His eyes widen, but he nods. "I think so."

"Then tell them to retreat. This battle is lost."

With a deep breath, he takes my hand and closes his eyes. All around us, our soldiers take to the sky or evanesce away from the battle. As the rebels realize what is happening, cheers erupt from below the hill. My heart sinks as I watch our army depart. When everyone else has gone, Charaide lifts me into his arms, and we lift off.

We regroup near the village where we saw the cannons. I speak to the villagers to let them know we mean them no harm. To my surprise, they bring food and blankets to the men, and a healer visits the wounded.

Cliste and my uncle wait for me in the center of the camp, their faces hard as stone. I suspect they've been arguing over my order, but I trust my brother with my life. He hasn't steered us wrong yet.

"We should have stayed and fought," my uncle says as soon as I reach them.

"To what end?" I demand, crossing my arms. "Our men could not hold the line."

Brutach's mouth curls in disdain. "This is why the council never wanted a halfling leading an army."

"Perhaps your pigheadedness is exactly why we should," I retort, and he whirls around. Even I'm shocked at my boldness, but I manage to keep it off my face. "We stood to lose so much more than just the battle, Uncle. We held them off long enough to get the scouts and retreat." I gesture to the camp, where the wounded are being tended. "We will rest here, allow our soldiers to heal, and gather whatever intelligence we can. Then we can decide our next step."

"Our loss today will only fuel the flames of the rebellion." My uncle points his index fingers at me. "Mark my words, girl. This was a grave mistake, indeed." He stalks away, leaving Cliste and me staring after him.

My chest tightens at the same time my jaw clenches. Part of me worries I have done the wrong thing, while the other resents my uncle dismissing my motives. Win or lose, I don't believe anything is going to quench the flames of rebellion, but at least our retreat provides our army the chance to regroup so we can fight another day.

"I'm sorry." Cliste bows his head. "You shouldn't bear the brunt of my call."

"You made the right call, and as the leader of this army, I will absolutely bear it." I glance at him. "But I do wonder what hope we have now of winning this war."

"It's one battle and one that we weren't as well prepared for as we should have been." He kneels on the ground, pulling a map from his cloak. "We had every advantage, and yet still we lost."

"Well, not every advantage." I gesture to the men around us. "We still lack the numbers."

"I know you see war as whoever has the most people left wins," he replies dryly. "But that's not really how it works." He points at the map. "The first time we attacked, we had the element of surprise. I think, were we to attack this camp again, we could approach from a different vantage point." His eyes meet mine. "We'd lose the high ground, but you did a lot of damage to their camp. They may be too distracted with rebuilding to realize we're there until we strike."

I pull the map closer, surveying the area he's pointing at. It's near where we'd evanesced to burn the camp and find the missing scouts. While it could be a better position for ensuring a surprise, we'd already taken that avenue to save our soldiers.

"They'd expect us there," I say. "Granted, there weren't many guards on that side of the camp, but since that's where our small group entered last time, I expect security will be bulked up."

"Perhaps we should have brought more men with us." Marto joins us and crosses his arms over his chest. "You did quite a bit of damage while you were there." His eyes gleam with whatever he's thinking. "Maybe we're coming at this the wrong way."

"How do you mean?" I furrow my eyebrows.

"Shadowroot tactics." He rolls his eyes at my blank stare. "Pop-up ambushes. Sabotage... much like setting fire to the camp. Breaking down their defenses from within." His lips curve in a sinister smile. "It's too bad your father didn't survive the attack on the castle." I give him a sharp look that he ignores. "Humans are well-versed in that type of battling. It's not exactly what you'd call civilized."

"Is anything about war civilized?" I look to Cliste for support, but he stares at Marto, a speculative tilt to his head.

"I've heard of something like that," Cliste says. "In Dad's old war books." He shakes his head as if in wonder. "There was one war, not in Father's home country but in one nearby, where such strategies not only won the war but the victors became famous for them." His face falls. "I wish I had those books with me now. They might help."

"We can certainly send a small band to the castle to retrieve them," Marto suggests. His gaze sweeps over our camp, lingering on the wounded near the massive bonfire being built. "It's not as if we're going anywhere anytime soon."

"I'd like to go with the group," Cliste says, avoiding my questioning gaze. "I know exactly where the books are and..." He swallows. "I'd like to see how Mom is doing."

My heart lurches in my chest. With everything going on, sometimes I forget why we're fighting this stupid war. My mother and other siblings are safe at the castle but only for as long as we hold back the rebel army. I wish I could join Cliste in visiting them, knowing full well it may be the last time I ever see them. But I can't. My place is here, preparing for the next battle.

"Wait until the morrow." When my brother looks ready to protest, Marto holds up a hand. "The men need rest and food. Then you can gather those who can evanesce. Take some of the more severely wounded with you." His expression turns grave. "They need healing powers we simply don't have out here."

Cliste nods before facing me. "Is there anything you wish me to pass on to Mother and our brothers and sisters?"

"Tell them..." My voice cracks as an image of my sister Elana comes to mind. The last time I saw her, she stood on the safe side of the drawbridge, waving goodbye with her handkerchief in one hand and her other dashing the tears off her cheeks. I clear my throat. "Tell them all is well and we will return to them soon."

He raises an eyebrow. "You want me to lie?"

I glare at him, and sparks fly unexpectedly from my fingers. We both drop our gazes to my hands, but the magic dissipates as quickly as it came on.

"I want you to give them faith to hold on," I say as evenly as I can. "I don't want to cause them any more undue worry." I wave toward the soldiers. "For now, we are beaten but not defeated, and we will rise again."

His face betrays his skepticism, but he inclines his head before walking away to determine who will join him. I stand with Marto, surveying the progress of the building of our camp. Our men are tired and weary but so happy to be alive. Even the wounded manage to crack jokes with our healers, and a pang hits me in the chest.

"I'm going to hunt," I announce, hurrying away before Marto can respond. I grab my quiver and bow before tossing on my cloak and pulling the hood up to hide my face. Thankfully, Charaide is nowhere in sight. I need a few minutes on my own.

As I enter the small batch of trees near the village, which barely counts as a forest, I feel the aching in my chest ease. It's not *my* forest, not even close, but it still gives me a sense of peace. I breathe in the deep, woodsy scent of pine and the muted decay of fallen leaves. Nothing has ever felt quite like home as much as being surrounded by trees.

Tears spring to my eyes, and I let them fall, streaming down my cheeks in salty currents. It's too much—leading this army, fighting the rebels, the weight of my entire family's future resting heavy on my shoulders. I curse Laochard for leaving me with this then bite my lip with regret. He didn't *choose* to leave. I'm not being fair.

With a sigh, I crouch to the ground. I told my brother I was hunting, so I best get to it if I don't want to return with nothing but a tearstained face to show for myself. Though within this small expanse of trees, I doubt I'll catch anything larger than a squirrel. I close my eyes, listening for the slightest sound in the trees. Silence. Not even the crunch of a leaf underfoot or the sigh of a breeze through the trees.

My eyes fly open. It's almost *too* quiet. Unnatural. My nostrils flare, but all I smell are the trees and earth and leaves around me. There's a stillness here that makes my hair stand on end. I strain my eyes, seeking the danger that lurks in the misty shadows.

Astreilles.

A whisper comes in the wind. I shake my head, sure I've imagined it.

Astreilles.

My mouth goes dry. There's a familiar, raspy quality to the voice, but I can't tell if I'm hearing it with my ears or… inside my head, the latter of which terrifies me.

Come to me, Astreilles.

I swallow as my stomach tightens. My foot moves of its own accord, and I stand. I stare at my feet.

Astreilles.

Again, I take another step as if that voice is controlling my movements or perhaps is pulling me toward it. I sink to my knees, grasping at the roots around me. I will not yield to whatever strange power is compelling me to go.

A whisper of a chuckle caresses my ear, and I shiver, closing my eyes and digging my nails into the bark. *Come.*

The word is both a request and a command, and my body moves again without my permission, but my hands remain locked around the roots. At least part of me is still under my control.

The wind picks up, pushing against my back, beckoning me to follow it. I grit my teeth, planting myself more firmly against the ground to withstand the pressure.

Astreilles. The seductive quality of the voice gives way to growing impatience. Whomever or *whatever* is calling me isn't used to resistance.

A feral smile pulls at my lips, and I lift my face to the wind, which has suddenly stopped pushing me toward the source of the voice and is instead twirling around me so fast, I fear it might upend the tree.

"Do your worst!" I scream.

The playful, cruel chuckle is gone, replaced by a cold rage. The wind blows in violent gusts, but the earth rumbles beneath me as my feet appear to be swallowed whole. As I cling to the tree trunk, random twigs and branches encircle my arms as if the tree is hugging me back. I have no idea what is happening, but whatever it is, it's keeping me safe.

"Astreilles?" This voice, familiar and kind, breaks through the wind like a torch in the fog. The gale falls still. My body sags into the earth with quiet relief. I lift my head to find Charaide, his beautiful blue eyes locked on mine, his brow furrowed.

"What are you doing here?"

I can't answer. My chest hitches with sobs as I try to extract myself from the roots, but my fingers refuse to loosen. My body still isn't convinced the danger is gone. So I stay there, crouched on the ground, clutching the bark like a lifeline.

Charaide crosses the space in two strides before kneeling in front of me. "What happened?" He pulls me into his arms.

The warmth of his chest grounds me. My fingers, one by one, finally release. I wrap my arms around him like he's the only thing holding me to this world.

"There was... a voice," I gasp. "A-And wind, so cold. It was calling, beckoning me to join it."

He draws back just enough to see my face.

"I didn't hear anything," he says, his brow furrowing. "But I did notice the rise in the wind." His eyes search my face. "What did the voice sound like?"

"I don't know." I frown. "It was raspy and familiar. But..." My lips tremble. "I can't place it."

Or perhaps I just don't want to. While the voice was sinister, it was also seductive. My body moved toward it of its own volition, but a part of me *wanted* to follow it.

"I'm surprised you heard anything at all," says another voice —soft, low, and unmistakably *not* Charaide's.

We turn. Caillea stands just beyond the clearing, her pale cloak almost luminous in the twilight. She steps forward slowly, keeping her hands visible as if not to frighten us.

"That wasn't a normal wind." Her eyes never leave mine. "That was something older. And your magic didn't just react, Astreilles. It *answered*."

I look down at the tree roots that I've pulled from my arms, the dirt still clinging to my skin like a shell. "I didn't conjure anything," I whisper.

Caillea nods. "Exactly."

CAILLEA WALKS to the camp with Charaide and me. Despite my encounter with the strange voice, I insisted on continuing my hunting trip, and Charaide and Caillea insisted on accompanying me. Together, we brought back several squirrels and rabbits.

Charaide and I don't speak about what he witnessed in the woods. Our argument about telling the others remains between us and the trees. He thought they should know that I'm being haunted by something powerful and sinister, but I was afraid it would bring further questions to my authority and leadership. I don't want anyone to doubt me, not when I would be leading them into another battle in the near future. If they don't trust me, they won't trust my judgment, and that would hurt any chance we have of protecting the kingdom and my family.

Caillea kept silent during our argument. I'm not even sure why she insisted on returning to camp with us, and I can only imagine what Brutach will say when he sees she's joined our ranks.

I set our kills down by the fire and kneel to clean them. Caillea leaves to speak with my uncle, and Charaide heads off toward our tent, presumably to brood.

One of the soldiers approaches, his eyes wary, and I lower my knife. He sinks to the ground beside me and skins a rabbit. We work in silence, but it feels companionable.

"What's your name?" I ask as we skewer the meat on sticks and hand them to the men standing by the fire.

"Arantheo," he says, his gaze darting to me then back to the last of the squirrels.

"Thank you for your help, Arantheo." With a grunt, I push off the ground. My legs are numb from kneeling for so long, and I bend to brush off the dirt.

"Thank *you*, Princess... for bringing us this bounty."

I start to scoff. A few forest creatures are hardly a bounty, but there's such deference in his voice, I can't bring myself to speak. Instead, I give an awkward nod before carrying Charaide's and my share of the meat to our small fire.

As I suspected, he's sitting alone, scowling at the flames, when I approach, and I swallow a sigh. Clearly, he's still stewing about my insistence that we don't tell the others. Without bothering with a greeting, I shove his stick toward him then sink to the ground before roasting my skewer. He grunts his thanks, which I suppose is the best I can hope for, and follows my lead.

It never used to be this difficult with Charaide. Things were effortless when we were children. If we had a squabble, we either made up quickly or forgot whatever caused it by the next day. But now, between the attraction I feel for him and the constant threat to my life, what was once easy is now strained.

When the meat is roasted, I decide to go eat somewhere else rather than continue sitting in this uncomfortable silence. Charaide doesn't even flinch when I stand and walk away. An ache throbs in my chest, but I ignore it, telling myself that he needs to cool down. Once this war is over, things will go back to normal, or at least, they'll improve... or so I hope.

I find Cliste sitting on his own, and I give him a tentative smile as I approach. "May I join you?"

He waves his hand to the log across from him before biting

into the meat. I lower myself to the log and follow suit, silently wishing for a spice or marinade to make the meal more palatable.

"Makes you miss the palace, doesn't it?" He chuckles, and I gather my distaste is clear on my face.

"Sometimes." I shrug. "Though a pinch of salt would go a long way."

He nods. "It's funny the things you miss when they're gone." Shifting in his seat, he arches his back. "My bed at home isn't as soft as I would prefer, but it's heaven compared to the cold ground."

"Well, hopefully, we'll be victorious soon," I say, feigning optimism.

He lowers his skewer and raises an eyebrow. "You don't really believe that, do you?"

I take another bite to give myself a moment before I answer, giving a cursory glance at the soldiers sitting nearby. My position is precarious. While I would never lie to my brother, I cannot be seen as having doubts. There's too much at stake.

"I believe with the right strategy and approach, we have a good chance," I say, keeping my voice steady.

His brow furrows as he picks at the meat as if he's lost his appetite. I force myself to keep eating, ignoring the lump in my throat. Another awkward silence ensues, and I'm not sure I can take it. I seem to be causing strains in all of my relationships. *At what point did winning and portraying myself as a leader become more important than being honest and up front with the people I love?*

"Have you given any more thought to what we spoke of before?" he asks, his voice low.

"You mean about abdicating and going to the human world?"

His reply is an infinitesimal nod as if he, too, is afraid to admit his deepest fears. "After today's battle, I've been thinking about it more." He stares into the flames, but I know that's not what he sees. While I missed most of the battle when I was setting fire to the camp, I saw enough of the remnants to gather how gruesome it was.

"No one would begrudge you your choice, Cliste." I sigh. "But if I may ask a favor..." Wary eyes meet mine. "Would you at least stay and help me strategize until it is clear there is no hope?"

His face tightens as if in pain, but he nods. It's no small thing. The longer we fight, the longer this drags on, the more likely it is that we won't survive to see the end. We have targets on our backs, and I hate asking him to stay with me, but I need him. Beyond his clever brain and brilliant strategizing, he's my brother and the sibling closest to my age. I cannot do this alone.

"Will you promise me something in return?" He gazes at the fire, and it is my turn to be wary. "Will you consider joining me when the time comes?"

I stare at the meat on my skewer, my appetite gone. This is no small ask either. I don't dream of the human world the way he does. As much as I have no desire to be queen or to fight in this awful war, this is my home. It's all I've ever known. To leave it, to abdicate, has more significance to me. Laochard is gone, and our other siblings are too young to take the throne if something were to happen to our mother.

"Just... consider," he continues as if he can read my thoughts. He likely can. My face tends to betray me so often that faery telepathy is not required.

"I'll keep an open mind," I finally say. "But I won't make any promises."

He raises his hands as if to ward me off. "That's all I ask."

"Are you ready to return to the castle tomorrow?" I change the subject, hoping to avoid any discussion of his plans. Technically, what he is suggesting is treason, though our mother would never begrudge him his choice. Brutach, on the other hand...

"I am." He unfolds his legs from under him and stretches out.

"I wish you could join me. Mother won't take my word for it that 'all is well,' as you put it."

"Then you'll have to be more convincing," I tease.

"I was never a good actor." After tossing the empty skewer into the fire, he leans back, surveying me. "But you seem to have stepped into your role here."

"Shoved into it, more like." I keep my eyes on the flames, refusing to meet his glare.

"So you claim, but it suits you."

I flick my gaze to him briefly before returning to the fire. "I'm not sure if that's a compliment or an insult."

"It's neither. Simply an observation."

"I'm not much of a leader," I reply, tossing my stick into the heat. The flames catch it, and sparks shoot up into the air.

"Not in the accepted practice, no, but that doesn't mean you don't possess leadership qualities."

I can't help staring at him, my eyebrows raised. "The 'accepted practice'?"

He leans forward, face dancing between shadow and light from the flames as the sun sets behind him. "Laochard commanded loyalty through force. You draw it through something quieter. They trust you because you throw yourself into danger with them. Not because it's wise," he adds with a look, "but because it's honest."

I can hear the derisive undercurrent to his words, his disapproval of me putting my life on the line, not just for what I risk but for what my death would mean for him.

Before I can speak, he continues, "You listen, even when you don't have the answers. You don't pretend to be stronger than you are. That earns something force can't." He takes a deep breath, fixing me with an unwavering look. "And most importantly, you acknowledge your weaknesses and let others lead when appropriate."

I swallow thickly. "Then you know about Marto."

He nods. "Brutach disagreed, but I understood why you did it. You knew the other men trusted Marto, and you were willing to put your pride aside to let him take the lead." He chuckles. "Marto reveres you, though I doubt it's love." His body shifts, his spine straightening. "Not like Charaide."

Warmth floods my cheeks as I duck my head. "I have no idea what you're talking about."

"Don't you?" His eyes light in amusement, but he doesn't press. It's one of the reasons he and I have always been close. Laochard would have crowed to anyone who would listen had he learned the truth of my feelings for my best friend. But Cliste has a quieter soul, like me. Perhaps that is why he is so determined to go to the human world. A priesthood like he envisions may allow him the peace and tranquility he so desperately wants.

I stand, not bothering with a response. None is needed. "You should get some rest. The castle is far, and I know how much you hate to evanesce."

He grimaces. "I would rather fly if it wouldn't call attention."

"Or take several days," I retort with a laugh. My eyes grow misty. "Give my love to Mama."

He pushes off the ground and pulls me into a warm embrace. My heart fractures, and a part of me wishes he could remain in the castle, safe with the rest of my family.

When we part, his eyes are wary. "Don't go into the woods alone again." He walks away without explanation.

A shiver runs up my spine. *What did he sense in that brief moment?*

CHAPTER

FOURTEEN

"You've returned," the raspy voice says.

I squint into the room. The vibrant colors are dazzling, blending in that same strange way that they did before. It blinds me, and I lift my hand as if to shield my eyes, but it's no use. My hand is, once again, translucent, and the light from all of the colors shines right through it.

"You'll get used to it after a while."

Spinning around, I search the room for a shimmer, but there isn't one. The room is the same, with the floor-to-ceiling windows on the one side, curtains blowing in an endless breeze, even though the air around me is stagnant. Or is it that I can't feel the breeze because I am not physically present? The thought unnerves me.

"Why am I back?" I ask, closing my eyes against the brightness. It's foolish to waste energy searching for the shimmer again. Staring at it only gives me a headache, and I'm sure to wake up with enough aches and pains from sleeping on the hard ground.

"I have the same question," the voice responds with a hint of amusement. "I didn't expect to see you again so soon."

"If I knew how I was doing this, I would have picked a place with better company," I retort, crossing my arms. The same sheer white *nightgown adorns my body, and I shiver against the chill, but rubbing my hands over my arms provides no friction or warmth.*

"You'll grow more accustomed to that as well if you keep returning."

Footsteps sound behind me, but I don't open my eyes. The pounding of my head has dissipated now that I'm no longer staring at the blindingly bright colors.

"Why are you here?" I ask, trying to refocus the conversation.

"This is my safe haven," the voice replies, and I'm surprised by how melancholy it sounds. "I come here to find solace." It chuckles quietly. "And usually to be alone, but you seem to take great joy in being an unexpected guest."

I start at the choice of words. Not unwelcome or uninvited, just unexpected? "Perhaps I need someone to teach me how to stay in my own body."

"Or perhaps something is drawing you here," the voice purrs. It's seductive and sensual, and the next shiver that flows through me has nothing to do with the chill.

"To kill me, I'm sure," I say, taking a step back. This is a mistake, as my back hits something hard behind me. I whirl around, opening my eyes, but again see only a shimmer.

"I told you, Princess, nothing can harm you here." The shimmer steadies me with unseen hands before moving away.

"So you claim, but I suspect you're not above trying to harm me."

There's a shift in the air as if the shimmer is shaking its head. "Not here. As I said, this is my safe haven." The weight of a stare lingers on my face. "And I suppose it's yours now too."

"The forest is my safe haven," I say.

"In your physical body, yes, but what of your soul?"

"Am I dead?" I cover my mouth. I didn't mean to speak.

A rough laugh comes. "Not yet."

I step toward the window, hoping to escape the brightness burning my eyes. Outside this bright room is a dark abyss. I can't tell if the light in this room is so blinding that it erases any trace of light or if it really is pitch-black outside. My feet move of their own accord, beckoning me to move closer.

"I wouldn't go out there if I were you," the voice rasps. "It's not safe."

"But what can harm me when I'm not even physically present?" I ask this as much to the strange being before me as to myself.

"You'd be surprised." The air shifts again, like someone taking a breath. A sudden heat warms my cheek, as if a hand has cupped it, and I stagger away. I blink, and the shimmer is across the room. "My apologies. I did not mean to startle you."

I peer into the brightness, trying to see through it and around it. My eyes adjust, but the shimmer doesn't take any discernible form. "Why can't I see you?"

The silence becomes pregnant with words not spoken, and I realize that the shimmer has knowledge it hesitates to reveal. I pull myself to my full height, hoping to portray a more foreboding presence. "Answer me!"

A sigh whispers through the room. "It's... complicated."

I lean against the window frame, which feels unnatural since neither I nor the frame is physically present. "Try me."

After a moment's hesitation, the shimmer glides toward me. I brace for impact, but it stops just short of reaching me.

"I created this place," the voice says. "And so I can take whatever form I wish. I assume your mind has not been able to place the form I chose, so it remains a blur."

"A shimmer," I correct.

It barks a laugh. "That's new and hardly an apt description of me. I would have expected a shadow."

I cock my head. "Because you're evil?"

Though it's hard to make out, I could swear the being flinches. "I suppose I've been called worse." It—er—he moves beside me and flicks the curtain. I assume the shimmer is male based on the rough, deep voice. "But no. It's how I operate. A shadow in the world, never fully allowing myself into the light."

I stare out the window. The pure darkness I saw earlier was misguided. As my eyes adjust to the brightness of the room, I can make out a swirling mist, shadows and light, battling for dominance.

"How do I control it?" I somehow know he will understand what I mean.

"Practice." He turns, and the weight of his stare causes me to lower my eyes to the floor. "And a damn good teacher."

I steel myself, fighting with a need to stop leaving my body without my consent while at the same time not wanting to ask the thing that frightens me for help. "Can you teach me?"

The being before me goes impossibly still. "I don't think that would be wise."

"And why not?" I add an edge of haughtiness to my voice to hide the mixture of relief and fear.

For a second, the shimmer clears, and I catch a glimpse of a face, one so familiar I lean closer, trying to make it out, but just as soon as it clears, the image clouds again. "Because in the physical realm, I'm destined to kill you."

My eyes fly open, and I stare at the inky sky spattered with stars. My heart pounds in my chest, and the rush of blood roars in my ears. I take a breath then another, trying to calm myself. It was only a dream. I shake my head. But it wasn't. Not if the raspy voice at the center of it was to be believed.

I close my eyes, willing myself to call up the glimpse of the face I saw. If I can identify it, maybe I can figure out who the shimmer is in the physical realm and why they intend to kill me.

Beside me, Charaide snores, and I'm comforted by the sound. Perhaps this means he's not still angry with me, though I suspect it has more to do with our normal routine. The ground is cold and hard, and I shift, trying in vain to find a comfortable position. Part of me wants to get up and prepare for the day, but the sky is still so dark, and despite how restless I am, I need my rest.

But sleep evades me. I sit up, taking in the rest of the camp. Cliste will leave at dawn, and I don't know what will happen while he's gone. *We have no immediate plan of attack, but will we need one of defense? Will the rebels choose to attack us now, since we were forced to retreat?* I take a deep breath, willing my pounding heart to calm. With the damage I inflicted on their camp, I can only hope it was enough to keep them busy for a few days, giving us time to regroup, though it will never be enough.

I stand and stretch. I'm not on the roster for keeping watch tonight, but it's clear that sleep will remain evasive for some time. *What better use of my wide-awake status than to give reprieve to whoever is on duty?* I walk to the center of camp, stepping around sleeping bodies. Brutach is nowhere to be found, and I suspect Cliste is resting up for his trip home tomorrow.

When I can find no one to tell me the time or the shift change, I wander to the edge of the camp. Marto stands amongst some other soldiers talking in low voices while keeping a watchful eye on the forest beyond. I step on a twig, cracking it under my weight, and they all spin toward me. Marto's wary expression fades into an easy smile, and he leans against a tree.

"Couldn't sleep, Princess?"

The way he addresses me causes my spine to lock in place. It reminds me of the voice in my dream. I stare at him for a moment. *Is Marto the shimmer?*

"Astreilles?" he asks when I don't respond. "Are you all right?"

Forcing a smile, I nod. "Bad dream."

What if it wasn't a dream? A small voice asks the question I've been avoiding since my first visit to that impossibly bright room. I still believe astral projection is a myth, but there was something eerily real about the dream. *Is the voice awakening an unknown ability within me?* I shiver. Nothing good can come from that voice.

Marto leans toward me, his easy smile widening. "Maybe I can take your mind off of it."

I roll my eyes at his suggestive tone and gesture to the men. "I can keep watch if any of you need a break."

They glance at each other, and a couple of the men nod before going off to grab a bite to eat or relieve themselves. I keep my eyes on the forest, fighting a desire to trigger the voice again and my natural self-preservation telling me to run far from the darkness swirling among those trees.

Marto stays, though neither of us speaks. His presence is oddly comforting. He's not overly protective of me like Charaide is or constantly questioning my authority like my uncle. It's one of the reasons I trusted him to lead both the scouting mission and the one to save the scouts from the rebel camp.

"You're not what I expected," Marto says, bringing me back to the present.

"And what did you expect?" I try to keep the curiosity from my voice.

"A timid little girl afraid of her own shadow."

The words are blunt though not surprising. I'm a princess, after all. A halfling born into a privilege I don't deserve. Of course he would expect me to be spoiled, incapable of actual combat. Eyebrow raised, I assess him. "And now?"

He grins in a mocking way. "You are definitely more than a girl."

I roll my eyes. I should have known he would turn it into another innuendo. "I'm not afraid of my own shadow either."

"But you *are* timid," he observes.

I don't bother arguing. He's not wrong, after all, though I would consider it more being cautious than timid.

"Or at least, you pretend to be timid."

I jerk my head toward him. "What's that supposed to mean?"

He shrugs, and the nonchalance sets my teeth on edge. "Just that I think you're capable of more than you let on."

"I haven't tried to hide my capabilities."

"Haven't you?" He leans back and purses his lips. "I've been around awhile, and I've not seen a faery wield fire like you do"—he sneers—"especially not a halfling."

I lift my chin in an attempt to appear haughty and unbothered by his assessment, but inside, I'm reeling. I'd always thought of Marto as an ally, a reluctant one, perhaps, but still on my side. But now, something in his tone stirs a flicker of doubt. *Does he see me the way the rebels do? Or is it more complicated than that?*

"If that's how you see me, then I question your choice to fight with me." I spit the words out through my teeth.

His smirk falters. Just slightly.

"I—" He hesitates, blinking like he's been struck. The weight of my words seems to land somewhere between his chest and his pride. He drags a hand over his face then looks at me and swallows. "That wasn't fair." He pauses, and his voice drops. "You're right. I'm sorry, Astreilles." He bows his head. "If I'm being honest, I envy that power."

I take a step back, unsure of his sincerity. "My power is nothing compared to yours." I gesture to the camp. "To that of every fae here. As you say, I'm just a halfling."

His eyes close, and I catch the slightest wisp of regret on his face.

"I didn't mean it like that."

I fix him with a hard stare, unblinking. "That's exactly what you meant."

A sheepish smile pulls up his lips. "Fair." He straightens. "But I meant what I said. I envy you the power of fire." Shaking his head, he moves to a nearby campfire. "So much destruction lies in the palms of your hands. I wonder you don't take the throne for yourself."

Dropping my gaze to the ground, I say, "If I'm being honest, I don't want it."

He doesn't immediately respond. When the silence becomes unbearable, I glance up at him. His eyes narrow as if he's assessing me again. With a wave of his hand, he motions me away from the group. I hesitate, not wanting to abandon the post. My eyes stray beyond the tree line to the foreboding shadows deep in the forest, and my feet turn of their own free will. Before I can take another step, Marto catches my hand and pulls me along with him. I don't try to shake him free, instead clinging to his hand as if my life depends on it. With another glance at the woods, I shiver. Perhaps my life *does* depend on it. Whatever is drawing me to those shadows can't have good intentions for me.

We walk to the north corner of the camp, where a small fire has been left mostly unattended. A few soldiers sleep nearby, but otherwise, we are alone.

Marto releases my hand, and I perch on a stump. He sits beside me, warming his hands in the dying flames.

"Why don't you want to be queen?"

I close my eyes. Maybe it would have been better to go to the forest than to have this conversation. It's like an echo of my earlier discussion with Cliste, and it's a subject I've avoided with Charaide.

"What does it matter? My mother is queen, and she's got many years ahead of her. The throne isn't something I'll have to worry about for some time."

His silence twists my stomach, and I can almost hear his thoughts even without the gift of telepathy. If the rebels target my mother and succeed, then I will have to worry about the throne much sooner. But I can't risk such thoughts, not so soon after the deaths of my father and brother. I can't bear the idea of my mother joining them, not now.

"Then let us speak in hypotheticals."

I glance at him out of the corner of my eye, suspecting that if he doesn't read my exact thoughts, he can sense the tenor of them. "Why does it matter to you so much?"

"I should think that would be obvious." He leans back and stares at me. "If I'm going to put my life on the line to save your family and the line of succession, I deserve to know why a member of that line doesn't want the job."

Damn. He has a point, but the answer isn't so simple. "I'm not much of a leader." It's an excuse and one he unfortunately sees right through.

"Hogwash." His eyes bore into mine. "You forget, I've fought with you, twice, and you are more of a leader than your brother ever was."

I flinch, both because of the reminder of Laochard and also due to the harsh comment. My heart aches.

"My brother was a fierce warrior—"

"But not a great leader," Marto cuts me off. "He had his moments, to be sure, and owned the battlefield, but I've never seen someone lead like you do, with your heart. You pulled us out of a battle not because we were struggling to hold the line but because you could see what holding that line would cost us, even if we were successful." He shakes his head with a quiet laugh. "Fighting this war... It feels more like an impulse, not to protect —" He smirks. "You're hardly a damsel in distress, but it's more, a desire to prove myself to you. To earn your respect as a soldier."

I scoff. "You've fought in many battles before me. You have nothing to prove."

"Perhaps not, but you inspire that in me." He gestures to the camp behind us. "In many of the men, whether you see it or not." Then he leans back. "But you still haven't answered my question. Why don't you want to be queen?"

My hope that he would drop it crumbles, and I take a deep breath. "Leader or not, I wasn't raised to be queen. Laochard was next in line, and it was a relief to me. He was always the strongest of my siblings. When he died..." My voice cracks. "Suddenly, this huge responsibility was thrust onto me, and I haven't been able to process what it means for me, for my future."

For a moment, neither of us speaks. Then Marto flicks his wrist, and sparks fly out of his fingers, rekindling the dying embers of the fire.

"I never had any siblings. My father died when I was a baby, and my mother raised me on her own. But the way you speak about Laochard... it makes me think I might have liked to have a brother. Maybe then I wouldn't have felt quite so alone in this world."

Something about his tone wraps around me, and I lay a hand gently on his arm. "I'm sorry. For the loneliness. And for never asking."

He shrugs and grins in his usual way, but this time, it doesn't quite reach his eyes. "Anyway, we weren't talking about me. We were talking about you." He nudges my knee with his. "Haven't you been raised to take the throne your whole life?"

I bow my head, the weight of running a kingdom pressing down on my shoulders. "I was raised to be a royal. I learned all the pomp and circumstance that comes with that role, but it's never come naturally to me. I'm not a great speaker or strategist. My skills with a bow and arrow are better suited for hunting than battle." I worry my lower lip with my teeth, staring into the flames. "Of course, if the rebels are successful in abolishing the entire line of succession, my lack of leadership skills won't matter in the end."

"You can't think like that," Marto counters. He stares off into the distance before continuing, "The rebels are misguided."

"Why do you say that?"

"They see you and your siblings as inferior, and they question your mother's judgment in marrying a human. But they fail to see how much potential lies within halflings." His gaze lands on my wrists, where the marks left by my iron bracelets are still visible. "Admittedly, I haven't met many halflings. So many of them return to the human world, hide their abilities, and live mostly normal lives. The few that stay are forced to wear those wretched bracelets, which suppress their powers. As a result, we've never seen what they are capable of, though I know most full-blooded fae view them as less than." He smiles sadly. "I've struggled with that myself. But you've made me rethink my own prejudices. And your fire ability makes me wonder what else you can do."

"I can't even evanesce," I say, unable to keep the bitterness from my voice. "I doubt I have much else to offer magically."

"Don't you think it's time you found out?"

I want to say no, but a small part of me, the part that wonders why the tree reacted to me clinging to it, makes me want to learn as much about my magic as I can.

"Perhaps you're right." I keep my voice nonchalant.

But inside, I realize that the only way I'm going to ever learn to harness my magic is by finding a teacher. And I know just the person to fill that role.

Hours later, my limbs tremble from exertion, and my eyes sting with exhaustion. But Caillea, ever serene, simply tilts her head and lifts her hand in silent instruction.

"Again," she says softly, not unkindly.

I exhale sharply, frustration curling at the edges of my tone. "We've been at this for hours. Aside from my flames, I haven't been able to produce even the most basic faery magic you've asked me to attempt."

Caillea only watches me, calm and unreadable. "Then let's stop asking it from your head and let it come from your body."

I blink. "I don't understand."

"You're thinking too much." She gives me the smallest smile. "Magic doesn't always come through logic. Sometimes it needs quiet."

I close my eyes and attempt to still the thoughts racing in my brain. I imagine a box, tucking each worry inside—the war, my siblings, my mother, the strange voice in the forest, Charaide's silence. I breathe, slow and deep.

A rustle in the brush draws my attention—Charaide. Of course. He leans against a tree just outside the clearing, arms crossed, watching silently. Guilt prickles under my skin. We tried training together once, and now I'm out here with Caillea, near the place where I last heard that terrible voice.

I open my mouth to explain, but Caillea lifts a hand. "Stay in it. You're close."

Reluctantly, I shift my focus inward again.

"Feel the heat in your core," Caillea murmurs, "the ember of something ancient. Let it rise through your chest, down your arms, to your hands."

Warmth sparks in my fingertips. When I open my eyes, two flames glow gently in my palms. I guide them toward the pit Caillea prepared, and they leap like eager dancers to the wood.

She smiles, nodding once. "Well done. You're starting to feel *with* the magic, not just reach for it."

"Not bad…" Charaide's voice is quiet from the tree line.

I glance at him, startled, but Caillea speaks first. "Your power responds strongly to fire. But perhaps there's more than just one thread to follow."

"She can wield water," Charaide says, startling me. "I broke into the apothecary and stole the elixir to break her bracelets. I didn't think it was fair that I had magic and she didn't. But once it was off, she couldn't control her magic, and she set my curtains on fire. When she realized what she'd done, suddenly, there was a wave of water dousing the flames." Charaide's lips lift in a small smile. "I'll never forget the sizzling sound as the fire went out."

Warmth creeps up my neck, and I duck my head. I'd forgotten that incident or perhaps banished it from my memory. It wasn't my finest moment, even if there wasn't any permanent damage. But the reason for the flames was one I would never forget. Charaide and I had wrestled for the bracelet, as I was so scared I would be in a lot of trouble with my grandfather for removing it. Charaide pinned me to the ground, and the look he'd given me made me think he was going to kiss me, and well, my hormones got the better of me.

Caillea regards me with interest. "Do you need a source, or is it something you build inside yourself? Like fire?"

I shrug. "It wasn't like I intended to set his room ablaze or put out the fire I started."

"Well, why don't we test this theory?" She gestures to a stream nearby. "Come."

I sneak a glance at Charaide, his full lips pressed into a grim line. The idea of going closer to the voice, the one I couldn't seem to resist, fills me with panic. I hold out my hand, and after a moment of staring blankly, Charaide takes it. Maybe his presence will be enough for me to withstand the thrall of the voice in the forest.

Lucky for me, the stream is not as deep into the trees as I feared. It's small, more of a creek than a stream, but I bend beside it, listening to the flow of the water and letting the cool liquid run over my fingers.

"Let it come to you," Caillea whispers. "Not as a tool. As a companion."

Coolness seeps into my palms, crawling up my arms like ivy. When I open my eyes, the water has risen into the air, encircling me like a veil. I breathe in sharply, stunned.

"It's responding," she says, thoughtful. "Not because you're controlling it but because you're connecting with it."

I guide the water gently, letting it arc above us before returning it to the stream. My body sags with effort.

"Extraordinary," Charaide says, lifting his hand and touching the stream. The water drips down his fingers, but otherwise, his movements cause no interruption to the flow.

"You're attuned in a different way than most," Caillea says carefully. "Not because of lineage or training. Just... unique, as if nature *responds* to you instead of you controlling it."

I glance at my hands then up at the trees. "Then why does it feel so unpredictable?"

"Because some forms of magic don't like being caged." Caillea crouches beside me and places her hand on my shoulder. "But you can learn to move with it. It just takes practice and getting out of your own head."

"Just not today." Charaide steps between us. "She's exhausted and needs to rest."

I don't argue. Every muscle in my body aches, and I can't help but question Caillea's words. *If I'm connecting with elements through my power, why does it take so much effort?*

Instead of pressing the issue, Caillea smiles. "We'll pick back up with this tomorrow."

As I rise, Charaide offers me his arm. Caillea walks beside us, and for once, I don't feel like my magic is something broken. It's ready to work with me and just wants to be understood.

But then the shimmer's words return to me. *Will my magic be enough to save me from the destiny he promised?*

CHAPTER

FIFTEEN

THE NEXT FEW days pass without incident. I'm praying that means the damage I did to the rebel camp was significant enough that they haven't had a chance to regroup. But every day that passes without Cliste's return makes me anxious.

I approach my uncle's tent, trying to ignore the pounding of my heart. We've had the same argument several times, and I'm tired of conceding. The rebels will have had time to plan and strategize, even while rebuilding their camp, but we have no real plan for our next move. As I take a breath before storming into the tent, I promise myself that this time, I won't allow my uncle to dissuade me.

"Astreilles," Uncle Brutach calls. "How lovely to see you."

"Uncle." I prepare for another battle. "You've put me off long enough. We need to determine our next move before the rebels ambush us."

He holds up a hand. "I'm one step ahead of you, my dear." As he moves aside, I see Marto and Cliste's second in command sitting at a makeshift table in the center of the tent. "We were just about to send for you."

I blink and shoot him a wary glance. His face is impassive, betraying nothing. I take the seat he indicates, and he sits to my right.

"Let's get my niece up to speed, shall we?" Brutach says. The men around the table give silent nods, and my uncle turns to me. "Cliste has sent word that he returns on the morrow. We'll send a scouting party to assess the rebels' activity." His smile is measured, almost diplomatic. "After all, we saw what happened when we underestimated them last time."

I swallow my retort and incline my head, indicating for him to continue. Inside, I'm torn. On the one hand, I'm glad my brother is returning, but on the other, I wish he could have stayed with our mother a bit longer. Still, we need those books if we're going to embrace Brutach's strategy.

"Marto has offered to lead the band again, but I would prefer if you would stay here. I hear you've been working with your magic." He leans back, folding his hands in front of him. "It's wise to explore what assets we can rely on. Especially ones that surprise us."

My gaze drops to the floor. Even when he's praising me, it never quite feels very complimentary. Brutach always seems to know where to hit hardest so that his praise leaves me questioning my very existence. Someone shoves back their chair, and I jerk my head up. Marto's face is bright red.

"With respect, sir, I think you underestimate what she's accomplished. Her magic may still be finding its shape, but I've seen few command with her clarity at such a young age. She doesn't just lead with power, she leads with purpose."

Warmth spreads through my chest. It's one thing for Charaide to defend me, but it's quite another for one of the men I've been charged with leading to do so.

My uncle doesn't even blink. Instead, his cold glare meets Marto's heated one. "I didn't realize the admiration for my niece extended beyond Charaide." He clicks his tongue. "Take care, Marto. Charaide has all the devotion of a guard dog, but tread near that which he thinks is his to protect and he may bite."

Despite the callousness in my uncle's words, Marto doesn't flinch. "I recognize her dedication to the cause. I suggest you do the same."

But Brutach just waves a hand and changes the subject. "Once we have the books Cliste set out to recover, we will need some of the men to read over them, learn the techniques the humans used in their wars, and figure out how to adapt them for our purposes."

"Do we expect the rebels will attack us anytime soon?" I ask. "Have we had any intelligence on that front?"

"All's quiet for now," Marto replies, meeting my eyes for the first time. Despite his defense of me, something in Marto's gaze catches me off guard. It isn't quite affection, but there's a reverence, maybe even admiration. It almost resembles my reflection in the mirror when I let myself think of Charaide. But with Marto, I'm not sure what it means.

"And we'll know more when we get to the camp," my uncle says.

I nod. "When will the scouting group leave?"

"As soon as I can prepare them." Marto stands, moves to leave, then turns back, his eyes on me. His teeth chew on his lower lip, and I suspect he has more he wants to say.

"Why don't I go with you?" I jump up from my seat. "I'd like to wish the men well before their journey."

Ignoring the knowing sneer my uncle gives me, I hurry out of the tent with Marto. When we've put some distance between us and any listening ears, I stop him.

"I could tell there was something you didn't want to say in front of the others." I cross my arms. "Out with it."

Rubbing a hand over his face, he nods. "Charaide and Caillea have been arguing all morning. He would prefer to evanesce somewhere safer to do your training. But Caillea doesn't think it's wise, and personally, I'm not sure your uncle would approve of you leaving the camp." He raises an eyebrow. "Charaide says you're not safe in the woods."

With a sigh, I plop down on a nearby stump. "He's right to worry, though I can't imagine I wouldn't be safe if both Caillea and he are with me."

"Is there some sort of creature there?" When I don't immediately respond, he kneels in front of me, forcing me to look at him. "If there's danger so near our camp, the men and I deserve to know."

"There's no danger to anyone but me," I say, shaking my head.

His eyebrows pull together. "I feel like you're speaking in riddles."

Resigned, I recount my experience in the forest the other day, silently cursing Charaide for this betrayal. His concerns may be valid, but practicing somewhere else was something we could have discussed privately. There was no reason to worry the others.

When I finish my tale of insanity, he sits back on his heels, rubbing his chin. "And you said you've heard this voice before?"

"Yes, but I can't place it." I run a hand through my hair. "Where I know it from is on the fringes of my memory. If I could only hear it again, maybe I could determine its owner."

Before I've even finished speaking, Marto shakes his head. "The voice is only calling to you, and from what you've said and what little Charaide would tell me, it sounds as though you aren't able to resist its thrall. Better for you not to go seeking it."

I push off the stump and rise to my full height, glaring down at him. "I would think that I've proven I'm no damsel in distress."

A wry smile pulls up one corner of his mouth. "You're also not an idiot who puts herself in danger unnecessarily."

The smile catches me off guard, but as his words hit, I bow my head, grumbling. He has a point, as much as I hate to admit it.

"But who's to say the voice won't just follow me and wait for me to be alone?"

He shrugs. "It may, though I would assume the source would be nearby. Still, since we know for sure it called to you in the woods, it's best not to return there." He pushes up from the ground and holds out his hand, which I accept. His skin is warm and callused against mine, so unlike that of Charaide. Soft where Marto's is rough, as if there is a stark contrast between our privileged lifestyle and that of a true warrior.

The thought brings me up short. While I've known many privileges, the constant hatred for being what I am has never made me consider just how different my life has been. Even now, a callus has begun to form on my fingers where I pull back my bow. At one time, archery was something I did for fun or to hunt. But now, it's something I do to survive and to protect those I love dearly.

Marto doesn't release my hand as we cross the camp to the edge of the wood. Charaide and Caillea are waiting for me, and neither looks happy about it. While Caillea hides her irritation behind a dazed smile, Charaide stands with his back to the forest and his gaze darting back and forth along the camp. When he spots us, his tense stance relaxes, but as he focuses on our joined hands, some other emotion I can't place darkens his features.

As if sensing Charaide's change in demeanor, Marto drops my hand. "Her uncle will never permit her to leave the camp, and if he sees you evanesce with her, he'll have your heads." Marto nods to the trees. "Take her to the clearing and then depart from there. Everyone will assume you've gone to practice, and no one will blink an eye."

Caillea presses her lips together, clearly not happy with this plan, but doesn't protest. Charaide offers his arm, but before I accept it, I take Marto's hand and squeeze it gently.

"Please be careful," I say. "And tell the men I wish I were going with you."

That wry smile returns. "Believe me, they all wish you were coming as well, if for nothing else than to see what crazy scheme you come up with next."

We laugh, then Marto bows his head before turning and walking away. I watch him, my heart in my throat, and pray to whatever deity may be listening that they don't meet with an ambush.

THE NEXT THING I KNOW, Caillea has whisked us away from the clearing, and I'm stumbling away from her in a familiar setting. I look around me, breathing deeply for the first time in days.

"My forest," I whisper, feeling more like myself than I have since this whole ordeal began. "You brought me home."

"We can't stay long," Charaide says, coming up beside me. "But I thought you might be more comfortable practicing unfamiliar magic in a familiar place."

"I suppose, if we must leave the safety of the army"—Caillea sighs—"then there is no better place for you to go." She faces me. "Shall we?"

With a nod, I step into the center of the clearing and close my eyes. The goal is to work on wind today, but something about the soft moss beneath my feet and the smell of damp earth filling my nose convinces me to focus on a different element. I plant my feet, breathing in the place I've felt connected to all my life.

Charaide moves to the edge of the trees, and Caillea steps back, giving me room, and I focus on my magic. I can feel the flame ignite in my belly, and I briefly pull it into my hands before extinguishing it. Fire is easy; it comes the most naturally to me. Then I focus on the firm ground beneath me, the way the dew on the grass seeps into my clothes. I draw the water into my feet, up my legs, into my core, then up through my shoulders to my hands. My fingers spritz the droplets around me.

But how to control the earth? Fire is a part of my soul, and water is a part of my body. Earth is solid and immovable. When I think of earth, I think of Laochard and his strength. I think of Charaide and his steadfastness. They both wield the power of earth, though in different ways. I allow my gaze to travel over the forest and the ground before me. Earth is rock and tree and dirt and stone. I concentrate, trying to find a way to reach it, but I sense nothing.

I crouch low and place my hands on the moss, letting my fingers sink into the soft green. The familiar scent of damp earth and bark fills my lungs, grounding and steadying my senses. Unlike the fire that pulses with urgency or the water that rushes in my veins, the forest hums quiet and deep, like a heartbeat just beneath the soil.

I close my eyes, not to force anything, not to prove anything, but just to be here. Present. Known. And for the first time since this war began, I feel a part of something greater, something ancient and enduring.

A warmth unfurls in my chest, not the burn of power but the ache of homecoming. The moss shifts beneath my palms. A low tremble builds from the ground, subtle at first, as if the forest is reaching up to meet me in response, in recognition.

"What was that?" Charaide asks, and I open my eyes to find him staring, open-mouthed, across the clearing.

I glance at Caillea, but her expression is neutral, giving nothing away. She inclines her head as if to encourage me to try again.

"I'm not sure yet," I murmur and allow that familiar ache to expand. The rumbling starts again, so I push my fingers deeper into the ground, pouring forth that longing for home, that need for the familiar, into the dirt, into the core of the forest.

Around me, the trees begin to shake. Charaide calls out in alarm, and his feet slap against the mossy forest floor as he races toward me.

"Wait!" Caillea calls.

He skids to a stop, his breath coming out in heavy pants. I focus on the ground, pushing more energy into it as the forest comes alive around me. The trees sway faster, and the smaller animals race from the clearing, seeking shelter from the shaking earth.

I cut off the energy flowing out of me, and the shaking ceases. A hush settles over the forest, warm and watchful. The branches above sway gently, not from wind but as if brushing back my hair with familiar fingers. Still crouched to the forest floor, I look at Charaide, who stares at me in shock and wonder.

"Did you do that?"

With a laugh, I nod, standing and shaking the dirt from my fingers. "Not bad for a halfling, eh?"

His eyes are wide. "I've worked the earth my whole life, but even I've never seen it answer like that." He breathes out slowly. "Imagine the impact you could have in battle."

A sinking feeling hits my gut. Yes, the power to cause an earth-quake could split an enemy's line. The images come fast and unwelcome—rebel soldiers scrambling back to escape the fissure I create in the field, some of them falling in, plunging to their deaths. I swallow bile.

"Maybe this is a power we keep to ourselves for now," I say, my voice barely above a whisper.

By this time, Caillea has joined us. "Your power is more than your magical abilities. You care deeply, and it reflects not only in your unleashing but also in your restraint." She takes my hand. "It is wise to weigh the consequences of using your gifts to destroy." With a gentle tug, she guides my hand back to the earth and smiles. I release a small amount of magic, afraid I might hurt her in such close proximity. "When you can also use them to create."

A small stem slithers from the earth as I pour out a little of my magic at a time. Soon, leaves sprout from the stem, and a tiny rosebud forms. As I cut off the stream of power, the rose softly opens its petals. Caillea releases my hand and nods as if I've just proven a theory correct.

Charaide frowns at the flower. "But think of how much more valuable you would be to the cause, to your uncle, if you used your power to destroy the rebels once and for all."

I wince at the mention of Brutach. *If he knew that I had this power, what would he ask of me?* I trust my uncle with my life, yet I fear how he might use the knowledge of my power to further our efforts. I've enjoyed leading my own faction, remaining on the sidelines, and following his lead with Cliste's strategy. If he knew I could do this, I would be sent to the front lines to protect us all. It's a burden I'm not sure I'm ready to bear.

It's also not something I'm quite sure how to explain to Charaide. For years, I've lamented being a halfling and how much I wish I could just fit in somewhere, anywhere. Now I have a chance, and I expect my hesitation won't make much sense to him. But we're at war. It was one thing to want to fit in when times were peaceful and I just didn't want to be an outcast. Having the fate of so many on my shoulders over-whelms me. I want to have powers that allow me to be more "normal" amongst the fae while also allowing me to simply blend in.

"Ast?" he asks, and I realize I haven't responded to him.

"I'm more afraid of how much more of a threat I'll be to the rebels," I say, which is at least partially true. "If they found out, I'd only have a bigger target on my back."

He nods, and the tension in my shoulders eases, though a gnawing sense of guilt churns in my belly. I hate lying to him.

"We should get back," I continue when he doesn't respond. "I don't want Brutach to know how far we've strayed from camp."

"Not just yet," Caillea says, a strange gleam in her eye. She nods to Charaide, and he offers me his arm.

I wrap my hand around it, raising an eyebrow. With a sly smile, he leads me into the trees. The feeling of coming home deepens as we walk the familiar paths of my forest, our place. Caillea follows us at a respectful distance, and for the first time in a long time, I feel safe.

I give a contented sigh and lean my head against Charaide's shoulder. "I needed this."

"I figured as much." Charaide chuckles. He stops and turns toward me, his hands brushing gently over my shoulders. His touch is meant to reassure, not possess. I step closer, instinctively drawn to the quiet steadiness of him.

"Ast." There's a gruffness in his voice that betrays something —not quite fear but not quite hope.

"What is it?" I ask, but before he can answer, a rustle in the woods breaks the moment apart.

Caillea appears by my side, her eyes wild with fear. She puts a hand on my arm as if ready to evanesce us at a moment's notice, but I shrug her off.

"Is someone there?" I call out, my voice surprisingly steady. "Show yourself!"

Astreilles, a voice whispers, and I shudder. It's the voice from before, the one that beckons me in a way I can't seem to resist. Even now, my feet turn toward it.

Charaide's gaze darts between my face and Caillea's. "Is it the voice again?"

I nod, not trusting myself to speak, or perhaps it's that I'm unable. Something about that voice renders me powerless. If only I could figure out why.

"We should go. Now."

Come to me, Astreilles.

Gritting my teeth, I lock my knees, but my legs lurch forward of their own accord. Only Charaide's death grip on my arm keeps me from running toward the voice and whatever sinister plans it has for me.

Caillea grabs my other hand, and I feel her preparing to evanesce.

"Wait." I yank free of Caillea's grasp and carefully pry Charaide's hand from my arm. His eyes widen in alarm, and he reaches for me, but I hold up a hand. "Trust me."

I take a few cautious steps forward, allowing the strange thrall of the voice to pull me toward it. All the while, I use all of my senses to try to make out its source. The familiar rasp, the quiet chuckle. I *know* it in a way I can't explain. If I could just place it, perhaps I can remove its power over me.

But the trees are thick, and the sky is overcast. Shadows shift among the branches, but I can't tell if they are from animals or whatever monster is attached to that voice.

I let out a frustrated growl as I run to the edge of the clearing. "Come out, you coward!"

A soft chuckle, like a whisper on the wind, caresses my ear. Rage churns in my belly like fire. If I must burn my whole beloved forest to the ground to seek the source of my torment, I'll do it.

I raise my hands, preparing to summon my flames, when a strange sensation builds in my chest. It's not quite a burning, more like a comforting heat.

The voice calls to me like a tide, but I don't answer it. Instead, I respond to the ache in my chest that is tired of running, tired of being afraid. And as that ache builds, so does the warmth within me.

"Astreilles!" Charaide calls from behind me, but his voice is strained with worry.

I glance at him. His face is stricken with fear, but Caillea's is triumphant. They're both staring at my chest. Following their gaze, I'm amazed to see a bright light emanating from within me. I put a hand over my heart, and the light spreads from my core to my fingers and toes until I'm lit up all over.

The light is so bright, it chases away the shadows of the forest. I peer through the trees and catch a glimpse of a familiar dark cloak covering a patchwork of skin.

"It's you," I breathe, the words catching in my throat like a gasp. The fear that's lived in my spine every time I've heard that voice rushes forward, but something else presses in too. Recognition. And confusion. *How can the voice that frightens me also feel so familiar?*

His honey-gold eyes lock on mine, and what I see in them isn't malice. It's something softer. Unsteady. Almost... afraid.

"It's you," he echoes, voice raw with disbelief. Then he stumbles back, vanishing before I can react.

The light that pulses through me suddenly goes out, and the shadows of the forest return. I stand there, awestruck by what just happened, but Caillea doesn't hesitate. One moment, she's across the clearing with Charaide, and the next, she has a hand on both of us, and we evanesce away.

I collapse on the ground in a heap before pulling my legs into my chest and curling into a ball. Everything hurts, and I feel completely drained. Tears spring to my eyes unbidden, and my breath hitches in my throat.

"Who was that?" Caillea kneels beside me.

"I don't know," I admit. "But this isn't the first time I've encountered him."

She nods sagely. "I've glimpsed stitched creatures like him before, Astreilles. Fae cobbled together by grief or vengeance, wearing a face that isn't their own."

Her hand touches my arm, but Charaide shoves her aside. He kneels on the ground and tries to hold me.

"You're safe, Ast. You're safe." His voice cracks, betraying the fear he's trying to hide.

I want to lean into those comforting words, wrap myself up in his embrace, and forget about the voice, the war, and everything weighing on my shoulders.

But I can't. We went to the forest to escape the voice and practice my magic. Yet the voice still found us, and now I've unlocked a power I've never seen before and do not understand.

CHAPTER

SIXTEEN

I SPEND the rest of the day avoiding everyone, especially Charaide. He tried to talk to me after we arrived at camp, but I told him I needed to see my uncle then proceeded to hide whenever I saw him coming. As a result, I've moved throughout the camp, directionless. I wish I had traveled with Marto and the other men. At least then, I would have something to keep my mind off what happened in the forest.

The memory of the moment when I caught sight of my assailant continues to haunt me. I'm relieved to finally know the source of the voice that has haunted my nightmares, but I can't understand why he's stalking me. *And more importantly, why am I so drawn to him?*

I can't explain what happened in the forest or the strange light that radiated from within me. But that isn't the question that plagues me the most. *Why was my assailant so taken aback by the power? What did he mean when he whispered, "It's you"?*

Before we parted, Charaide pressed me to tell my uncle, but I'm not ready. While Brutach has encouraged me to practice my growing powers, he won't be happy we strayed so far from camp.

Besides, I don't want to tell him or anyone else about the new power that manifested there. At least, not until I have a better understanding of it myself. It came on so naturally, like fire, that I can't help wondering if it was more instinctual than something I created. It's almost as if the thrall of my assailant somehow ignited it within me.

I stake out a place far from the tent I've shared with Charaide and burrow under various blankets and furs, trying to shut out the world. But sleep evades me. Or perhaps it's more accurate to say I evade it. I'm terrified of falling asleep. *What if I dream of my assailant again? What if he finds me alone and vulnerable and slits my throat while I slumber?* So even as my eyes burn with the need to close, I force them open, keeping my ears tuned to every branch cracking and every harsh laugh from the camp.

Sometime in the wee hours of the morning, I lose my battle, but when I wake to sunlight streaming through the trees, I'm relieved to have slept dream-free. I'm tired and achy from lying on the hard ground and not getting enough rest, but I'm so happy to see another day dawn that I don't allow myself time to dwell. Cliste returns today, and hopefully, so will Marto and his scouting troop. I pray they will have the information we need to meet the rebels in battle once more. This waiting game has taken a toll. I'm ready for the next fight.

I scramble out of my makeshift bed and scoop my blankets into my arms. The camp is starting to awaken, and the grumbles I hear confirm I'm not the only one who had a rough night of sleep. Everyone is restless.

When I arrive, Charaide is cooking eggs over the fire near our tent. His gaze briefly meets mine, but otherwise, he doesn't acknowledge my presence. The air between us is tense with all the things we've left unsaid.

Part of me wants to have it out with him, but I know it's likely to span multiple conversations. Besides, my brother should be arriving soon, and I want to be with Brutach to greet him when he does.

So I toss my blankets into the tent and stalk off toward the center of camp. My uncle is having breakfast with some of the men, but neither Marto nor Cliste is in sight. I grab a plate of eggs and meat before taking a precarious seat on the stump to Uncle Brutach's left.

"Any word from Cliste or Marto?" I ask before digging into my food. It dawns on me that I didn't eat dinner the night before, and I'm ravenous.

"Cliste will be here within the hour, but I have not heard anything from Marto."

"No news is good news, I suppose," I say.

Uncle Brutach fixes me with a steely gaze. "Not in this instance, not with what's at stake." He finishes his breakfast before setting down the plate and turning to me. "Yesterday, I was going to discuss some ideas for how to plan our next attack but couldn't find you."

I choke on a bite of eggs, and my uncle hands me a mug of water. Swallowing thickly, I clear my throat. "Charaide and I went into the clearing to practice."

"I went to the clearing," my uncle counters. "You weren't there."

Damn. When no one approached me after our return, I thought we were in the clear. My uncle raises an eyebrow as he waits for me to respond. There's no getting out of this. I rack my brain for a plausible excuse for why I disappeared, but nothing comes to mind.

"Caillea evanesced Charaide and me to the forest near the castle." I steel myself for the angry tirade.

"You abandoned not only your post but your men for, what, a private rendezvous?" His eyes narrow, his voice sharp. "Tell me, was that worth the risk?"

I jerk my head up with a frown. "You really think so little of me?"

"You didn't answer my question," he replies, not missing a beat.

Dropping my gaze to the ground, I push the remains of my breakfast around on my plate. "We did not intend to be gone long enough for anyone to notice. But it wasn't what you think. I was practicing my magic by experimenting with different elementals."

"If you think disappearing without a word makes you look like a leader, you're sorely mistaken, even if it was to practice your powers." But the anger rolling off him stems a bit. "That said, how did it go?"

I consider my next words carefully. My uncle is familiar with my fire magic, and Marto may have mentioned that I healed one of our soldiers after the last battle. But only Charaide and Caillea know about the water magic, the earth-moving, and the strange light. And I intend to keep it that way.

"We practiced my fire and healing magic," I say, still not meeting his eye. "Caillea really wants me to learn air, but I'm struggling with that one."

"Possessing more than one type of elemental magic is rare." My uncle eyes me with a look that hovers between surprise and calculation. "Given your... mixed heritage, I admit I didn't anticipate quite so much potential."

I keep my gaze steady and say nothing. Defending myself risks betraying the significance of my powers.

"Still, it's good that you're practicing it, as it may come in handy in battle."

Again, I remain silent. The idea of unleashing my earth power against the unsuspecting rebels still twists my stomach. But the thought convinces me more than ever that I need to keep any other elemental power a secret. The last thing I need is to be used as a weapon.

Luckily, I'm saved from any further interrogation by a commotion on the other side of the camp. I stand, hoping Cliste has returned or Marto and his men. Uncle Brutach sets his empty plate aside and strides toward the noise. I follow, heart in my throat, and pray for good news.

"Move aside, move aside," he commands as he nears a tight circle of men. "What's the cause of all this racket?"

"It's Marto, sir," one of the men says, his face grave. "It appears he's been struck with an iron arrow."

A collective gasp sounds around me, then the air is still save for Marto's moaning. I shove my way through the crowd before kneeling beside him. An arrow sticks out of his side. The only evidence of the iron is the blackened blood staining the ground beneath him.

"We need a healer!" my uncle bellows, staring down the men still circling us.

"There's no one here with that skill, my lord," another soldier says, running a hand through his blond hair. "We need to send him to the castle with the rest of the severely wounded."

I return my gaze to Marto. His face is ashen, and his moans grow softer. A glance at my uncle confirms my worst fears. There isn't time to evanesce Marto to the castle, and moving him will only make things worse.

"Then we need to bring a healer here," Brutach commands.

The men exchange uneasy glances. I understand their hesitation. Marto may die before anyone arrives to aid us.

I glance around wildly until my gaze lands on a pale face.

"Caillea." My voice trembles as I beckon her forward. "Can you help him?"

With a nod, she steps toward Marto, but my uncle moves between them. His lips press into a hard line.

"Your grandfather exiled her for a reason," he says, blocking her path. "We can't gamble a soldier's life on her unpredictable magic."

"You know she's our best option," I counter, meeting his glare with my own. "And Marto doesn't have time to wait for your approval."

Brutach's jaw clenches and unclenches as he considers my words. "It'll probably come with a price." But he shifts to the side, allowing Caillea to assess Marto.

"An iron arrow must be removed cleanly," she murmurs then meets my gaze. "You can do this."

I blink. "Me?"

She nods. "With water. Guide it through him. You've done this before."

I swallow. *Not with so many people around.* Her lips curl in an encouraging smile as if she can read my thoughts.

Taking a deep breath, I kneel beside Marto and close my eyes, reaching for the stream near the northern edge of the camp that we've used for washing. My fear for Marto surges, and with it, the water comes as if in answer to an unspoken prayer. I guide it to the source of Marto's pain.

The arrow moves, inch by painful inch, as if resisting. I grit my teeth, my fear giving way to determination. As if in answer, the water's flow steadies, gently carrying the arrow out of his body without further tearing.

Gasps echo around me as the arrow slips free and clinks to the ground. The rest of our army had seen me wield only fire. I hope this doesn't draw a bigger target on my back.

I collapse beside him, chest heaving, but Caillea moves in like she's done this a hundred times. She closes her eyes and hums an unfamiliar tune as an ethereal light flows from her hands, surrounding Marto. It's not quite like the light I produced in the forest but similar in a way. I watch in fascination as the blood pouring from his open wound slows to a trickle and the skin around the wound appears to meld together. Marto's labored breathing eases, deepening as if he had fallen asleep. His face is so peaceful, the pained expression evaporating like it was never there.

"How...?" I start, but Caillea shakes her head.

"We all carry a thread of healing within us," she says. "Some through touch, some through song." Her gaze meets mine. "And some through water."

Brutach watches, his expression unreadable. Finally, he turns to the others. "Report. What happened out there?"

I blink as I refocus on the situation at hand. In all the chaos of Marto's injury, I'd completely forgotten why he'd been sent on a scouting mission in the first place.

"We were ambushed," one of the men says. "It's like they knew we were coming. The rebels were prepared. Their camp looked like it'd never been scorched." He shakes his head. "I've never seen anything like it."

"But they're still there, then?" my uncle asks. "They haven't moved on."

"No, but several additional men have moved in. They've doubled in size."

I swallow, closing my eyes and trying to wrap my head around this news. The rebels already had close to triple our numbers. *With such a large army, what chance do we have?*

"Then it is all that more imperative that Cliste return with your father's books," Uncle Brutach says to me.

I nod, though I can't help hoping Cliste will choose to defect. Despite my telling him how much I need him here, a large part of me hopes he'll ignore my pleas and escape to the mortal realm. And if he's smart, he'll take my siblings with him.

My heart lifts and sinks all at once when Cliste returns, arms full of Father's books. I hurry to meet him and hold on a little too long when he pulls me into a hug. The rebels' growing numbers have haunted me all day. I'm not sure how many more moments like this we'll have.

Behind me, Brutach's voice cuts the air. "Show us what you were able to find."

Cliste gently steps around me, calm despite whatever grim news he's already sensed. "Father kept many war texts." He places a thick volume on the table. "This one, *The American Revolution*, might be our best hope. He was oddly obsessed with it, considering he was born in a country south of there. But I believe his human parents moved there at some point." He shoots me a wry smile. "Perhaps they thought the fae couldn't follow them."

I laugh in spite of the stress weighing on my shoulders. Humans like to believe they can escape the things they don't understand. But the fae realm lies parallel with theirs, with many different portals to pass from one point to another. Near our castle, there's a portal that enters the human realm on an island in my father's home country, but if I travel across the sea, I can enter the human world in countries that speak in languages I don't understand. But my father translated many of their stories, and the tales they tell of the fae folk are very similar.

"He once told me his fascination was due to it being a war of the underdogs, of ordinary men toppling an empire," I say, my chest aching at the memory. "He admired that, even if he never said so directly."

"I'm not interested in fairy tales," Brutach snaps. "Get to the point."

Cliste opens the book. "Their victory relied on stealth. Surprise. They used the land to their advantage."

I glance toward the woods. "The rebels know the land better than we do."

"Some of our men grew up among them," Cliste counters. "They know the trails, the terrain. If we teach them the tactics—"

"Assuming they stay," I say.

My brother touches my shoulder. "They've stayed this long. That counts for something."

I force a smile, but I can't find the same optimism. The image of Marto's gaping wound hasn't left my mind since he arrived back at camp. Even though he's going to be fine, I'm terrified about who will be hurt next.

Brutach grunts, flipping through the rest of the books. "Once Marto's recovered, he'll train the men in these methods. In the meantime, Astreilles, you should strategize with Cliste. We can't send any more scouting troops without risking casualties. We need options."

Cliste leads me outside. I pause, inhaling the air like it might be my last breath. He watches me, his expression unreadable.

"We can still leave," he whispers, and I squeeze my eyes shut, not wanting to let go of this moment of peace.

"I can't." My voice breaks on the last word. "You know I can't abandon Mama and our siblings."

"We can take our siblings with us. And Mama…" He sighs. "Maybe if we're gone, the rebels…"

I hear what he doesn't voice: Would the rebels be satisfied if halflings were no longer in the royal bloodline? Mama could remarry, though I can't imagine she would want to. Or if she didn't, that would move Uncle Brutach to second in line.

Sometimes, I can't help wondering if his heart is really in this war. *Wouldn't it be easier for him to just let the rebels win? Why is he fighting so hard to protect the royal bloodline?*

I push the thought aside. Whatever his ambitions, he loves his sister, and he values order. That's likely why he tries to guide me despite his often brash manner in doing so.

"Come on," Cliste says. "Brutach is clearly in a mood, and I'd rather not be on the wrong end of it." Inside his tent, he opens his book and flips to an image of men with painted faces, hiding in forests.

"Did Father mention these warriors?"

"No," Cliste replies. "But that is where many American soldiers learned their attack techniques."

"It's too bad we don't have a band of warriors like these hiding somewhere in the kingdom," I say.

"Perhaps we do if we only knew where to look."

I nod absentmindedly. My mind is still mulling over what my brother said earlier, about the men knowing the land.

"Did all of the colonists rebel against the crown?"

Cliste bites his lip. "Some of them remained loyal. Some switched sides, but most followed their conscience." He gives me a meaningful look. "I have to believe our men will do the same."

I don't answer. He sounds so sure, but survival makes people loyal to coin, not crowns.

LATER THAT AFTERNOON, my eyes are burning from reading through the book, studying what worked and what didn't for the Americans. All the while, in the back of my mind, I question some of the recounting in the book. After all, it's the victorious who write the history books, so everything is always a little skewed to one side or the other.

Still, it's not difficult to see why these tactics are successful. They rely on cunning, stealth, and sneaky attacks that the other side doesn't see coming. We've done that to some degree, but it hasn't helped us on the larger battlefield. Torching the rebels' camp did little more than delay them from charging after us when we fled. But nonetheless, we fled.

A throat clears near the entrance of the tent and causes us to jump. Caillea stands just inside, her arms crossed and her expression unreadable.

"I've been looking for you," she says, nodding to Cliste before turning her attention fully to me. "It's time."

Cliste raises an eyebrow, but I simply begin gathering my things. Caillea doesn't wait for me to catch up as she strides through the camp with purpose, weaving through soldiers and equipment as if this place holds no more significance than a pebble on a path. I jog to keep up.

We leave the camp and make our way to a quieter grove just outside the perimeter. It's not quite the forest where I feel most at home, but the hush of the trees and open sky eases something tight in my chest.

When we reach a small clearing, she finally turns to me. "Today, we try air."

I blink. "Shouldn't we start with something I already know? Like earth?"

She shakes her head. "Earth responded to you because you listened. Wind requires something else. Not just strength but surrender."

"That's helpfully vague." I don't even bother to hide the sarcasm.

Her lips curve in the same knowing smile. "Magic doesn't like rigid instructions. It listens when we speak to it with our truest voice."

With all the seriousness of a child playing pretend, I shut my eyes, trying and predictably failing to follow her wonderfully useless advice. The breeze is faint, brushing the hair at my temples. I focus on the space between breaths, the moment when air fills my lungs and the moment it leaves.

"That's it. Let the air flow through you. Don't try to hold onto it."

Her riddles are starting to get on my nerves. My breaths come faster as my irritation grows, and as it intensifies, so does the breeze. I raise one arm, and the air follows with a gust of wind. When I bring the same arm down, the current switches direction, echoing my movement.

"Good," she says. "Now ask it to dance."

Dance? Just when I'm about to open my eyes and ask if she's lost it, a memory of my father springs to mind. I'm small, and he twirls me around and around in his arms, spinning faster with each revolution. An ache grows in my chest, and I lift my arms to relieve it, turning in place.

The wind sharpens into a gale. Twigs and leaves rise with it, swirling in a gentle vortex. I open my eyes, and a funnel cloud hovers above me in the clearing.

My breath catches. The tornado is beautiful but tenuous. The moment I try to push it further, it falters.

"You're overthinking again." Caillea moves closer. "Wind isn't about control. It's about freedom. Unlike the solidity of the earth or the fluidity of water, always filling the space it inhabits, air has no master. It extends beyond our wildest imaginings to the places we can't reach, even with our wings."

I close my eyes again. *Freedom.* The word has many meanings for me. Freedom from the responsibilities of the crown, from the authority over an army that I never wanted, and freedom from a hated existence I didn't choose. I embrace that freedom that I so desperately covet and begin to spin, letting my desire, my hunger, guide me.

When I spin again, it's not with purpose but with presence. The wind rises with me, surrounding me completely. I'm lifted off the ground not by my wings but by the air itself as if I've become weightless.

I open my eyes and meet Caillea's gaze across the clearing. Her smile is small but real.

"That was something else," she murmurs.

I land gently but whole. "It felt different from the other elements. Less power. More trust."

"Exactly," she says. "Not all strength looks like fire."

I don't respond, but something inside me shifts. Maybe I don't have to master every element like a weapon. Maybe it's enough to learn their language. To listen first and move second.

And somehow, that thought, that possibility feels like hope.

CHAPTER
SEVENTEEN

We're set to launch micro-attacks at the rebels. I've spent days with Cliste's books and training with water and fire with Charaide, keeping earth and air hidden. Guilt tightens in my chest —these woods pulse with purpose now, not peace.

Marto, Cliste, and I are leading separate groups to confuse and divide the rebels before we engage them directly on the battlefield by week's end. Excitement and fear war within me. Our track record against the rebels hasn't been stellar. For every step forward we take, they seem to push us several steps back. On the other hand, most of the poor interactions took place when the rebels expected us. We've kept our plans secret, telling only the men involved. Even Uncle Brutach is on a need-to-know basis. It's essential to our success to keep everything quiet.

Once we've destabilized the rebels, we'll bring the whole of our army back to the hill to fight. The hope is that in the confusion and hysteria, they'll either retreat or surrender. It's a long shot, but I'm praying this will be the end of the war. Brutach tells me this is a pipe dream. The rebels will never give up so easily.

Though I've enjoyed learning from Caillea, Charaide has

offered to practice with me. We sneak into the forest to focus on my earth and air powers. They are key to our disruption plans. Everyone assumes that I will just be setting fires to the camp again and maybe flooding the lower ground to make it harder to traverse in battle. But Charaide has convinced me to test my powers from a distance. The earth power is easy, which I suspect is due to Charaide. Watching him wield this power has helped me see how it can be used for both creation and destruction. With practice, I've sent rumbles through the ground and created small fissures for incredible distances. Air, on the other hand...

I sigh in frustration as, once again, the tornado I try to create is little more than a stiff breeze, barely lifting any of the twigs and leaves nearby. Of course, my frustration has caused my fire magic to misbehave, and I'm constantly putting out gales of fire to avoid setting the whole forest aflame.

"It's no use," I say, shoving my hair out of my eyes. "If I'm not at the center of it, I can't infuse the power necessary to bring the funnel to its full-force potential."

Charaide stands off to the side, rubbing his chin. "At least you've improved with earth, but wind is beyond me. Perhaps we should have brought Caillea."

As if speaking her name was her summoning, Caillea herself steps into the clearing. Charaide breathes a sigh of relief, but my back stiffens. Despite her assistance with honing my magical skill set, her way of speaking sets my teeth on edge. Her words always seem to possess some deeper meaning that I can't grasp. Like the riddle she told me when we first met: *Beware the creation. It will be your destruction.*

"Astreilles," Caillea breathes as her eyes meet mine. "Why did you not tell me you were practicing today?" She waves a hand. "Come now. Show me what you've learned."

My magic has already been drained so much this morning by

my feeble attempts to produce a tornado that I'm not sure I can conjure anything more. But I grit my teeth and focus my mind.

Lifting my arms, I spin, faster and faster, until Caillea gasps then squeals in delight. My feet lift off the ground as the wind gains speed, whipping me around like a doll. I push harder, building the strength of the whirling air around me. Leaves and twigs are brought up from the ground, and they graze the fingertips of my outstretched hands.

"She's a true wonder," Caillea says. "You're so lucky to have her."

My chest seizes—not with pride this time but with raw need. I pour every ache I've felt over the past several weeks into the wind. And suddenly, thunder answers. The wind around me grows colder, and something flashes beyond my eyelids.

I snap my eyes open and lift my chin. Above me, a storm cloud rumbles, and slashes of lightning hit the forest floor. Charaide and Caillea jump back, mouths agape. *Well, this is new.* I've never called thunder and lightning before, just wind.

Charaide raises a hand. "Ast, breathe. You're feeding it too much power. You need to slow the storm. Let it pass through you."

His words resonate, but it feels so good to let go. To feel that wild pulse of magic building inside me, answering to my every thought. A part of me hungers for more.

But then my gaze meets Caillea's, and her eyes flicker with concern. Not fear—something softer. Something that tethers me back to myself.

I take a calming breath, and my heart slows. The winds fade as I harness my emotions once more. When my feet finally touch the ground, I feel alive and whole in a way I've never felt before.

But somewhere deeper... I wonder what it would feel like if I didn't stop.

Marto evanesces Charaide and me to the bottom of the hill under cover of darkness. The rest of my small team appears behind us, silent and sharp-eyed.

Above, the rebels lie in wait. They expect us to charge the high ground, but we have other plans.

With a finger to my lips, I motion us forward. We crawl through the tall grass, clad in dark, mottled green. It's excellent camouflage as we vanish into the terrain.

From the hilltop, the rebel voices drift down, loud and careless. They're overconfident, as if they've already won.

"When they arrive, take whatever man you want," one says, raspy and vile. "But the princess is mine. No one touches what belongs to me."

My heart stutters. That voice. I know it. It haunts my nightmares and stalks my awakenings. I freeze. *He's here.*

Charaide shifts subtly, angling his body between me and the sound. "Astreilles," he hisses, grabbing my hand. "We have to keep moving."

I nod but can't stop listening. Why does he want *me*? The way he speaks about me... It's not politics. It's personal. And it seems like a game for him. He's like a cat toying with its prey.

We reach the edge of camp and wait. Marto's team should be circling behind. I scan the field. Then—

A flash. Shouts.

"Now," I breathe.

Chaos erupts. I summon fire to my palms and hurl it into the nearest tents. Flames catch, but they're ready for me as buckets of water douse the fire.

My lips curve in a smirk. Too bad for them. Water obeys *me*.

I lift my arm and crook my finger at the water, beckoning. The water answers. It turns away from the flames and flows... *To me.*

Gasps of disbelief rise from the rebels as I thread the water along the ground. Although there's not enough water in the buckets to flood the camp, I feel the pulse of a reservoir beneath my feet. The flow of it churns in my veins, and I draw it toward me. It bubbles up from the ground, pouring into the camp. And the flooding begins.

I shape a boundary around my men. The water surges through the camp but leaves us untouched. Across the field, the rebels' eyes grow wide, and one turns to flee.

"She's doing this!" he yells. "Stop her!"

But it's too late. The water obeys only me. I bite the inside of my cheek to keep from smiling. *Call me a veilcling imposter now.*

The thought brings me up short. My pulse pounds, and the heat of my rage claws up my spine. But this isn't about revenge. It's about sending a message. Let them fear what comes next if they don't put an end to this rebellion and stop this terrible war.

I stop the rising tides, and the water begins receding slowly. The rebels seem to sigh with relief until the water stills and a sudden hush falls over the camp.

I glance sideways. My uncle stands on the edge of the chaos, one hand extended. The receding water begins to shimmer—then crack. It freezes solid in an instant, locking boots and bodies in place. A few soldiers cry out, caught mid-step in the ice.

Brutach lowers his hand, expression unreadable. I stare across the plain to see the rebels burning through the ice, preparing to charge again.

Charaide meets my gaze and inclines his head. I take a deep breath. If fire and water didn't break them, maybe it'll take an *earth-shattering* revelation. I take Charaide's hand, and together, we plant our feet.

As the rebels charge, we hold steady and wait for the perfect moment. The ground vibrates. Their feet pound against the ground, the sound echoing through me.

At my signal, Charaide and I kneel, hands pressed into the soil. The rebels' steps falter as if they wonder whether we're surrendering.

I lift my head and stare into their eyes as Charaide and I release our energy as one. The ground rumbles. A roar fills the air, and the slight tremors give way to severe shaking. Cracks form beneath their boots, and some of the men tumble into the fractured earth.

An image of my father's severed head sparks in my brain, and I cry out in agony as more magic pours from me. Tents collapse. Poles snap. More rebels drop to their knees.

Charaide touches my arm. "Ast, that's enough. Astreilles," he hisses. "Enough."

I clench my jaw. Not yet. They're still fighting. I need to make them stop. I need to make them *see*.

But Charaide doesn't give up so easily. He grabs my shoulder and hauls me away from the earth. Once the connection is lost, the tremors cease, and the ground settles.

"Marto and Cliste have accomplished their part and are ready to return to camp," Charaide whispers in my ear. "We should join them."

I know he's right, but adrenaline courses through my veins. "We've got them on the run. Let's finish this once and for all."

"No, Ast." He grabs my arm and pulls me to him. We're nose to nose. "You've done more than your part. Leveling their camp wasn't part of the plan, but it will make them distracted when we return with the whole of our army."

"I don't need an army!" I snarl, trying to shake him off. My measured approach is no longer as satisfying as it once was. Suddenly, I want blood. I want revenge for my father and brother. "I could finish this. Right now."

His gaze bores into mine. "You could. But at what cost?"

His words hit something raw in me. I stagger back, the fight going out of me and with it, the power I've summoned. Risking my own life is one thing, but I won't do that to my men.

"You're right," I say, defeated. "I'm sorry."

By the time Marto and the rest of our group have joined us, Brutach is already gone. I frown. He wasn't supposed to come on this expedition, though I can't deny his use of ice was well timed.

"Don't worry, Princess," Marto says as he claps me on the back. "We will win this war in due time."

I force a smile. But Charaide's words haunt me. *But at what cost?* Today, I let my emotions get the better of me. I let my pain almost drain me entirely of magic. *The next time I meet the rebels on the battlefield, will I be able to stop?*

Pushing those thoughts from my mind, I nod. "Good job, men. Let's go home."

CHAPTER

EIGHTEEN

"Welcome back," the voice rasps.

To my surprise, the fear I usually feel doesn't come. Instead, a hot rush of anger floods my veins, and I clench my fists at my sides.

"Why have you brought me here again?" I demand, spitting the words out through gritted teeth.

A soft chuckle is my reply. "Why do you continue to accuse me of something I have not done? The question you should be asking, Princess, is what or who draws you to this place?"

I shake my head, seeing red despite the colorless surroundings. "I'm so sick of your riddles." I stomp toward the door. "If all you plan to do is taunt me with nonsense, I'd much rather return to camp."

"Nonsense?" The tone is sharp, then a whisper of a laugh blows past my ear. "You call what you don't understand nonsense. Interesting."

Rolling my eyes, I continue moving away from him. When I reach the door, I grasp the handle, but it doesn't twist. I pull and push, trying to get the door to open, but my efforts are futile. In my frustration, my fist collides with the wood, and I don't even get the satisfaction of seeing a dent in the frame.

"Now, now, Astreilles," the voice coos. "We don't want to break anything here. It's not polite."

"Screw politeness," I seethe, spinning on my heel and searching the room. "And screw you. Why don't you show yourself? Stop being a coward, hiding in the shadows, and face me!"

A pregnant pause. "You're not ready for that."

"The hell I'm not. I'm here, am I not? Summoned by you once more for whatever sick game you're playing." I raise my hands. "Clearly, I'm not afraid."

"Perhaps you should be!"

The rage in the voice catches me off guard, and I stagger back.

Swallowing, I force myself not to shudder. Show no weakness. *I shake my head. "Figures. All talk and no action."*

"You want action?"

The room disappears, and I find myself on the hilltop. I reach for my arrows, but my quiver isn't there. I clench my jaw. Fine. My magic is stronger than my aim anyway.

With my eyes closed, I pull the energy into my hands, and the heat of the flames dances on my fingertips. I open one eye a fraction, hoping to catch my assailant off guard.

"Nice parlor trick," he whispers close to my ear.

I spin around, but no one is there. "Show yourself!"

He gives another quiet chuckle, and a breath grazes my cheek like a warm breeze. I turn again but am met with only emptiness. It's then I realize I'm by myself. Not only are there no rebels to fight, but where are my men? Where is Cliste? Charaide? Marto? I lower my hands, the flames extinguishing. Have they abandoned me?

The quiet, raspy laughter builds around me, coming from everywhere and nowhere all at the same time. Covering my ears, I run down the hill, hoping to meet with a familiar face. But there's nothing. I'm completely and utterly alone.

"No!" I cry out, shooting up from my bed. *Where am I?* Blinking, I take in my surroundings—the canvas of the tent, the soft snore of Charaide lying beside me, the murmur of the men's voices outside, and the scent of burning wood.

I bury my head in my hands. It was a dream. Just a stupid, silly dream. *But why? Why does my assailant haunt me so?* I'd hoped once I determined the source of the voice, I would feel more in control, but instead, I'm as fearful and confused as ever.

Lying back on my pillow, I stare at the ceiling of the tent. *And how did he know how to tap into one of my worst fears?* Standing on that hill, alone... With no one to fight with or for me. It's something I've buried deep within me. I've never told anyone about it, not even Charaide, but somehow, my assailant knew.

I close my eyes, though I know that sleep won't return. It's probably for the best. I don't need another dream like that psyching me out right before our battle tomorrow.

Shifting to my side, I pummel my pillow a few times to plump it up before laying my head back down. Charaide faces me, his mouth slack. He looks so peaceful, with his tousled hair and soft features. I envy him. I can't remember the last time I've known such peace.

SLEEP CONTINUES to elude me as the colors in the tent change with the approaching dawn. The darkness lightens to a pale violet then warms to a pinkish-orange hue before the bright light of the sun lifts over the horizon. I blink against the daylight, dog-tired but ready to face our enemies.

As I scramble out of bed and put on my armor, my dream haunts the back of my mind. *Will I finally come face-to-face with the man who stalks me even in my sleep?* Part of me fears it, but a larger part is ready to face him once and for all. It's the only way I'll ever know peace, regardless of how it ends.

Charaide groans beside me, stretching in his makeshift bed.

His tousled hair falls over his eye as he searches the tent for me. When he sees me dressed, he rises from the ground, working out the kinks in his back from sleeping rough.

"What time did you wake up?" he asks, his voice hoarse.

For a moment, it takes me back to my dream, and I stare at him, unable to speak.

"Astreilles?"

I snap out of my daze and focus on sliding my quiver onto my back. "Before dawn. Couldn't sleep."

"More nightmares?"

With a nod, I pull my hair out of my face then braid it down the side of my head.

He stands and touches my hand, his eyes softening. "Want to tell me about it?"

"Not right now." I finish the braid and push it over my shoulder. "Later. After we win this battle."

He smirks. "Someone's confident this morning."

"I'm trying to be," I admit with a sigh. "If for no other reason than to give the men a boost."

After shrugging into a shirt, he touches my shoulder. "You did good last night. I'm sure the rebels aren't going to be prepared for a full-scale battle thanks to your efforts."

"Cliste and Marto deserve credit too," I say, though my insides warm at his words. I watch him dress, pulling on his boots and adorning himself with his sword. My heartbeat picks up speed, and I swallow a wave of desire. When this is all over, maybe I can finally tell him how I feel. If anything, having him by my side through all of this has only made me love him more.

Footsteps sound outside the tent, and the flap is lifted, revealing Cliste. "You ready for this?"

I nod and follow him out, Charaide on my heels. Throughout the camp, men prepare to leave, and my heart jumps to my throat. While I know this is what we've been preparing for, I still can't help wishing there was another way. I don't want these men to risk their lives for me, for my family.

"Astreilles"—Uncle Brutach approaches us—"we should leave before the sun is too high in the sky. The rebels will have been working through the night to repair their camp. Best to catch them when they're exhausted."

He makes no mention of his sudden appearance during our clandestine mission against the rebels. I decide not to call him out on it in front of the others, but I'm curious why he chose to join us and how he knew exactly where we would be.

Marto joins us just as Brutach finishes his speech and meets my eye. "Ready when you are, Princess."

Swallowing my fears, I square my shoulders. "Prepare the troops. We'll leave within the hour."

Cliste and Marto nod and take their leave. Charaide goes to gather my battalion.

"I was quite impressed with your performance last night," my uncle murmurs when we're alone.

I bristle at his choice of words. "I was just doing my part to aid in the attacks."

He crosses his arms, fixing me with a look. "Why did you hide your earth magic?"

"I didn't hide it," I protest, even though we both can see through the lie. "It's not the element I feel most connected to." My uncle likely believes I mean fire magic, and I don't correct him. Charaide and Caillea are still the only two who know about the air. "Besides, you weren't even supposed to be there."

"I wanted to gather intelligence while the rebels were distracted," he says, no sense of remorse in his tone. He raises an eyebrow. "You should consider tapping into the magic again today. You never know when it may come in handy."

I don't respond, keeping my face blank. Only Charaide knows my plans for using my additional elemental powers, though we hope to keep air magic a secret for as long as possible.

The weight of Uncle Brutach's gaze causes me to sweat, but I don't let him see. Thankfully, my men arrive soon after, and he moves on, barking orders at soldiers who have not joined their squadrons yet.

I lead my men to the center of camp, where Cliste and Marto have gathered their troops. We will all evanesce together to the woods outside the rebels' camp. I don't trust that the rebels have given up the high ground, and I want us to have some cover until the rest of the army arrives.

Cliste and Marto move to meet me, their faces grim. I swallow my fear, determined not to let it deter me from the mission. We will succeed. I must believe that.

"Are you ready for this, Princess?" Marto's lips pull up in his signature smirk.

"As ready as I'll ever be."

"Let's go, then," Cliste grumbles, and I sneak a glance at my brother. While he was more than happy to lead small groups in the skirmishes before, his enthusiasm waned. But I get it. The strategies we used last night were fast and efficient. Little likelihood that the trend will continue today with the battle we expect to wage.

I nod and turn to Charaide to give the signal. One by one, the men disappear around us. Marto grabs my hand, and a moment later, I stumble onto the ground near the hillside. I immediately sink to my knees, and all around me, the men are doing the same. We listen, straining our ears for the familiar noise from the camp. We hope to determine where they are, how close, and whether they know we're here.

But all I hear is... birdsong. The wind whistles through the trees in an eerie silence.

With caution, I slide up the hill on my belly, careful to keep out of sight, but the exercise is unnecessary. The hilltop is empty, and as I peer into the valley below, I find the camp is as well.

I stand, shaking my head in bewilderment at the sight before me. It's abandoned as if the rebels vanished overnight. The waters I conjured have left muddy puddles throughout the camp and the valley. Torn canvases sway in the breeze, and the smoke from doused fires trails leisurely into the air.

"They're gone!" I shout, not bothering to be quiet.

Cliste, Marto, and Charaide clamber up the hill behind me before surveying the area around us.

"That's impossible. They must be hiding nearby," Marto says, but he searches the woods on the other side of the clearing in vain. There's no one here.

"I'm going to go down," I say, making my way toward the other side of the hill. "See if I can gather any clues about where they went."

"We'll go, too, take different points, and see if they're hiding nearby. I'll go this way." Cliste points at the east side of the hill. "Charaide, why don't you go west, and Marto, go back down and have the men search the forest behind where we arrived."

Everyone splits off in the direction he told them, with me heading south toward the rebel camp, or what was left of it. I move cautiously, keeping an arrow nocked in my bow and turning in slow circles as I move through the field. Even if the rebels have gone, there still may be danger here, and I'm fully exposed.

When I reach the outskirts of the camp, I crouch low, darting among the tents as quietly as possible. Maybe they've left someone to warn the others that we are here, that we will be coming after them.

But as I continue deeper into the camp, I feel increasingly alone. I search the tents and firepits for any indication of where they've gone, all the while fighting a growing sense of unease. An entire army wouldn't just abandon all their things and disappear into the night. There's no way our attacks convinced the rebels to give up their fight. *So where are they, and what are they planning?*

"There's no one here," I whisper to myself.

"I wouldn't say no one," a raspy voice says behind me.

I spin around and aim my arrow at a familiar cloaked figure. His face is hidden, but his arms, crossed in front of him as he leans against a post, are exposed. I stumble back in revulsion. The skin on his arms is a continuation of the patchwork I've seen on his face. It's... unnatural, like someone has clumsily sewn pieces of skin together.

He chuckles, that familiar rasp sending chills up my spine. After pushing off the post, he stalks toward me, and I scramble away, drawing my bow.

"Stay back," I warn, trying to keep the quaver out of my voice.

"Now, now, Princess, I thought we were past all this."

"What do you mean?"

He sidles up beside me, all casual and nonchalant as if I don't have an arrow aimed at his throat. I try to catch a glimpse of his face, but he keeps to the shadows, making it impossible.

"What I mean, sweet princess, is that after our chats on the astral plane, I thought we had put all this hostility behind us."

I blink. *What the hell is he talking about? The astral plane?* Shaking my head, I refocus. He's speaking in riddles, just like in my dreams.

"Ah, there's the problem," he whispers. "You still think they're dreams."

"Get out of my head!" But even as I shout at him in defiance, my stomach drops, and my skin grows cold.

"You've been astral projecting without even knowing it. Fascinating. Though I suppose it makes sense. You, unbound by worlds. Me"—he gestures to himself almost wistfully—"stitched together by magic too dark to travel far. The human realm would tear me apart."

There's a strange awe in his tone that I immediately don't like.

"And here I thought your elemental powers were the most impressive thing about you."

A stray breeze lifts my hair from my shoulders, serving as a reminder that I'm here, not in my tent, not asleep. Reality tugs at the edges. This isn't a dream.

"H-How do you know about my powers?" I cringe as I stammer. This is no time to show weakness. While I can't see his face, it's like I can feel him smirking in the darkness.

"I've been watching you." He moves around me in a wide circle, never touching me but also never allowing me to get a good look at him. It's frustrating and intriguing at the same time.

"I suspect you've barely tapped into your capabilities," he continues. "So many are trying to 'train'"—he lifts his hands and makes quotes with his fingers—"you who don't even realize your potential." He shifts closer to me but angles his face in a way that allows him to remain in shadow. "I'd love to see what you can *really* do when you unleash it."

Riddles and lies, that's all this man seems to spout. "You act like you know so much about me."

"Ah, but I do, dear princess," he rasps. "I've watched you much longer than you realize."

The blood in my veins freezes, and my mouth goes dry. I wet my lips, willing the churning in my belly to cease. My arrow has never faltered despite his constant movement. I've turned in a slow circle, my bow taut and my arrow aimed perfectly. But why I haven't fired it, I couldn't say. It was as if he holds some sway over me.

"You're curious," he says, reading my mind.

He must be fae. There's no other explanation for his uncanny ability to know what I'm thinking.

He laughs. "I don't need telepathy to know what you're thinking, Princess. It's written all over your face."

With a growl of frustration, I pull my bow ever tighter. "Why are you here? What do you want with me?"

Cocking his head, he studies me. Or at least, I think he does. It's hard to tell when his face remains concealed.

"Shouldn't you be asking me where the rebels have gone?"

"It's on my list of questions," I retort. "But as they aren't here, *you* are my primary concern."

He bows his head. "All right, then what about 'Who are you?'" He gives a whisper of a laugh. "Isn't that how these things usually begin?"

Is he serious? Fine. I'll play this stupid game if it means I might get some answers. "Who are you?" I'm unable to keep the mocking tone from my voice.

"I'm called Kythrall."

His name doesn't conjure any sudden revelations or familiarity. "Why are you here, Kythrall?"

For the first time, he shifts in a way that allows the light to illuminate his mouth. His lips pull back over gleaming teeth, and I'm reminded of a wolf. An involuntary shudder travels down my spine, causing my aim to falter.

"The war, the rebels, they're all just noise. I'm here for you, Princess."

His words drop through me like winter's chill—intimate, impossible. I draw breath. "Here... *for me?*"

CHAPTER

NINETEEN

I STARE AT HIM, waiting for an explanation, but he offers none.

"And what do you want with me?" I ask, my annoyance plain.

"So many things," he whispers. "But I suppose I should get around to what I was hired to do."

I exhale sharply. "Which was?"

He steps into the light, and his honey-gold eyes gleam. "To kill you."

My heart stutters. I want to run, but I can't move. I'm frozen from fear but also because I'm caught in his gravity. His words sink in. *The rebels hired a mercenary for me?*

Before I can speak, he shakes his head. "The rebels didn't hire me."

"Then who?"

"Someone who prefers to remain unknown." He twirls his dagger.

Pain twists in my chest. *How many people hate me for who I am? How many despise me for something I didn't get to choose?*

He watches me with a knowing expression. "I agree. It's terribly unfair."

I lock down my thoughts as best I can. Unfortunately, I still have a face that tends to betray every emotion. His smirk deepens.

"Do your worst," I growl, raising my arrow.

"Oh, I won't be killing you here." His tone is almost fond. "It's too easy. And I've enjoyed the chase too much to let it end so soon."

I stumble back. "Then what do you want?"

He leans against the post, spinning the dagger. "To talk. Like we do on the astral plane."

What the hell? "You're insane."

"Perhaps," he allows. "But I've watched you. Long enough to know you. You intrigue me."

"I'm a halfling." I shrug as nonchalantly as I can. "Nothing special."

"You're rare." His eyes narrow. "That trick with the light in the forest... How did you do that?"

I don't answer, mostly because I don't know. I've never replicated that power, not that I've tried. It terrified me.

"You never wanted this." His voice is low, almost reverent. "Leading armies, shouldering crowns. Yet here you are, risking everything for your family."

His eyes meet mine, and his expression shifts ever so slightly. The hard menace gives way to something softer beneath the surface.

A light breeze kicks up scents of charred wood and overturned earth. It brings me back to our surroundings. I allow my gaze to sweep over the abandoned camp for any other danger. But once again, it's like we're in a quiet cocoon of our own, where no one else can reach us.

"Why didn't you run when your brother suggested it? Why do you stay here when you'd be safer in the human realm?" His smirk fades. "Especially now that you know you'd be safe from me."

"How do you know about that?"

He scoffs. "I pay attention. But you didn't answer my questions."

I look away. "I have a duty, a responsibility to my family and my kingdom."

"One that you don't want."

"Was it your lifelong dream to be a mercenary?" I retort.

To my surprise, he bows again, and this time, his tone is solemn. "No, but it's what I was created to do."

Interesting choice of words. Not born but... created. I sneak a glance at his arms again, the strange patchwork of sewn-together skin that doesn't match.

"What are you?" I breathe, realization hitting me for the first time. This is no ordinary fae standing before me.

"A mercenary," he replies, a note of humor in his voice.

"That's what you do," I whisper. "Not what you are." I take a deep breath. "You said you were created, not born?"

"No, Astreilles, I wasn't born." His use of my given name catches me off guard.

"Then—"

"Astreilles!" a familiar voice yells nearby. Charaide has come looking for me, and my shoulders droop in relief, but I keep my gaze on Kythrall.

"Ah, I see your boyfriend has come to spoil our fun." He pushes off the tent pole and moves around me. "I suppose we'll have to pick this up another time, when you're alone."

"There won't be a next time," I say, nocking the arrow, but even as I take aim, I hesitate.

He smiles as if he senses my uncertainty, his sharp teeth catching the light. "Do you really think you can kill me in cold blood, Princess?"

"It's not cold. It's survival."

Charaide's voice draws closer. I can't wait any longer. It's him or me, and I choose me.

"I've not attacked you," Kythrall replies with a chuckle.

"You've admitted that it's your plan."

"Perhaps you'll prove more useful alive."

The way he says it strengthens my resolve. "You won't." I let the arrow fly.

But he's already gone, vanishing into the shadows behind the tent and leaving me with nothing but smoke and questions. I lower my bow, but my thoughts don't still. His words echo.

A shiver crawls down my spine. The threat was clear, but it's the implication that clings. Not every choice is between kill or be killed.

Sometimes, survival means strategy. Sometimes, it means using people I love. The thought unsettles me more than the encounter itself. Because deep down, I know that I would do anything to protect my family. Even if it means shredding everything that's good about me.

"There you are," Charaide says as he enters the tent behind me. "Why didn't you respond?"

I summon a fireball and head in the direction Kythrall just disappeared. "I was a little preoccupied."

Charaide follows me. "With what?"

"He was here." I glance at Charaide. "The man who attacked me at the castle. The one who has been stalking me in the forest, whispering my name? He was here."

His eyes widen. "What? You should have called for us!"

"There wasn't time," I retort, maneuvering around the remnants of a fire. My handiwork, I'm sure. Had I known I would be chasing a ghost, I might have been a little more judicious in my attack.

"What did he say to you?"

"A whole lot of nothing," I mutter under my breath as I climb out from under a fallen beam. Turning in a slow circle, I check the area for any sign of the mercenary, but he's gone. Perhaps he *is* a ghost.

"You were missing for quite a long time for the conversation to be that short."

With a sigh, I focus on Charaide. I'm not being fair. He doesn't deserve my dismissive attitude.

"We did talk for a while. I meant that he didn't tell me much that was useful." The rest of the camp is empty. Pity since I wish I had something to fight.

"What *did* he tell you, then?" Charaide crosses his arms.

"He said he was hired to kill me," I begin, ignoring his hiss of anger. "But he wouldn't tell me by whom. Just that it wasn't the rebels." I frown, gazing at the tent where I last saw Kythrall. "Though it makes me wonder. When my grandfather died, news of his death spread far and wide despite Brutach's attempts to keep the secret. Caillea told us there was a rebel spy amongst us, but then the rebels attacked the castle, and in the chaos, there was no time to investigate the claim." I turn to Charaide. "Do you think the spy and whoever hired the mercenary are one and the same?"

He scrubs a hand over his face. "I guess it's possible, but who could it be? I can't believe any of the men we've fought with these last few weeks are capable of such a betrayal."

"I agree, but there's no other explanation for this, is there?" I wave my hand at the empty camp. "Someone clearly tipped off the rebels to our planned attack. And now, we have no idea where they've gone." I shake my head. "If it is the same person, it must be someone close to me."

Charaide cocks his head. "Why do you say that?"

"The mercenary... He knew things about me. I think he's been watching me for far longer than we were aware."

"What do you mean?"

"Like... conversations I've had, private discussions with my brother. He knew about them. In great detail." I start to tell him about dreams that apparently weren't dreams, but I stop. There's no way for me to relay that information without sounding crazy. I'm not even sure I believe what Kythrall told me about the astral plane. That another plane exists isn't necessarily a surprise. After all, we have a realm that overlaps the human realm. Why wouldn't there be other realms into which we've never set foot? But it's a legend amongst the fae, not something I've ever taken seriously. Until now.

"Wait, if he was hired to kill you, why hasn't he done so? He's had multiple opportunities."

"He said I 'intrigue' him," I say, unable to keep the bitterness out of my voice. "And that I may be more useful to him alive, though I can't see how. He doesn't get paid if he doesn't deliver my head on a platter, I'm sure." I grab a rock from the ground and pull out my blade before sharpening it on the rock's edge. "But maybe I can use that."

"Whatever you're thinking, forget it," Charaide says. "It's too dangerous."

I gesture with my blade to the remnants of the camp. "What about any of this *isn't* dangerous? We're at war, Char. If he doesn't get me, the rebels will. At least if I take him out, there's one less bounty on my head."

"The price won't go away. It'll just transfer to a new mercenary. You're lucky to have found one who seems to have a conscience."

"I don't think he spared me because he cares," I reply dryly. "He knows about my powers, and he suspects I've barely scratched the surface." I glare at the ground. "He wants to use me for his own purposes, just like my uncle would if he knew the extent of my magic."

Charaide doesn't respond, which says more than if he had tried to deny it. It's one of the many reasons I've kept some of my more potent magic to myself. If other powers manifest as strongly as air, my uncle likely wouldn't need an army to defeat the rebels. As much as he loves me, I doubt he would hesitate to use me if it meant protecting the crown. Even if it destroyed me in the process.

"Come on," Charaide says after a moment. "The men are wondering where we are."

After taking one last look around the camp, I follow him. Aside from what I learned from Kythrall, the visit to the camp was pointless. I see no sign of the rebels or where they've gone.

When we meet up with the men, Marto steps forward. "Your uncle demands we return to our camp immediately."

"Is there news of the rebel army?" I ask, hopeful that perhaps my uncle's spies have had word of their movements.

"He didn't say."

Without giving me a chance to ask anything else, Marto takes my hand and evanesces Charaide and me back to our camp. Uncle Brutach is waiting for us. His lips are pressed in a grim line, and my stomach flips.

"It's true, then?" he asks. "The rebels have left?"

I nod. "The camp was empty." Charaide shoots me a look, but I ignore him. I'm not ready to tell my uncle about my encounter. "It's not clear where they went."

"We'll have to start from scratch, then. Send scouting troops to ascertain their location." He raises an eyebrow. "Anything else I should know?"

Charaide's glare burns a hole in my back, but thankfully, my uncle remains oblivious. "No, sir. Nothing else to report."

"Good." He waves a hand, and I'm dismissed.

"What the hell was that?" Charaide hisses as I make my way to my brother's tent. "Why didn't you tell him about the mercenary?"

"Because I don't want to worry him unnecessarily." The men

are restless, and it takes effort to maneuver around the groups of them cursing the rebels for disappearing.

Charaide grabs my arm. "Astreilles!" He spins me around to face him. "What are you planning?"

"Right now? I want to warn my brother. It's not safe for him or any of my siblings."

Charaide's eyes widen, and he releases me. "But you said the mercenary was only there for you."

"Why would someone hire a mercenary to take out one member of the royal bloodline?" Shaking my head, I start moving through the crowds again, with Charaide on my heels. "My guess is he's being paid a hefty sum to take us all out."

He gasps. "What about the queen?"

The thought trips me up, and I stumble. I've been so focused on my siblings that it hadn't crossed my mind that someone would want to kill my mother too. I couldn't understand it. While my mother had done something apparently unthinkable in marrying a human, she was a full-blooded fae. Her legal right to the throne was never in question. *Is it possible someone found her marriage so repulsive that they won't allow her to live either?*

This was a complication I hadn't anticipated since I'd started plotting how to save my siblings. Cliste already put the idea in my head with all his talk of the wonders of the human realm. We are halflings. We may always be othered by humans, but my siblings' magic is suppressed. They will be less detectable as long as they wear their bracelets.

Which is why it is imperative to get them away. Perhaps in the human realm, we can find a safe place to live in peace. Here, we are all sitting targets, waiting for a strange creature to pick us off one by one, with powers far beyond what I've ever seen from other fae. And if he's been watching me, I suspect he's been watching my siblings as well.

An army, I could fight. But this? One man slipping past walls, into my dreams, into my thoughts... How do I fight that?

"I don't know if my mother is part of his contract," I finally say. "I was under the impression it was the halflings the rebels objected to. That if my mother consented to marry a fae, she could redeem herself." I spat the last words out. They left a bitter taste in my mouth nonetheless.

"Shouldn't you warn her?"

"There's no time!" I quicken my pace. Cliste's tent isn't much farther. "I need to get my siblings out now. I should have done it sooner." The idea of Kythrall getting anywhere near my sisters in particular chills me to the bone. They're so dainty and fragile, he could dispatch them without a second thought. "We're lucky he's been so single-mindedly focused on me. They've been unprotected this whole time."

"I don't know that I'd call a castle with a full royal guard 'unprotected,'" Charaide says dryly.

I glance at him with a sharp look. "He's already proven more than once that he can slip into the castle undetected."

When we reach Cliste's tent, he's not alone. Several of his men are standing around a table and peering at a map. He glances up when we enter and waves us over.

"We have an idea of where the rebels have gone," he says, gesturing to the man on his left. "Tell Astreilles what you told me."

"Good day, Princess," the man begins with a bow. "I'm Aric and just recently arrived from the castle." He points at the map. "Based on some intelligence we've gathered from our spies throughout the kingdom, I believe the rebels are heading east toward the castle proper. We suspect they will wage a full-on attack in the next day or so."

"We need to get our army back to the castle before they do."

Cliste's eyes blaze. "To protect Mama and our brothers and sisters."

It's worse than I feared. My stomach clenches, and I fight a wave of nausea. Flames spark from my fingers, drawing the attention of every man around me. Focusing on my breathing, I manage to quell my panic, at least for the moment.

"I need to talk to you," I say, surprised by how steady my voice sounds. "Alone."

My brother raises his eyebrows but doesn't argue. He dismisses the soldiers, and soon, it is just him, Charaide, and me.

I turn to my best friend with pleading eyes. "I need a minute with my brother."

His eyes widen. "But, Ast—"

Holding up my hand, I shake my head. "Please."

With a frown, he stalks out of the tent. My heart sinks as yet another thing comes between us, but I don't have time to dwell. Family comes first.

"What is it?" Cliste asks. "Did you find out something new?"

"Someone hired a mercenary to kill me," I say, not bothering to soften the blow. His eyes bulge, but I don't give him a chance to say anything. "Probably all of us. It's not the rebels, or at least, that's what he says."

"You spoke to him?" He stares at me like I've grown two heads.

"He was at the rebel camp when I went to investigate." I avoid Cliste's gaze. "Anyway, he's likely with the rebels. The castle guard may be able to hold them off until we get there, but this fae is cunning, Cliste." My stomach churns. "Though I'm not sure if he's even pure fae."

Tilting his head, Cliste frowns. "What do you mean?"

I explain the strange patterns on his skin. "He also said that killing was what he was 'created to do.'" I stare at the map, trying to keep my voice steady. "At first, I thought it was just a strange choice of words, but what if he meant it exactly as he said it?"

"You're not making any sense."

I run a hand through my hair in frustration. "You weren't there. You didn't see how he was. Nothing about him was normal." Closing my eyes, I take a deep breath. "Father had a book. He said it was written by a human some time ago. It was about a man who was created from pieces of other... humans." I open my eyes and squint as if I can manifest the book with my mind. "It had a strange name."

"It's probably back at the castle," Cliste says, "though it sounds made-up to me."

"It wasn't a real account." I feel heat rising in my cheeks. "It was just a story."

"Then it's not important." He points at the map. "We need to focus on what's tangible. If this mercenary is with the rebels, we need to move now. Bring the men to the castle and save our family."

"No, we need to get our siblings out of there."

"And go where?" He waves his arms over his head. "There's no safer place for them than the castle."

"There is." I give him a hard stare.

He frowns, but a moment later, his expression clears. "You mean...?"

"The human realm. It's the only place they'll be safe." I lower my head. "It's the only place *we'll* be safe."

"But you said—"

"I know what I said!" Clenching my fists at my sides, I work to keep my temper in check. "I was wrong. This isn't an enemy we can defeat. The army can't protect us from this mercenary." When I look at him, his face tells me he's not convinced. "Trust me. He is powerful in ways I can't explain."

"From what I've heard, so are you."

"My magic is growing, yes, but I need time, and that's something we don't have right now."

He's quiet as if digesting everything I've told him. He studies the map, marking off the journey he expects the rebels to make. They'll be on foot, as they have too large a number to evanesce in any orderly fashion. Not to mention all the things they'll be bringing with them.

"What about Mama?"

A lump forms in my throat, and I work to swallow it. This is the hardest part of my plan, and I prepare for the protestations I expect Cliste to make. "We go without her."

His mouth drops open. "What the hell, Ast?"

Tears prick behind my eyes, but I blink them back. "She'll be safe with Uncle Brutach. They don't want to kill her." My voice cracks. "Just her sullied offspring."

Sinking onto a tree stump, he puts his head in his hands. "Did he actually *say* that, or are you just assuming?"

I replay the conversation in my head. "Technically, he only admitted to being hired to kill me." I kneel beside my brother. "But it wouldn't make sense for the rebels to go after Mama."

"Yes, but you said he wasn't hired by the rebels."

He's right, but I still can't wrap my head around a world where anyone would want to kill the queen. She has every right to the throne. And she is young, especially for fae. If she remarries, she can create a whole new bloodline.

"Look," I say, pushing away the conflicting thoughts, "I can't promise that he wasn't hired to kill all of us, including Mama. But what I *do* know is that he plans to kill me, and so I don't think it's a stretch to assume you and the rest of our siblings are also on his list." I take a deep breath. "Uncle Brutach and the royal guard can protect Mama. Hell, she has magic of her own to wield. But we need to save ourselves."

Cliste stares at his hands, not responding. I open and close my mouth a dozen times, unsure what to say next. Sitting here doing nothing is making me antsy. I want to be moving, bringing our men back to defend the castle and whisking my siblings away to safety.

"If we leave her behind, what if we never see her again?" he whispers, the pain clear on his face.

My heart pangs at his words. *If we do this, will we ever be able to return? Or will our home, our family... everything we love be lost to us forever? Charaide. Will I ever be able to tell him I love him?* This time, when the tears come, I let them fall.

"Let's talk to Brutach and Marto." He stands but avoids my eyes. "It's time to go home."

CHAPTER
TWENTY

After our conversation, Cliste and I waste no time in spreading the word. The men work to break down the camp quickly so we can set on a path home. We'll evanesce as much of the way as we can to try to beat the rebels back. Marto and some of his men have already left, but on their own, they won't be able to hold the castle for long.

In all of the chaos, I haven't had a chance to really talk to Charaide, and for that, I'm grateful. I'm not sure how to tell him I'm leaving or how to say goodbye.

That's not to say Charaide hasn't tried to speak with me. As soon as I left Cliste's tent, Charaide grabbed my arm and asked what we had decided. But all I told him was that we were leaving and needed to break camp immediately. Despite his best efforts, I've managed to work as far away from him as possible as I help clear tents and pack food. I'm afraid if I find myself alone with him, I'll confess everything, including my feelings for him. *And then what? Where does that leave us?* There's a good chance I may never see him again.

I drop the bag I'm packing as the pain in my chest becomes

unbearable. I wonder how I'm supposed to walk away from him, from Mama, from... my life. I've never left the faery realm for more than a few days at most. My father took us for brief excursions to the human world, and I've learned to blend in, but it'll be different this time. I can access my magic now. And we may be stuck there forever. *How will I hide my powers?*

My brother and I have spent the better part of the last few days together. For someone who recently begged me to come with him to the human realm, he's rather disgruntled about going. Surely he didn't really think Mama would abandon her people and join us. She's full-blooded fae and queen, after all. Besides, she wouldn't be able to hide her effervescence for that long. It's the thing that gives full fae their glow. Like sunlight catches in their skin and magic laces through every breath. Beautiful but painfully obvious. The kind of thing humans notice. The kind of thing they start whispering about.

My father used to tell us stories about what happened to fae who stayed too long in the human realm. Their magic behaved strangely there. Elemental powers still worked but just barely. Just enough to pass as luck or a trick in the wind. But deeper magic never worked as well. Glamour faded. Enchantments slipped. Eventually, humans caught on. What began as harmless curiosity eventually led to witch hunts and persecution. People fear what they don't understand, and that fear turns cruel fast. Though I suppose the same could be said for the fae based on how they've treated my kind.

And death holds harder in the human realm. Time moves differently. The more I consider my father's stories, the more Kythrall's words make sense. If he was created, as he claims, whatever dark sorcery stitched him together wouldn't hold across the veil.

But that's one gift of being a halfling. Being half human allows us to blend. We don't glow, at least not as brightly. We pass for human when we need to.

The tent flap lifts, and Charaide enters the tent behind me. I don't look up, and I force myself to focus on my task.

"Are you going to avoid me for the rest of this war?" His tone is harsh, though it sounds more like it's from pain than anger.

I close my eyes and take a deep breath before facing him. "I'm not avoiding you. There's just a lot going on."

Crossing his arms over his chest, he fixes me with a steely gaze. "Bullshit, Ast."

Damnit. Sometimes, I wish he couldn't always see right through me. "Believe what you want." I spin back to my bag and continue tossing things into it with more gusto than before.

He comes over and places a hand atop one of mine. I wince at his touch. My emotions are so raw, I feel as if he can see the scars across my heart bleeding anew.

"Talk to me." His voice is pleading, and I know that if I meet his gaze, his eyes will be my undoing, so I keep mine trained on the ground. He takes my bag and guides me to a chair before kneeling in front of me. Despite his best attempts to get me to look at him, I stay resolute, staring at the ground.

"For goddess's sakes, Ast. What are you hiding?" Now he's angry, which makes this a little easier. I would rather match his anger than face his pain.

"I'm not hiding anything," I retort, letting my frustration color my voice, hoping he'll misread its direction and storm off. No such luck.

"You're lying to me." He runs his hand through his blond hair. "Or you're lying to yourself. At this point, I can't tell."

Both. To him about hiding something and to myself about having a chance at saving my siblings. Deep down, I know we'll be lucky to make it to the castle at all, let alone before the rebels arrive. For all I know, the mercenary went ahead of the rebel army and my siblings are already dead. I take a calming breath, trying to steady my racing heart.

"Damn it, Ast, talk to me!"

My resolve crumbles, and I raise my head to meet his gaze. I don't know what expression is on my face, but it must be bad because in the next second, he pulls me into his arms.

"It's going to be okay." He strokes my hair, his voice soothing.

I want to believe him, but I know so much that he doesn't. And I can't risk him telling the men or my uncle. My siblings and I have a small chance of saving ourselves, but we'll lose even that if we divulge our plan. Best if everyone just assumes I'm worried about fending off the rebels.

"We need to finish packing," I say, wiping a rogue tear that has escaped. "Brutach wants to leave at sundown."

Charaide searches my face, and I try to put on a brave one, but I'm so tired, I doubt I'm successful. With a reluctant nod, he pushes off the ground and holds a hand out. I take it, allowing him to lift me from the chair.

We make quick work of packing up the rest of the tent and breaking it down. As Charaide rolls the canvas and ties it off, I can't help taking in every detail. The way his hands move so deftly over the ropes. How his biceps bulge under the weight of the wooden stake as he pulls it from the earth. I memorize each movement because I don't know when I'll next have a chance to see him, and I want to remember as much as possible.

Cliste arrives then, rolled-up maps in his hand and his lips pressed into a grim line. "It's time."

The sun is setting over the horizon, and my heart jumps into my throat. But I nod, not allowing my emotions to show on my face. If there's one good thing that came from my unfortunate meeting with Kythrall, it's that he taught me how much I need to control my expressions. No more wearing my heart on my sleeve.

It has only made me a better target, more vulnerable to anyone who might exploit those emotions.

After gathering the remaining men, we head out and evanesce as far as we can. Soon, we're moving through the countryside, heading toward the castle and my beloved forest. How I wish I could have one more hour to enjoy it, to savor the sanctuary that I may never see again. But it's a risk. Kythrall knows my weakness for the woods.

WE ARRIVE at the edge of my forest just before daybreak. Everyone is tired and hungry, so we stop briefly to rest, not wanting to wake the village and rouse the alarm. I decide not to stop with the rest of the men but to venture a bit farther to say goodbye to the place that was like a second childhood home, since I may never see it again.

After a glance around the camp to make sure no one is paying me any mind, I slip through the trees, keeping to the shadows. The forest is quiet, unnaturally so, as if the trees are waiting with bated breath to see the outcome of the battle that will soon be waged. I sigh, stealing along through the underbrush until I reach the creek.

The last time I was here alone was when I went hunting. Before the rebels, before Laochard, before Father. So much has happened in such a short time, I feel as if I've yet to have a moment to breathe, to grieve. Even now, as I face the possibility of leaving my home for good, I don't have the time or the peace to do so.

As I allow my eyes to sweep the lightening wood, I commit it to memory. I want to be able to recall every detail. The barren branches above me, stretching out black and gray in the darkness. The quiet sound of the brook beside me, babbling along without a care in the world. The damp, earthy scent of decaying leaves and moss.

A twig snaps somewhere nearby, and I crouch, hiding behind a boulder. My gaze darts from one shadow to the next, hoping for an animal, but instinct tells me I'm not alone. Maybe Charaide came to find me. Or maybe Kythrall is already here, waiting for me, where he knows I can't resist going.

"Astreilles…" That familiar voice rasps, and my blood goes cold.

I shut my eyes, which is as silly as an ostrich burying its head in the sand. *As if that will hide me.* He can read my mind, which is more likely to give me away than any sound I make. I bring up mental shields, praying they'll be enough.

It was so foolish to come here without my bow and arrows, with nothing to defend myself. Well, nothing except my magic. *But is that anything against him? Perhaps… If he was created, not born, that means he's not pure fae, right?* Maybe…

"Would you like to test that theory?" His breath tickles my ear, and I jump away.

My heart leaps into my throat. *How did he find me so easily?* His magic must be stronger than I realized.

"Oh, it's not that," he drawls, leaning against my boulder hiding place. "You and I are connected in ways even I don't understand."

"What do you mean?" My voice sounds stronger than I feel, a thin veil over the truth. Because part of me realizes we have more in common than I would ever like to admit. Neither of us is wholly fae nor wholly wanted.

"I'm not entirely sure myself." His gaze roves over me in a way that makes my skin crawl—except for the traitorous heat that blooms where his eyes linger. "At first, I thought it was just a coincidence, you not only showing up in the astral plane but in the place I had created to be alone. Like maybe my efforts to learn more about you had drawn you to me." Lifting his hand, he picks at a nail, which bends unnaturally away from his finger. "But now, I think it's more than that. I can feel your shields, and I was prepared to fight my way through them..."

"And so you did?"

He shakes his head, the hood covering it moving down, exposing more of his face. The shadows deepen the lines of his patchwork skin. I swallow my bile and work to keep the horror from my expression.

"I didn't have to. They just... melted away." He waves his hand in the air. "Like snow in the sun."

Nothing he says makes any sense. "Are you here to finally kill me and collect your payment?" If only I had the power of telepathy, I could call my brother or Charaide to my aid.

His eyebrows furrow, and he stares at the ground. "I'm supposed to, but I'm not sure I can."

"I'm defenseless." I snort, even if we both know that's not entirely true. "No bow or arrows. Not even a dagger in my boot." My mind conjures an image of Charaide and the way it felt when he pulled me into his arms. He only meant to comfort me, but it felt like the start of something more. A heaviness settles over my shoulders, and my breath shallows. I should have told him how much he means to me.

I love you. I send the message with every ounce of my being and hope he will somehow receive it despite my lack of telepathy.

"That's not what I mean," Kythrall replies, lifting his gaze to meet mine. His honey-gold eyes search my face as if he's hoping to find the answer to some unasked question there.

I don't have time to piece together whatever the hell he's thinking. My fear and anger churn in my gut, a wild energy that begs to be unleashed. But as he steps closer, everything shifts.

A jolt sears through my chest, and suddenly, I'm somewhere else. A hallway of stone. Damp walls closing in. Chains bite into my raw wrists. My mouth opens and screams in a voice I don't recognize— hoarse, guttural, and unending. Every nerve is on fire. The air stinks of blood and rot. Someone laughs, loud and maniacal, but I can't make them out.

It lasts only a heartbeat. I blink and I'm back in my body, back in the present. The fire still builds in my hands, but the fury behind it falters. Across from me, Kythrall watches, his eyes wide with surprise and something else. And I realize that it was *his* memory I saw.

"What was that?" I whisper.

He doesn't answer. His mouth opens then closes. For once, he has no quip, no smug retort, just a flicker of something raw and fractured in his eyes, as if whatever just happened surprised him too.

"You weren't supposed to see that," he says softly. His voice, usually so low and menacing, sounds different this time. Almost like... shame.

My heart twists unexpectedly, but I crush the feeling. Whatever that was, whatever he went through in that moment, it doesn't change what he is. It doesn't change what he's done or what he came here to do.

"I didn't ask to," I snap. "And I won't let it distract me."

He lifts his head slightly, but there's no challenge in the motion. His silence dares me to choose.

So I do. I raise my hands. The fire comes easily now, no longer wild and untamed but honed, forged from everything I love that he's threatened. I release it with a cry, the flames roaring toward him like a wave breaking free.

He dodges, the leaves crackling in the spot where he stood. Frustrated, I gather another fireball into my hands, but he's too quick, tackling me to the ground. I see red, and I radiate heat along every inch of my skin. He cries out, yanking his arms away from me and waving them around to put out the flames.

"Astreilles, wait. I don't—"

Not giving him a chance to finish, I press my hands to the ground, and it rumbles beneath them. His face pales, and he staggers away from me. I think I can make a run for it, but as soon as the earth stops quaking, he's on me again, pinning me down with his knee on my chest, knocking the breath out of me. Without oxygen, my flames become a harmless smolder.

I struggle to break free, but his hold is too strong. The creek bed calls to me, and I go still, focusing my energy on pulling the water toward us. But he realizes what I'm doing before even a droplet touches his boots. He rolls us over, away from the snaking liquid, and pins me against a tree, his eyes blazing as if daring me to pull my fire magic again and risk setting the whole forest aflame.

This is it, then. I have no tricks left up my sleeve. Without the ability to spin, I cannot call on the wind, and I'm not sure it would do much to stop him. I stare into his eyes, my chest heaving as the fight drains out of me.

"Be quick about it," I spit through my teeth.

His eyes light with humor, but he unsheathes a dagger from his hilt and presses its tip to my throat. I lift my chin in defiance, staring him down. No one will say I begged for my life. After everything I've been through, I deserve a soldier's death.

"Are you a soldier, Princess?" he whispers, his hot breath brushing my cheek. "Or are you just a poor innocent who got caught up in a political war?"

Before I can respond, an arrow flies past my head. Kythrall glances behind us and groans. A smirk pulls up one side of his mouth.

"Your boyfriend has arrived to ruin all our fun."

My chest caves in on itself as fear and relief fight for dominance. To see Charaide one last time before I die is a blessing and a curse. He's no match for Kythrall, and I suspect the mercenary will delight in killing us both, slowly.

"Charaide," I call, trying to sound calm while my heart hammers away in my chest. "Stay out of this."

As if in response, another arrow flies, and this time, it rips a piece of Kythrall's shirt before sticking in a tree behind us. I stifle a sigh. Charaide is a great many things, but an archer is not one of them. It doesn't help that the sun has barely begun its descent in the east and he's, quite literally, shooting in the dark.

Kythrall pulls me away from the tree, spinning me around to face Charaide with the knife still against my throat. "Do you really wish to risk your love's life in this way?"

"Let her go."

"How did you find us?" Kythrall asks, ignoring Charaide's demand. "Still brooding over your little spat? Hoping for a quiet moment to patch things up?" His tone drips with mockery.

My stomach plummets. He'd been watching, not just now but earlier. Closely enough that he could sense the tension between us. Which means he also heard the conversation we had and saw Charaide comfort me. I thought we were alone, that we had a moment to ourselves, but of course not. Not with Kythrall. He's been shadowing me like a curse that won't lift.

"Oh, I've never left you, Princess," he coos in my ear, sending chills down my spine. "The rebels are a bunch of halfwits who have little hope of accomplishing their aims. I knew better than to wait for you at the castle."

"Stop reading her mind!" Charaide's voice seems to echo across the forest.

I lift my gaze to him, and it's as if I'm seeing him for the first time. He glows among the shadows of the dawn. Sometimes, I forget that he's a full fae, but in this moment, he could be nothing else. I blink as his light burns my eyes, but I can't look away. *Does he hide this side of himself around me? Or have I just been blind to how brightly he shines?*

"But her thoughts are so delicious," Kythrall says, his raspy voice taking on a bitter tone. The wavering man from moments ago has been replaced by a cold and calculating killer.

Or so I assume. But there's something off in the way he says it. It's almost... wistful, like he's envious of how I feel about Charaide. But I push the thought away. After all, Kythrall's still a mercenary with a dagger to my throat, and that's not exactly a winning way to make friends.

"Don't act like you've never read her thoughts," Kythrall continues, "searching them for some inkling of how she feels about you."

I stiffen, but Charaide shakes his head. "I respect her too much for that."

And the cold thread of doubt that had begun to worm its way into my stomach dissipates. Still, it doesn't explain why he is so different now.

"He hides his true self to make you more comfortable." Kythrall cackles beside me. "As if you haven't lived your whole life amongst the fae." He leans forward, glaring at Charaide. "Do you really think her so self-conscious? Has her power over the last few weeks taught you nothing about your so-called best friend?"

Charaide's jaw clenches. I widen my eyes, hoping that he'll see that I don't buy any of the drivel that Kythrall is spewing. He's trying to turn us against each other so Charaide will leave me to my fate.

"No response?" Kythrall shakes his head. "Typical. You don't deserve her."

Heat radiates in my belly, a feeling I've had only once before. I latch onto it, letting it build as light begins to flow from my core throughout the rest of my being. Kythrall cries out and releases me. I don't know how long I can maintain this strange power I don't understand, so I begin spinning, building into a tornado and dragging twigs and branches into my funnel cloud.

Kythrall falls backward, his jaw slack, but whether in awe or horror, I can't tell. But I don't have time to consider because in the next revolution, Charaide runs toward Kythrall and tackles him to the ground. Kythrall pulls a blade from his boot, but before he can wield it, I maneuver closer and suck the blade right from his hand. It dances precariously in my swirling wind, and I contort my body as I try to catch it.

Beneath me, Charaide pummels Kythrall, not once reaching for a weapon of his own. I don't have time to dwell on the reason for this, as my hand finally closes around the hilt of the dagger, and I slow my spinning until my feet come to rest on the ground.

Charaide is holding Kythrall much in the same position I was in a moment ago. He pushes Kythrall forward, eyeing the blade in my hand.

"Kill him, Astreilles," Charaide says, his breathing heavy. "Kill him and be done with this."

"Ah, but if you kill me, you'll never know who hired me." A sinister smile pulls at Kythrall's lips, and I shudder as the patches of skin appear to separate at the seams.

"I don't give a damn who hired you," Charaide seethes. "You're not going to live to see your payday."

"But I do give a damn," I whisper, the knife in my hand wavering in the air. I meet Charaide's gaze. "If we kill him, whoever hired him will just hire someone new. It's better if we know what we're up against."

"Clever girl," Kythrall breathes, and I hate the way his approval stirs something in my chest.

I glare at Kythrall. "I'm not a complete idiot."

"Never said you were, Princess. Only a fool would underestimate you."

"Isn't that what you've done?" Charaide tightens his hold on

Kythrall. "You thought you could take her alone in the woods. How's that working out for you?"

"I am curious," Kythrall drawls, completely unfazed despite his predicament. "Since you never answered my question, how did you find us?"

Charaide's eyes soften as he looks at me. "She called to me."

My mouth falls open, and the hand that's not holding the knife flutters to my chest. *Is it possible?*

Kythrall's eyes gleam. "The witch was right. You *have* just scratched the surface of your power."

I ignore him, focusing only on Charaide. If my message went through, then that means...

Reading my mind, he nods, a warmth fills his eyes, and his hold on Kythrall slackens. Which is just what the mercenary needs. A quick movement and Charaide is on his back as Kythrall sprints away.

Just before disappearing into the woods, he turns and stares at me. I try calling my magic to stop him, but my energy is too drained. His lips curl into that same sinister smile as he lifts a hand in a wave.

I'll be seeing you, Princess.

I shudder at the thought he plants in my mind. Then he's gone, and I'm on my feet before rushing to where Charaide lies on the ground.

"Are you all right?" My hands move over him to check for any wounds Kythrall might have inflicted in their scuffle.

"Goddess damn him." He holds his head in his hands. "I'm so sorry, Ast. I can't believe I let him get away."

"Shh." I pull him into my arms. "I'm just glad you're all right. That *we* are all right."

He lifts his head and searches my face. "Did you mean it? What you said—"

I nod, a lump rising in my throat. "I've wanted to tell you for so long, but I..."

He places his hands on either side of my face. "I know. With everything going on, I get it." His lips lift in a shy smile. "I love you, too, you know."

My heart swells so quickly it feels like it might crack wide open. Before I can think better of it, I wrap my arms around his neck and kiss him. When my brain finally catches up with my actions, I start to apologize, but I'm taken aback by the heat in his gaze. Wordlessly, he cups my chin and presses his lips against mine again. My hands slide into his hair, and his lips part with a sigh. It's everything I've ever wanted but nothing like I anticipated. It's soft and sweet and sensual all at once.

When we finally break apart, his smile is bright. "You have no idea how long I've wanted to do that."

"Really?" I ask, breathless.

He nods, pulling me closer. "I've wanted to tell you how I've felt for a while now, but after your grandfather died... there was never a good time." He rests his forehead against mine. "But lately, the way you've looked at me—I started to hope. Then when I heard your voice in my head and what you said... I knew. I knew I'd been a fool not to tell you sooner."

He kisses my hair. "I love you, Ast. I think a part of me always has."

My heart aches at how long I've waited to hear these words. The timing may be terrible, but this moment... it's ours. I tilt my face to his.

"I love you too," I whisper.

He draws me close, and I meet his kiss halfway. It's warm, certain, full of promises we may not get to keep, but I believe in them anyway.

For now, it is enough.

CHAPTER
TWENTY-ONE

CHARAIDE and I return to camp just in time to leave it. The sun is high in the sky, and the sounds of the village waking up penetrate the thick brush of the forest.

As we move toward the castle, I no longer regard this forest as my sanctuary. My eyes search through every bare branch and shadow, expecting to find Kythrall waiting for me. *Would he attack when I'm surrounded by soldiers?* I doubt it. He prefers to have me all to himself so he can play mind games uninterrupted.

I can't keep betraying my instincts.

With each step away from the creek where we fought, the memory I glimpsed in Kythrall's mind—the memory of his past— pushes me toward a choice. I break away from the column of marching soldiers and slip toward the edge of camp. There, I find Caillea tracing sigils in the dirt with a long wooden staff. She looks up, brow furrowing before I even speak.

"I need your help," I whisper.

Her eyes narrow. "Something's happened."

I nod. "There's a mercenary. He's been stalking me for weeks now. I saw him twice at the castle, and both times, he attacked me. Then I started seeing him in my dreams." I shake my head. "Only... they weren't dreams. He said I was astral projecting. And he told me that he was destined to kill me."

The more I speak, the more Caillea's eyes widen. "Why did you not tell me this before?"

"At first, I thought it was just a coincidence." Once I've started relaying the tale, it's like I can't stop. It explodes from me like a bottle of sparkling wine that has been shaken before being uncorked. I tell her how Kythrall was hired to kill my siblings and me, not by the rebels but by someone else.

Her lips press into a thin line. "As I suspected, there is a spy amongst you. Someone close enough to know your family's every move. Someone who knew exactly who to target."

I swallow the dread rising in my throat. The spy is the least of my concerns. "But that's not the most important thing," I hurry on. "The last time I saw him, there was a moment where we... connected. I saw something. A memory. Not mine. *His.* There were stone corridors and screams that made my blood turn cold." I shudder as I replay it. "And a pain so deep I felt it in my bones." I meet her gaze. "It lasted only a moment, but when we fought afterward, it was like he knew me. Like something tethered us."

"He let you in."

I shake my head. "I don't think he chose to. It felt like... a crack in the world, and I fell through it." My teeth worry my lower lip. "He also said something that I can't explain. That he was created, not born. And his skin, it's like a quilt of different creatures."

She's silent for a moment as if absorbing what I've said. Finally, she sighs. "There are whispered tales of beings stitched together with dark magic. Magic that binds flesh and fuses bones in a most unnatural way. These constructs are born of grief or vengeance. Most of them break. They don't remember. They don't feel."

I wipe my clammy hands on my tunic. "But he does."

"Then he's something different." Her voice lowers. "Something dangerous."

My stomach twists. "Once he's done with me, he'll come for my siblings."

Caillea straightens her spine, her expression determined. "Then we'll make it impossible. I'll ward the castle walls. No one will evanesce against them without my knowing, not even a half-faded shadow."

"What about me?"

She rests a hand on my shoulder. "You stay guarded at all times, at least until we are sure your siblings are safe. No exceptions." Her expression softens. "That way, you can take your siblings to safety at the opportune moment."

I glance at her sharply. "How did you know?"

Her smile is sad. "Because it's the only way to save the kingdom and your family. At least for the time being."

"And you don't think it's the wrong choice?"

She shakes her head. "No, because I know one day, you'll come back to us."

I don't respond because I'm not so sure that's true. Instead, I make my way to the marching soldiers. Caillea follows, the rhythmic *thud* of her staff in the dirt the only evidence she's still nearby.

When I reach Charaide, he takes my hand and squeezes it. My lips curve in a grateful smile. I'm relieved to have a plan with Caillea to protect my siblings, but at some point, Cliste and I will need to plot our escape to the human world.

My smile falters. *When will I tell Charaide that I'm leaving him?* If I do it now, I risk exposing my siblings and me. Cliste would never forgive me for breaking his trust and putting our siblings in danger. But if I don't tell him soon, I may not get another chance.

The march through the forest is quick. The men are desperate to get home to something familiar. I'm looking forward to seeing my mother again and to spending a few precious moments with her. It pains me to know I can't warn her of her children's impending departure either. I hate knowing how blindsided and devastated she'll be when she learns we've abandoned her.

I consider what Caillea said about my return to the fae realm. I know, given the choice, Cliste will stay in the human world forever. *Would I?* Maybe Caillea sees a future where things calm down and we would be allowed to return. But it's hard to imagine a world where the rebels would welcome us back, even if we were no longer in line to the throne.

As we reach the edge of the forest, Marto, Cliste, and I hold up our hands, signaling to the men to stay within the trees. Together, moving with caution, we slip out from the shadows and into the light.

The castle rises in the distance, and the village is alive with activity. I strain my ears, wishing not for the first time that I possessed full fae hearing. My powers have surprised me, especially the latest one. I'm still trying to determine how the mental messages work. *Am I just so tuned in with Charaide that he was able to pick up my thoughts, even at a distance?*

"There's no sign of them," Marto says, his voice low.

Cliste nods. "Good. Then we've beaten them here, albeit barely." He turns to the forest. "Let's move. The sooner we can get behind the castle walls, the better."

We raise our hands, and the soldiers join us as we march through the village. The townsfolk hurry into their homes to get out of our way. Their faces soon appear in the windows, watching us pass, but otherwise, the last leg of our trip is uneventful. It seems almost too good to be true.

As we approach the gates, Cliste and I exchange a wary glance. The last time I crossed into the castle in a group like this, it was Mother's coronation, and we were attacked. While the rebels may not be here, they have allies that live in the moat. That they haven't attacked in our absence is a surprise, but perhaps they're waiting, biding their time until the opportune moment.

I lead the way across the moat, keeping one eye on the water. Its stillness is of little comfort. The creatures that live within its depths are known for stealthy movements. My heart is in my throat, but I press on. Just a few more steps.

A splash to my right causes me to jump. The mermaid stares at me, her eyes so blue I almost think I'm staring into the ocean itself. She grins, her teeth sharp and deadly.

"Welcome back, Princess," she says. "But don't get too comfortable." With that, she dives back into the murky depths.

Chills run down my spine, and I hurry the rest of the way across the drawbridge. The men move uneasily behind me, but soon, we're all safely behind the castle walls. Marto's troops stay in the village, some with their families, others to protect the villagers. We raise the drawbridge in hopes of stalling the rebels' attack for as long as possible.

"Astreilles! Cliste!"

My mother's voice brings tears to my eyes. I turn around to find her standing behind me with her arms wide. Our siblings cluster around her. She steps forward and wraps me in a warm embrace. For the first time since the start of this war, I feel safe, as if maybe everything will be okay.

One glance at Cliste and the warmth drains from me. His eyes bore into mine as he hugs our mother next. Those eyes hold a question, and I shake my head. We just arrived, and she's so happy to see us. Better to wait, to give her a night to enjoy us being home, before we rip her children away from her forever.

I turn away from his disapproving look to focus on my other siblings. Elana skips over to me and throws her arms around my neck. I laugh as I bend slightly to squeeze her waist. She's taller than I remember, and her smile almost erases the memory of her standing on the drawbridge, waving tearfully from the other side.

My other siblings wave shyly from behind my mother's skirts. I catch a glimpse of my reflection in the mirror and suddenly understand why they're keeping their distance. My face is smeared with dirt, and my hair is disheveled with leaves and twigs. I probably look like some woodland monster.

I turn away from my family and take in the castle. A pang hits my chest as my gaze sweeps over the grand staircase behind us, leading up to our bedchambers. The room feels emptier without Laochard's bolstering or my father's quiet laugh.

"Come now." Mother grabs my hand and leads us deeper into the castle. "Let's get you cleaned up. We've had a feast prepared in your honor, and I want you looking your best."

I follow her up the stairs to my bedchamber. The mirror is still cracked from my second encounter with Kythrall. I avert my gaze, not wanting any reminders of the one who is still out there hunting me.

A bath has already been drawn. Feidre arrives to help me undress, but I shoo her away. I need a moment alone with my thoughts, and I've been dressing and undressing myself for weeks. I promise to call her when I need help with my gown and shut the door behind me. It's the first time I've felt truly alone since we left.

The water is warm and luxurious compared to the cold springs I've washed in between battles. It takes more time than I would care to admit to wash all the dirt and grime from my body, but I feel better when I finally step out of the bath.

Feidre must have been waiting nearby, as she appears by my side with yet another green dress. I stifle a sigh because I'm sure my time with the army has done nothing to help my physique. If anything, I'm thinner, though perhaps a bit more toned. But she succeeds in draping the gown over my body in a way that allows it to flow elegantly down my frame. After fussing with my hair for the better part of an hour, she finally releases me, and I carefully make my way downstairs.

Several tables have been brought into the great hall, and the men filter into the room with tired smiles. We don't often host such large gatherings, and a part of me was hoping for a more intimate meal with just my family. However, the men have fought hard, and they deserve a quiet night dining with their queen. Especially since we don't know what tomorrow will hold when the rebels arrive.

Cliste and I take our seats on either side of Mother. Charaide sits to my left, and he grasps my hand as we wait for everyone else to settle in. His presence is a comfort as long as I don't think about the conversation we'll be having later. I've decided, now that we're back at the castle, it's time to tell him the plan.

Mother clinks her glass with her knife. "Welcome back. We are so pleased to see your faces and to have you within these walls once more." Her eyes alight on Cliste and me, and she smiles. "I know the war is not over, but I hope it soon will be. We are grateful for your sacrifice, and to show our thanks, we have prepared quite an evening for you."

She claps, and servers pour into the room from the kitchen, carrying trays piled high with food. I sneak a glance at Cliste and find his face as pale as I imagine mine to be. *How will this be viewed by the rebels when they learn of it? A celebration in the midst of a civil war?*

Brutach stands at the opposite end of our table and lifts his glass. "Thank you, dear sister. A toast to the queen!"

Everyone lifts their glass to my mother. I swallow the wine, hoping it will settle my nerves. Maybe if the men here remain loyal to her, the rebels will overlook this ill-timed feast. Besides, once the halfling heirs are gone, there won't be much reason for continued conflict. The rebels will have won in a sense.

The conversation around is lively. The men are happy to be

home, off the road, and having a fulfilling meal. Tonight, we'll all sleep in real beds, which will be a luxury after the hard ground.

After dessert, Charaide leans toward me. "May I steal you for a moment?" I frown, and he gives me a teasing grin. "I won't bite, Ast." His expression darkens, and he lifts my hand to his lips. "Unless you want me to."

My stomach flips, and I nod, allowing him to lead me from the dining room. He heads to the library and shuts the door behind us. Once we're completely alone, he takes my hands into his.

"Are you happy to be home?" he asks.

I nod, unsure why this question required such privacy. "Very." My gaze drops to the ground. "Though I suspect my joy won't last."

"You're worried about the battle?"

"Aren't you?" I ask.

"I believe the war is changing in our favor." He squeezes my hand. "The rebels will be brought to heel, and then we can look to the future."

A lump forms in my throat. "Char…"

"Wait." Pressing a finger to my lips, he smiles at me. "I know this is new and different for us. But I meant every word I said to you in the forest, Astreilles." He brushes my cheek. "I want to court you, properly, with the queen's blessing."

I stare at him, my emotions warring inside of me. *If I tell him, I lose him. If I don't, I betray him. Either way, my heart breaks.*

Tears sting my eyes, and I look away before he can see. "I don't think that'll be possible."

The silence is deafening. I take a deep breath to compose myself then glance over my shoulder. My heart sinks at his devastated expression.

"You don't…" He clears his throat. "You don't want me?"

"Of course I want you," I cry, throwing my arms around his neck and burying my face in his shirt.

His arms come around me, but there's hesitation. I squeeze tighter, trying to convey my feelings without words. But the message isn't getting through, and I know the time has come to tell him everything.

I step back, dread constricting my chest as I meet his eye. "You know I love you, Charaide. And if things were different, I would run to my mother without a second thought to ask her permission to court." As I shake my head, the tears stream down my cheeks, and this time, I don't bother trying to hide them. "But that's not where we are." I point at the door. "My family is in danger. There's an assassin who will not stop until we are all dead."

"We can stop him." Charaide moves toward me.

I stumble back, unwilling to be placated. "And another will just spring up in his wake." My head pounds as I try to find the words to get through to him. "Cliste and I have spoken, and we've decided to take our siblings to the human world."

His mouth falls open. "What?"

"Char, it's the only way to keep us safe."

Crossing his arms, he shakes his head. "I refuse to accept that."

"Then tell me another way. Tell me how I can protect my family without risking the lives of hundreds of others."

"We can find out who hired the mercenary and bring that person to justice. Kill them if necessary. Then they can't hire anyone else."

My answering laugh is bitter. "And how do you propose we do that? With the rebels practically on our doorstep and no idea when Kyth—when the mercenary will attack next?" I stare at him, begging him to understand. "And what if he goes after one of my younger siblings instead? Do you think I can live with myself if something happens to them?"

"Fine." His voice is low but firm. "But what about Cliste's plan? Why can't he take them? Why aren't *you* staying to fight?"

His gaze pins me. "Do you really intend to abandon your mother and your people?"

"The queen is hardly a damsel in distress," I retort. "Not to mention she has a whole army at her disposal." Taking a deep breath, I blow out my aggravation. It's not Charaide's fault that we're in this situation. I expected him to argue with me. It's why I've been dreading this conversation.

"Look," I continue. "Our hope is that if we're gone, if the halfling heirs are no longer in line to the throne, then maybe the rebels will back off." I close the distance between us then cup his cheek in my hand. "We're the enemy, right? To them, at least, we are unworthy of the throne."

"I don't think it's that simple."

"And you're probably right. But my siblings are safe in the mortal realm. Fae can't stay there long. You know our magic doesn't work quite right, and the mercenary confirmed he can't cross the veil." I bury my head in my hands. "I don't know what else to do."

"Stay with me," he says softly. "Don't run away from this, from us. And don't let the rebels deny you your birthright."

I turn away. "A birthright I don't even want?"

"I know you never thought you'd be next in line, but, Ast, you've always known there was a possibility."

I spin on my heel, heat rising in my chest. "Laochard was next in line. He should be leading this army. His future children should be the next heirs. I never wanted *any* of this."

Charaide places a careful hand on my shoulder. "Ast, I'm so sorry about Laochard." His lips press in a firm line. "But he's dead, and you have a duty to your mother... To your family. To your kingdom."

"I *am* doing my duty—to all of my family. My siblings need me now more than ever." I shrug him off. "I'm saving my siblings from a most certain death at the hands of a hired assassin." I move to the other side of the room, needing some distance. "As for my kingdom, they've proven time and again that they don't want me or my kind on the throne. So what better way to serve the people than to grant their most fervent wish?"

"Not everyone feels that way," he protests. His footsteps sound across the floor, but he stops several paces back. I can't blame him. My emotions are wreaking havoc on my powers. I balance a fireball between my hands as I work to control my anger and extinguish it.

"Enough of them do."

He sighs. "For argument's sake, let's assume your leaving does what you intend. The rebels withdraw, your mother is safe, and the kingdom is at peace." His hands are gentle on my shoulders as he turns me to face him. "What then? Will you stay in the human realm forever?"

I nod, and his sharp intake of breath tells me this was the wrong answer. But I can't lie to Charaide. Beyond my feelings for him, he's my best friend. It's better he knows the truth and hears it from me.

"Perhaps one day, we could return," I hedge, but it sounds hollow even to my ears. "Cliste will stay. He had plans to leave for good long before we considered bringing the rest of my siblings." Tears spring to my eyes, and I dash them away. "I told him it was treason to even consider. But now..."

Charaide steps back, and his throat bobs as he swallows. Tears well in his eyes, though he tries to blink them back.

"Then what are *we*, Astreilles? What is this *thing* between us?"

My chest constricts as I struggle to draw breath. I can hardly bear to look at him, let alone say the words we both know are coming. To be so close to having everything I wanted with him only for it to be taken away. Gods damn the rebels. And damn Kythrall to the bottom of the castle moat.

"You mean everything to me," I whisper. "But we can't be together. Not right now."

He closes his eyes, and with every tear that seeps from beneath his lids, my heart breaks anew. I go to him, throw my arms around his neck, and pull his face down to mine. Our lips meet, but it's not the warm promise of a first kiss. It's the cold goodbye of a last.

"Maybe I can come with you."

I shake my head, our noses rubbing against each other. "You know that's not possible. You're pure fae. No amount of glamor will hide you from the humans." I sigh. "Besides, you'll never be fully whole without your magic."

"My magic doesn't matter. I can't stand the thought of you vanishing into a world where I can't follow. Not now, not after everything we shared last night. I can't lose *you*, Ast." His voice breaks on my name.

My vision blurs with tears, the ache in my chest growing unbearable. "You won't." I place my hand over his heart. "As long as you love me, I'll always be here."

We stand there, holding each other in the darkening room. The shadows creep along the walls, and a cold chill runs down my spine as if something unseen is watching. I tense, but Charaide doesn't notice. For a moment, I imagine Kythrall on the edge of the library, unable to look away as we say our quiet goodbye. I don't know if that's true, but the sensation of his aura settles over me. It's a connection I can't explain, and it frightens me more than any dagger. I don't know if it's his shadow in the room or only the memory of his gaze that clings to me like smoke.

But if Kythrall *is* nearby, he gives us this moment. And for that, I suppose, I should be grateful. Inside, I seethe.

CHAPTER

TWENTY-TWO

THE NURSERY WING is quiet save for the hush of breath and the occasional rustle of blankets. I ease the door open and step inside. The soft moonlight pouring in through the window catches on scattered toys and crumpled quilts.

My siblings are tucked into their beds, peaceful in a way that makes my chest ache. Desslee has her arm flung across the mattress, her mouth open in a gentle snore. Elana's fingers clutch a corner of my old cloak like a lifeline. Meanwhile, my youngest brothers snuggle matching stuffed bears, a gift from the mortal realm from my father.

I slip into an old rocking chair and watch their sleeping faces, memorizing the lines of their innocence. A whisper of movement behind me sets my nerves on edge, and I stand, my hand on my dagger.

"I thought I'd find you here." Caillea's voice is low.

I glance at my siblings to ensure we haven't disturbed them. "They don't know what's coming."

"No," she agrees. "And it's better that way."

"Kythrall is closer than ever. I can feel him. We don't have long, and I can't risk him slipping in while I sleep."

Caillea steps beside me, her gaze sweeping the warded windows. "I've spelled the castle with the help of my replacement." Her eyes crinkle with her bemused smile. "Medea suggested we might reinforce our efforts with a bit of your magic."

She hands me her staff, and I stare at her in bewilderment. "Do you want me to draw runes with this?"

Her smile widens. "I thought you might infuse it with your light. The one that shone in the forest when Kythrall held you at knifepoint."

I swallow. "I don't know how to access that magic."

Instead of arguing or persuading, she simply purses her lips. "Try."

It seems a futile effort, but I close my eyes and focus on the memory of what that magic felt like. The warmth that seemed to radiate through me. The way it coursed from my core through my veins.

But nothing happens, and I open my eyes to find Caillea studying me.

"It responded to your fear," she says. "Perhaps if you channel that, it'll return."

I raise an eyebrow. "I was in a literal life-or-death situation." I gesture to my sleeping siblings. "That's hardly the case now."

"Hmm, but you are in a life-or-death situation. Your siblings need your protection." She steps forward and places a hand over my heart. "Tap into the fear you felt. Imagine your siblings are there with you and you're the only thing standing between them and a monster."

I'm not sure how, but her words fill me with a sense of dread. How easy it would have been for that exact scenario to have occurred. My mind conjures my worst fears—my siblings cowering behind me as I face Kythrall alone. I'm drained and tired, my magic barely hanging on.

Something pulses in my core. I glance down to see a light glowing from within.

"That's it. Now harness that energy and infuse it in the staff."

It takes effort, more than I've ever expended. This magic isn't like my elemental magic. It's more powerful and more unpredictable. It's almost as if it doesn't want to part from me. I grit my teeth and use my breath to expand the magic up my chest and into my arms. Gripping the staff, I take a deep breath and slowly release it, pushing my magic into the staff at the same time.

The wood glows as it absorbs the magic. I give as much as I can manage and release the staff. Caillea catches it before it clatters on the floor, and she smiles encouragingly at me.

"When you return, we will continue to practice this gift." She traces the runes she previously drew with the staff. They glow with my power. The floor hums with the soft vibration of her magic.

When she finishes, she turns to me. "It won't make the castle invincible, but it'll make it very unwelcoming."

I glance once more at my siblings. "That's all I need. Time."

Her gaze softens. "You're not the only one willing to fight for them, you know."

I nod, but something in me stays curled tight. Because I know, even if we succeed tomorrow, goodbye is coming.

***

THE NEXT MORNING, I'm physically well rested, but emotionally, I'm a wreck. Before leaving Charaide, I made him promise not to tell anyone about Cliste's and my plans. It wouldn't do us any good if our intent to leave became known to Mother or Uncle Brutach, let alone the rebels or Kythrall.

Charaide begged me one last time to reconsider, and the hope in his face was enough to make me promise to do so, even though I know I can't. It will break my heart to leave him. Beyond that, I *want* to fight Kythrall. To find out once and for all who hired him and kill them both with my bare hands. But if I fail, then I would cause Charaide far more pain than if he knew I was alive and well in the human world.

I dress in my armor and sling my quiver over my back. Staring into the mirror, I plait my auburn hair to keep it out of my face. Though Cliste had hoped to leave before the battle began, we agreed we couldn't leave our men without at least trying to turn the battle in our favor. But by nightfall, Cliste and I will ferry our siblings to the mortal realm. I can only hope that by dawn tomorrow, the war will be over, my family will be safe, and Charaide will forgive me.

When I arrive, the men are assembling in the great hall. I grab a quick bite to eat and join Charaide and Cliste at a table with my uncle. Cliste and Brutach talk of battle strategy, while Charaide keeps sending me pleading glances when he thinks he can get away with it. I wish he would stop. It's not like I wanted any of this, and his dying hope is making this harder. But then I feel guilty for thinking such thoughts. *Were the shoe on the other foot and Charaide was leaving me, wouldn't I be doing the same?*

"A word, Ast?" Cliste whispers to me after Brutach leaves the table.

I sneak a glance at Charaide and nod before following my brother through the hall to the library. Apparently, this is the room for clandestine conversation. I ignore the ache in my chest as I'm reminded of the conversation from the night before.

"I think we should leave in the middle of the battle, when the rebels are too distracted to notice."

I gape at him. "And abandon our men? No way."

He glares at me. "You underestimate our forces."

"Or maybe you overestimate them," I retort. "This is so much more our fight than it is theirs." I get right in his face. "And think of what that will do to Mama if we suddenly disappear in the midst of the fighting. She'll think we all perished in battle."

"Mama will understand, especially when Charaide explains everything." His eyes narrow, accusations building behind them. "Because of course, you told him, didn't you? After I specifically asked you not to?"

A flush creeps up my neck, but I turn away. I won't give him the satisfaction of knowing he's right. *Charaide wouldn't betray my trust like that, right?* Unless…

"Yes, your boyfriend came to me last night, asking, no, pleading with me to change my mind. Imagine my confusion then horror when I realized you'd told him everything. How could you, Ast?" His voice cracks on my name.

I glance at him from the corner of my eye, and his expression is menacing, but his eyes betray his fear. *So Charaide figured maybe he could make my brother see reason?* I scoff. This whole scheme was originally *Cliste's* idea, not mine. The threat Kythrall poses is the only reason I came around to it. Better to have Mama mourn our departure than to have her bury all her children.

"Fine." I lift my chin and meet my brother's angered gaze. "I did tell Charaide. He put me in an impossible position, and I felt I owed him the truth."

Cliste sighs. "I understand how hard this is for both of you. But it's because of your actions that I think it's imperative we leave sooner rather than later. This castle has eyes and ears everywhere. There's no telling who else might have heard our plans."

"Caillea and I strengthened the wards last night," I say. "We'll know if the rebels attempt to evanesce into the castle."

"Whispered incantations and desperate prayers aren't going to withstand the rebels bursting through the castle gates." Cliste shakes his head. "It's better if we leave in the midst of the chaos.

That gives us time to cross the veil and escape before the dust settles and everyone realizes we're gone."

My lower lip trembles, and I bow my head. *Does he even understand what he's asking of me, to leave everything in the heat of the battle and never know whether everyone I know and love survives the day?*

His hand slides under my chin and lifts my head. "I know it's hard. Believe me, if I thought there was another way, I would take it." He releases me and runs his hand through his hair. "And maybe once they learn of our disappearance, they'll finally stop this wretched war."

"Then we should alert someone when we leave," I say. "Because the sooner the rebels know, the sooner they may lay down their arms."

"Well, you already told Charaide. If you want to work out some signal with him to let him know, I suppose that will do fine." He frowns. "But wait until the last possible moment. Make it discreet and tell no one else."

Keeping my expression neutral, I nod. But inside, I'm screaming.

"I'll go and prepare our siblings," he continues. "It'll look less suspicious if I go, since you're supposed to be leading this army."

Again, I nod, unable to speak. He touches my shoulder briefly before leaving me alone in the library. With effort, I drag myself over to a chair in the corner of the room and sink into it, my head in my hands.

How did I end up here? I can't see beyond the moment we leave the fae realm for good, let alone where we'll go when we enter the human world. We know next to no one there. It'll be enough of a struggle to blend in, let alone find safe haven. I can't imagine what we'll even *do* once we arrive.

I've always had a clear path mapped out for me. As a princess, I have expectations I'm supposed to meet, and while I wasn't next in line to the throne, I still had duties befitting a member of the royal family. But now that I face the prospect of never seeing my homeland again, my future is as wide-open as it is empty.

After pushing to my feet, I leave the library and head to my bedchamber. I pack a small satchel with some clothes, books, and other things I may need. I wish I had something of Charaide's to take with me, but I don't even have a painting of his likeness. A rogue tear slips down my cheek. If he tries to stop me before I leave, I may not have the strength to go.

I slip the satchel onto one shoulder then crisscross my quiver on the other. After a moment's hesitation, I slide my sword and sheath onto my belt. Hand-to-hand combat isn't my strong suit, but I would be a fool to go into battle without the sword. With one last look in the mirror, I can't help thinking I look less like a fearsome warrior and more like a lost little girl.

But I'm not a little girl anymore. Because lost little girls don't lead armies or fight monsters in the dark. I square my shoulders and lift my chin. I may not believe in my abilities, but I'll fake it until I do.

CHAPTER

TWENTY-THREE

CHARAIDE and I stand together with the other archers on the tower. The misty morning haze obscures our vision, but in the distance comes the muted sound of thousands of stomping feet. They are coming, and we are ready. Marto and his men are somewhere beyond the walls of the castle, our first line of defense. But we don't expect them to hold very long.

In the dungeons beneath the castle, my siblings are waiting for the signal. When the time is right, Cliste and I will join them, following the tunnel under the moat that leads to the portal that will take us to the human realm. And then we'll disappear, perhaps never to be heard of here again.

"Are you sure you want to do this?" Charaide whispers for the thousandth time.

I give a curt nod. My nerves are already on edge enough without his constant second-guessing of my choice, though perhaps "second-guessing" is not the right word. The threat of Kythrall has forced my hand.

Pushing these thoughts from my mind, I force myself to focus.

I'm not leaving until I've at least done as much as I can for the kingdom I'm abandoning. The rhythm of the marching falters as if the rebels are trying to ascertain where we are in all this fog. I smile. It's not a natural occurrence, but no one has noticed. After playing around with my water magic last night, I discovered a new talent.

Fogging up the washroom was a lot easier than trying to create fog at such a large scale, but it worked. Unfortunately, I'm the only one who can see through it, but I can't be too precise in my aim or else others will know what I've done. The target on my back is already large enough.

Still, I take advantage of my situation and nock an arrow in my bow. I scan the men below, choosing my mark with care.

Charaide raises an eyebrow. "Why are you wasting an arrow?"

I don't respond, instead pulling back the string and letting it fly. A muffled scream causes Charaide's mouth to drop open, but I keep my expression neutral.

The rebels draw their swords, searching for the source of the arrow. They expect it's someone on the ground, and I stifle a laugh at how easy this is. If only I could share my unique vision with the rest of my men. But if I possess the power to clear their line of sight, I've yet to figure it out.

Marto's men are in position, and I begin clearing the mist ever so slightly to reveal how close they are to the rebels. To their credit, the only indication the rebels give of being surprised is widening their eyes. Otherwise, they move into attack position.

A command comes from behind the front lines, and the rebels rush forward, but Marto and his men are ready. I give the order, and a volley of arrows sails through the sky, taking out several rebels. But it won't be enough.

Fire lights in my hand, and I hold it aloft so my men can set their next arrows ablaze. It's a distraction, allowing Marto's men cover amidst the chaos of sudden fire and smoke. My archers and I continue raining arrows, but the rebels keep coming. They've increased their numbers tenfold since the last time we battled, and my heart sinks. Any hope I clung to of being able to remain here, with my family safe, evaporates.

But I'll be damned if I'm going down without a fight. While my men continue their efforts, I step away from the line of archers and begin to spin.

"Astreilles, don't!"

Charaide's too late, of course. I lift off the ground, spinning faster than I've ever spun before. My funnel cloud reaches up to the heavens, and I jump off the tower, flying toward the ground. The rebels scream, confused about why a tornado has sprung up when no thunder clouds darken the sky.

I cut a path through them, picking up men in my winds and tossing them like they're nothing. Of all the elements, I've come to appreciate the power of air the most. Perhaps it's because it was the most difficult to master, or maybe because it's my strongest asset.

Marto's men take advantage of the chaos I'm causing and charge through the rebels' front lines. Above me, arrows soar through the air, taking out swaths of enemy soldiers. From the battlements above the drawbridge, Brutach's battalion has unleashed its water magic. Large waves crest from the moat, crashing into the rebels and carrying all sorts of Merfolk sympathizers with them. Maybe we can win this thing after all.

"Astreilles," a dark, familiar voice calls to me.

I squeeze my eyes shut, vowing not to let Kythrall break my concentration. I'm surrounded by rebels on all sides. If I lose my focus now, I'm done for.

By this point, the rebels have realized that I am not a strange phenomenon of nature but a fae using elemental magic. They begin firing arrows of their own... at me. My winds knock them away like pesky flies.

I channel my frustration at Charaide into flame. It curls like hungry fingers into the coil of air. The rebels who had begun to close in on me jump back from the heat. Pushing faster, I race my ebbing magic to the castle, enemy soldiers closing in on my heels. Marto attempts to hold them off, but it's not enough.

As I reach the moat, I use what little energy I have left to propel myself over it and the wall, avoiding the drawbridge entirely. In retrospect, destroying the drawbridge might have been the smarter move, as then the rebels would have nothing to lower to aid them in breaching the castle.

Once I'm on the safe side of the wall, I slow my spinning, allowing all the debris my cyclone pulled into its orbit to scatter around me. No one pays me any heed as they bar the doors and work their magic to try to drive the rebels back.

A hand comes around my mouth while a strong arm encircles my waist. Before I have time to even attempt to react, I'm dragged into the library. Were I not so terrified by my inability to see my attacker, I might have found the room choice comical. The feel of rough skin, crudely sewn together, scratches my face, and my heart rate quickens. *He's come.*

"That was quite the show you performed for the rebels," a raspy voice murmurs against my ear.

If he has made it into the castle, then the wards Caillea and I cast have failed. *My siblings. Elana...*

"Come now, Astreilles. Surely you know me better than that." He releases me, and I stagger against a bookcase then whip around into a fighting stance. "Why would I dispatch the most vulnerable when their eldest sister is such a delicious challenge?"

"How did you get through?" I ask casually. "The rebels have yet to breach the gates."

"I've already told you that I'm not with the rebels." He picks at a nail. "They are merely a means to an end for me."

"But someone hired you to kill me. You say it's not the rebels, but I have no reason to trust you."

His face is half shadowed by his hood, but I see the glint of the light on his teeth as he smiles.

"I suppose that's fair."

"Have you come to finish what you couldn't in the woods, then?" Heat flares beneath my skin like fury caught flame, but little more than a spark appears. My magic sags within me like wet silk.

"A man's gotta eat, does he not?"

"Many men eat just fine without being killers for hire," I spit back. A heartbeat of fire ripples down my arms in response to my rage.

He leans forward, his grin widening. "Where's the fun in that?"

I shake my head in disgust. "I'm tired of your games. Let's just get this over with."

"Are you in such a hurry to die?" His tone has changed. The teasing lilt is gone, replaced by a bitterness I don't understand.

"I have no intention of dying." I lift my chin. "The sooner I dispatch you, the sooner my family will be safe."

A bitter laugh rumbles in his chest. "There are thousands of men just on the other side of this wall, and you think *I* pose the greatest threat to your family?"

"You're here, are you not? While they are still, as you say, on the other side of the wall."

He leans back as if assessing me. "Touché." Unsheathing his sword, he prowls forward like a predator.

But I refuse to be prey. I summon a spark from the marrow of my bones and aim the answering heat at his face. He dodges just in time, and the books behind him ignite. Gritting my teeth, I draw in water from the moat to douse them.

He laughs. "I'm impressed with your mastering of your magic. It's been quite entertaining watching you learn."

"Perhaps if you had accomplished your task when I was nothing more than a weak halfling, this fight would be over by now," I seethe, the floor rumbling beneath my feet.

"Ah, but you're a much worthier opponent now. It would have been a shame to kill you before you reached your full potential."

"What makes you think I've peaked?" Air coils around me like a protective serpent, and I pour all of my heartbreak into it, building its power before striking. He stumbles back but maintains his footing. His hood, however, falls behind his head, and I gasp in horror.

I've caught glimpses of his patchwork skin before on his arms and the little of his face I've managed to make out. But now that his head is exposed... *Grotesque* is too kind a word. His skin has a bluish tint, betraying its source. My stomach heaves, and I cover my mouth with my hand, forcing the bile back down my throat. Sharp black stitching crisscrosses the top and sides of his head, flowing down his cheeks. His nose is crooked, as if broken, and it dawns on me that it will never heal because...

"Because I am a patchwork of dead things?" His eyes flash. "Is that where your train of thought was leading, Princess?"

Words have abandoned me. Every instinct inside of me tells me to run, but I can't seem to tear my eyes away. He is terrifying and fascinating all at the same time.

"Did you not wonder, dear Astreilles, why I haunt your nightmares?" He laughs bitterly as he gestures at himself. "It is because I *am* the nightmare. A beast of your worst fears, pieced together into a monster."

"What... what *are* you?" I've seen terrible beasts in the forest, fae-like creatures that come out only at night, but never in my life have I seen one such as him.

"I am all of those beasts and none of them." He stalks toward me, and I scramble back, my heart pounding in my ears. "I was made of the flesh of others, my parts collected from throughout the kingdom and painstakingly pieced together to form... this." His hand clenches at his side.

I ignore the voice inside me screaming to run. This must end here. I cannot allow this abomination to continue threatening my family.

"An abomination is a good description," he agrees, and his face falls. "After all, I was created to be a killing machine."

The words of Caillea echo in my head: *"Beware the creation. It will be your destruction." Is* this *what she meant?* My stomach heaves again, and it's all I can do not to empty it. But showing that vulnerability here, in front of him, is something I cannot risk.

"The white witch saw me coming." He tilts his head. "Interesting. I've heard a prophecy as well, but I much prefer yours." His lips pull back in a terrible smile. "I suppose that confirms what we both know is about to happen."

"And what's that?" I manage to choke out.

"You lose. I win."

He lunges at me, and I have barely enough time to dodge the blow. But he's on me again, moving faster than lightning. *How is this possible?*

"Oh, did I forget to mention? My skin, which you find so disgusting, is a roadmap of every creature from this realm. But it's not just their parts I possess. I'm also imbued with their magic." He blocks my next fireball. "I was created to be unstoppable."

"With their strength must come their weaknesses," I retort, though it won't do me much good. I don't have time to figure out what those vulnerabilities are. It will have to be trial by fire, then, as many flames as I can throw at him at a time.

"Your elemental magic is effective against the rebels, but it's of little consequence to me." He taps his temple. "I have such magic of my own at my disposal."

In one fluid movement, I unsheathe my sword. A warrior cry rages out of my throat as I lunge at him, but he parries away my sword with a flick of his wrist. I stumble into a table.

After spinning on my heel, I face him again, my breath heaving from my efforts. I consider my options. He knows all of the magical tricks I have up my sleeve, and I'm clearly no match for him in hand-to-hand. But I do have one power that, while he knows about it, he can do little to stop.

Cliste. I channel my thoughts to my brother. It's a one-way communication, and I can only hope it works. *Gather our siblings and go. Now. Do not wait for me.*

Kythrall reaches for me, and I manage to dodge him, sliding beneath the table and scampering to the other side. Cinders crackle along my veins, feeding on fear. I run to the stacks, hoping he'll follow. If I can keep him distracted, if I can stay alive long enough, my siblings will be safe. That's all I want. My life is forfeit, but theirs... I pray to whatever gods may be listening to please get my message to Cliste and save them all.

I slip around the end of one row of bookshelves, my gaze darting around the room, searching for Kythrall. The room is silent except for my labored breathing. I take deep breaths, trying to calm my pounding heart.

What if Cliste doesn't get my message? The thought turns my blood cold. Charaide heard it, but he is fae, and Cliste is cut off from his magic by those damned bracelets. Maybe this power is only strong enough to reach those who already possess telepathy. I peek down another row of shelves, and the aisle is empty. Keeping my back to the books, I slide to the floor and pull Charaide's face into my mind.

Find Cliste. Save my siblings. Get them to the portal.

Rough hands grab my shoulders and slam me against the bookshelves. Volumes crash around me on the floor, and I scream.

The sewn-together flesh separates as Kythrall's mouth widens in an evil grin.

"Sending secret messages again, Princess?" He leans closer, whispering in my ear. "Your boyfriend can't save you now."

I press my hand against the bookshelf, and it rumbles beneath my touch. More books slide out of their homes, falling haphazardly. One hits Kythrall squarely on the head, and his hands loosen their grip. I shove him away and take off, desperate to stay one step ahead of him.

I'm not fast enough, and with one swift movement, he leaps into the air and lands in my path, his eyes dancing in amusement. I spin my grief into a storm, even as I accept that it will do little damage. But that's no longer my goal. I need to keep him occupied as long as I can.

"So that's your plan, is it?" His gaze pins me in place. "Abandon your kingdom, your mother, all to save your own hide?" He gives a quiet laugh as he grabs my wrist and pulls me to him. The feel of his patchwork skin against mine sends a chill down my spine, and I try to shake free, but his hold is firm. "Tsk, tsk. I thought you better than that, Princess."

"I'm still here, am I not? If you read my mind, then you know I've told my brother not to wait for me."

"And if I let you go?" he whispers. "Would you join them?"

"There's little likelihood of that." I twist away from him, but he clutches my wrist tighter still, the rough skin digging into mine. In one quick movement, he flips me around, and my back is pressed against him. His other arm wraps around my body. I struggle to break free, but it's no use. Every motion feels heavier, like I'm moving through water.

"What if there was another way to save your family?" His raspy voice rumbles against my back.

"What other way do you mean?" I ask, more to keep him talking than because I give a damn about what he has to say.

Suddenly, he releases me, and I stumble forward, catching myself on a bookshelf. I spin around, ready to engage again, but his demeanor has changed.

He places a hand over his chest and bows low, a grotesque echo of a knight before his queen. "Come with me, Princess. There's more than one way to end this war."

My stomach knots. *I can't have heard him correctly, can I?* "What?"

CHAPTER
TWENTY-FOUR

MY VOICE TREMBLES as I ask, "What?"

I know he's not serious. He can't be. Not after everything he's done.

Kythrall straightens from his bow, patchwork skin catching in the firelight. His honey-gold eyes gleam with something unreadable. "If you agree to come with me, I promise that not only will no harm come to you, but I will also spare your family. And I won't tell the rebels where they've gone."

My pulse hammers in my ears. The absurdity of his offer curdles in my gut, but underneath the revulsion, something darker stirs. Because part of me is tempted by what he's offering, and that scares me more than death itself.

"Why?" I ask, more to buy time than because I expect an answer. "If you don't kill me, you won't collect your bounty."

"There are some things worth more than money," he says, and there's a wistfulness to his tone that I don't quite understand.

"But what do you *want* with me?"

"To help you." He steps forward and reaches for me, but I back away. "I see so much potential in you. You've shown great power in just a few weeks. Imagine what you could accomplish if you weren't under constant threat. If you were allowed to flourish in a less volatile setting."

He sounds like Brutach, though with considerably more faith in my abilities.

"I'm not some weapon you can mold to your liking and unleash against your enemies."

His face contorts briefly in an expression of pain before a sordid smile takes its place. "I assure you, Princess, I do not need to mold you into a weapon. Your allies have done that well enough on their own." He lowers his head. "Besides, I know what it's like to be someone else's attack dog. I would never wish that on anyone."

For a fleeting moment, I see it, the future he's painting. Even while I try to deny it, I feel the tether between us. *Monster to monster. Outcast to outcast.*

But I shake my head hard enough to sting. "You're insane."

"And yet you listened." His lips stretch into that wolfish grin. "I caught that flicker in your eyes, Princess. That recognition. You can deny it all you want, but you and I are bound."

The air thickens around us, heavy with his words. I shake my head again as if I can dispel not only the offer but the desire to accept it. If he's right, if some unnatural bond exists between us, what will it mean if I tear it apart?

But we always have choices, and he chose to accept a bounty to kill me and everyone I love. As tempted as I am by his offer, I don't trust him to honor his word. Mercenaries are notorious for selling their souls to the highest bidder, and even though I am royalty, my coin will go only so far.

His eyebrows pull together. "As you have said so many times, I could have killed you at any point." His gaze softens. "In you, I see someone forced into war. Someone who was not born for it but has been shaped by it. You fight to protect, not to conquer. I've never met anyone like that."

My breath catches. I've known he's been watching me, but what I never suspected was how much he actually *saw* me.

"Help me hide you," he continues, voice taut. "Teach you what I've learned. Help you to hone the powers you possess, like astral projection." He lifts a hand as if to touch me but seems to think better of it. "Let me show you how to turn your fear into armor."

There is integrity behind his words, and I didn't expect that. And to my utter shock and horror, I find myself considering his offer. *But if I accept it, what will I lose?*

"You're offering me sanctuary," I say. It's not a question.

His nod is slight but unwavering. A light shines from his eyes as if he, too, is surprised I haven't immediately rejected his offer.

"Why?"

He steps closer, and the patchwork of his skin seems to soften in the warm lamplight. "I was created to kill, but I never wanted to destroy. You remind me there's another way. Maybe... Maybe there are things you can teach me too." He gestures to the scar on my wrist, a remnant the iron bracelets left, one that will never heal. "Like how you can hold onto your humanity in the face of such cruelty."

I avert my eyes because his sincerity is nearly more terrifying than his knife. And the weight of his gaze is heavier than the burdens I'm already carrying.

So I force a laugh, short and brittle. "Touching speech. You should write it down. Maybe you'll get a redemption arc in someone else's story."

He doesn't flinch and just watches me.

"You want to hide me in some forgotten corner of the realms, play house with your pet halfling?" I roll my eyes, because it's easier to pretend than to let him know how close he came. "Sorry. I'm not in the market for monster rehab."

The words taste sharp, but they're my armor. If I don't mock him, I might consider what he said. I might *want* to believe him.

His eyes flash. "I think I've more than proved to you that I view you as a worthy opponent. Why do you still doubt my integrity?"

"Because you're still contract-bound to end my life," I say dryly. "Thanks but no thanks. I'll take my chances with the humans." The brief reprieve in fighting has increased my magical stores, and a flare coils in my hand, hissing for release. The moment I let go, I whirl around and sprint toward the exit, praying I've stalled long enough. The door to the library swings open, and I stagger toward it, praying it's friend, not foe.

I crash into my uncle and throw my arms around his neck. Relief floods through me. He pats my back awkwardly as if alarmed by the sudden display of affection, then his hand stalls as he gapes in horror. I glance behind me in time to see Kythrall emerge, rubbing his head, his eyes darkening with anger.

"Go, Astreilles," my uncle whispers. "Rejoin your men on the wall. I will take care of this monster."

I can't leave my uncle to face this awful creature alone. Perhaps we'll fare better together. I shake my head, opening my mouth to protest.

"I said go!" Uncle Brutach's booming voice echoes throughout the room.

With one last look over my shoulder, I obey, running flat out as if my life depends on it.

When I reach the courtyard, my gaze flits from soldier to soldier, searching for Charaide, Cliste, and the rest of my siblings. I head toward the wall, where my men are still firing arrows, but Charaide is nowhere in sight. *Did he get my message?*

As I reach the platform, I grab one of my men. "Where is Charaide?"

The man shrugs. "He said he needed to help you. We were told to hold the line until one of you returns."

I stare over the wall at the chaos below. Marto's men are losing ground, and our arrows are no match for the onslaught of rebel soldiers still pouring in from outside the village. My attempts to stem the tide did little more than cause a slight reduction in their forces. Once they breach the castle, it's over. The battle, the war will be lost.

Torn between abandoning my post and saving my siblings, I stand frozen in indecision. If Charaide has left, then he likely received my message to ferry my siblings to safety. Uncle Brutach fights Kythrall, though I have no hope for his success. There's not much time, but perhaps...

Shouts rise behind me as I spin again, gaining the momentum to descend into the rebels' front lines. But they are ready for me, and they dive out of the way. This fits my aims perfectly. I land with my feet spread apart and touch the ground. The rumbles aren't noticeable at first, and the rebels stand, their eyes flashing in recognition and their greedy smiles taking me in. To them, I appear defenseless, armed with only arrows and a sword.

I pour all the confusion from Kythrall's offer into my magic. Cracks appear on either side of me, and those triumphant grins fade to horror as realization sinks in. It's too late to run, and the earth opens and swallows them whole. I press my palm deeper into the soil, channeling my grief and pain, and the cracks spread out from all sides, like a lightning strike in the earth. Screams fill my ears as the rebels fall. I struggle to control the direction of the cracks, risking my men as well as theirs. With my other hand, currents catch like invisible arms, carrying the royal soldiers to safety.

"Astreilles!"

I look up, and Marto runs toward me, his eyes wild with fear. Glancing behind me, I learn the reason for it. Kythrall has escaped my uncle, and he's heading straight for me. I jump out of my crouch and toss a fireball at him, knowing he'll dodge it but hoping to break his momentum.

"Astreilles!" Marto yells again. "Duck!"

I dive to the ground, tumbling into the dirt as an array of arrows flies overhead directly at Kythrall. They glance off him without even pricking his grotesque skin, but whatever magic he used to deflect has drained him, and he falls behind. I take advantage of this delay and spin my grief into a storm around me as I head for the moat.

When I reach it, the combination of water and air is more powerful than I ever imagined. My tears drip into the moat and swirl effortlessly into a waterspout. I shift my position and move to block the drawbridge. While I know I can't hold this forever, my delaying tactics haven't failed me thus far.

Marto's face breaks into an incredulous grin as he shakes his head, but he allows himself only a moment to gape at me before moving back into the fray. The rebels meet them sword for sword while arrows continue to fly from the castle behind me. But the mood has changed. The rebels are wary of me and what other powers I may possess.

Kythrall is making his way through the raging battle, his focus entirely on me. It's only a matter of time before he reaches the moat, and I'm not sure what I'll do then. *Face my death like a soldier? Find a way to kill an unkillable monster?* I weigh my chances of making it out of this alive. *Unlikely.* And yet I know I can jump the castle walls with enough momentum. There's still time to join my siblings.

As I watch the men fighting to push the rebel army back, I can't help wondering what kind of person that would make me. Perhaps I am a coward to seek sanctuary in another world. *What proof do I have that the rebels will stop this onslaught once my siblings and I are gone from this realm?* And the question that has plagued me since Cliste first brought up the idea of leaving: Can I go, knowing I'll likely never lay eyes on my home again?

"Astreilles!"

I turn in to the next revolution of my tornado and catch sight of Charaide. He waves to me, and I use the power of the churning water to propel myself to the top of my funnel cloud.

"Did you get them out?"

He nods. "Cliste is leading them through the tunnels now." His gaze strays behind me, and his lips press into a thin line. "Kythrall will not stop until he kills you." When he looks at me again, his face crumples with sadness. "It's time for you to go."

I glance behind me at the battle. Things are looking up for our men. The rebels continue to push forward. But the royal army is holding the line. It may be a futile hope that they'll be appeased by our departure, but it's the only thing I have to hold onto.

Charaide is right about Kythrall. I meet his gaze across the field, and his face is red with anger. It will not be long before he reaches me, and I can't keep this up much longer. If he's truly unkillable, my only hope of survival is to leave, now, before he catches me unawares again.

With the last of my magic, I leap onto the wall with Charaide, my funnel cloud fading behind me. I throw my arms around him in a tight embrace, tears streaming down my cheeks.

"I love you, Char," I whisper.

"Don't." He pulls me close and kisses me. "This is not goodbye. I won't let it be. We'll find his weakness, and then we'll end this together. You *will* come home to me."

I want so badly to believe him, but I've seen how determined Kythrall is. And now that I've refused his offer to be molded into his pet weapon, his unrelenting desire to kill us all is only going to increase. We'll never be safe here again.

But I don't say any of this because I don't want to dash Charaide's hopes. Perhaps he can dream enough for both of us.

Perhaps he'll find a way that we can be together, not here but somewhere else, in some other realm where we can be free to love each other. I let myself dream a little, too, even as it breaks my heart.

"Go, Ast." He releases me. "Go now, before it's too late."

Wiping the tears from my eyes, I take a deep breath as I stare into his face. I want one last unobstructed memory of him. Then I turn and sprint down the stairs, into the dungeons, and through the tunnels. I use the last of my magic to send a farewell thought to my mother as I race toward the rest of my family and my new home. A home I have yet to find but must create.

EPILOGUE

I STAND on the precipice of a cliff, wind whipping my hair as the foaming sea roars below. Cliste's hand finds mine, forming a lifeline across all that we've lost. Behind us, my younger siblings cling together, eyes bright with fear and wonder.

The danger is behind us, but the unknown future doesn't feel any less frightening. Cliste squeezes my hand with an encouraging smile. I try to return it, but my lips quiver as I fight back another onslaught of tears.

We survived, and we're safe... for now. The doorway to the human realm landed us on a beautiful island, my father's homeland. In his native tongue, it is called Isla Mujeres, which he told me means "The Island of Women." It's soothing, in a way. I feel less alone knowing that this is the place where my father was born. In some ways, this is where our broken family's story began.

"Welcome to your new life, Ast," my brother whispers, his face serene.

I envy his peacefulness, but inside, I'm a mess. My mind vacillates between wondering where we will go now that we're here and what is happening to our kingdom, to Mama, to Charaide.

Part of me wishes I could go back, or that I had never left in the first place, but as I look at my siblings, I know that my place is here with them.

"Mama will be fine," Cliste continues, and I wonder if he's trying to convince me or himself. "Uncle Brutach will protect her." He clears his throat when I don't respond. "How was the battle when you left?"

"I took down a handful more rebels before slipping off the battlefield," I say, voice raw. "It bought us time." I squint at the distant mainland. "Maybe it'll be enough to end the war."

Cliste nods, but I haven't quite convinced myself. There are so many things I wish I had done differently, starting with finding a way to kill Kythrall.

If I hadn't left, perhaps I could have asked the sorceress. Caillea predicted his arrival and warned me to be vigilant. I hadn't heeded her warning until it was too late.

Kythrall spoke of a prophecy, too, one I never heard in full. Maybe one day, I'll wish I had.

"We should go," Cliste says, turning to our siblings.

"Where?" I gesture to the island. "We know no one, and we have no money."

"We know someone, though I doubt he'll be happy to see us."

My heart stutters, because already, I know what name he won't speak. "You don't mean…"

He shrugs before herding our siblings toward the heart of the island. I shake my head, struggling to believe that *this* was his grand plan all along.

When faeries steal a human, they leave one of their own. It's hardly a fair trade. While the faery offspring is usually born without magic, it still holds onto its otherworldly physique. The human world, with its lack of magic and its distrust of anything different, is cruel and deadly to its natural inhabitants, let alone anything that appears too *other*. The changeling rarely survives.

But my father's substitute still lingers here. Forty years human, yet little human warmth remains.

"Great," I mutter under my breath. "We get to learn humanity from Father's hermit cast-off."

I watch my brother lead my siblings through the garden of sculptures, past the cave where the portal lies. I turn back to the sea, a silent promise sweeping through me.

I will return. This is not forever. I will return. To Mama. To Charaide. And I will take my rightful place upon the throne.

A Throne of Shadows and Spies, the next book in The Halfling Princess Chronicles, is available for preorder at all major retailers. Read on for a sneak peek.

Enjoyed this story? Check out my cozy fantasy serial, Elder Enchanted, on Substack. Think elder care facility but with fae. It's quirky, fun, and a bit parody based on my day job. Check it out here.

SNEAK PEEK OF A THRONE OF SHADOWS AND SPIES

IF ONLY I could find a portal and speak to him. But Cliste's warning repeats in my head. I scowl at the ceiling. Nothing about this seems fair. First, I'm forced to flee my homeland with my siblings in an effort to save all our lives and attempt to bring peace to said kingdom. Then, I'm chased to what should be a safe haven by the same rebels that forced me from my home. And on top of all that, I'm already wary of humans because of my halfblood status, but apparently, they're more likely to judge me by my Hispanic heritage than the fact that I've got barely concealed wings growing out of my back.

An idea strikes me as I roll to my side and gaze out the window. The sun has sunk low on the horizon and the tall buildings surrounding our hotel are cast in shadow. If I can't find a portal to speak to Charaide, perhaps I can use my other power to reach him.

I'm still not sure that this other power is real and not just a dream. But at this point, I'm desperate to try anything. Closing my eyes, I try to imagine myself at the castle. I picture the way the room looked when I was with Kythrall. The ethereal quality of the lights and air. Taking a deep breath, I let it out slowly and imagine my soul exiting my body on the same breath of air.

A moment later, and I'm standing in the brightly lit room. I'm both elated and disappointed at the same time. It's thrilling to know I have some semblance of control over this power now, but I didn't end up where I wanted to be.

"You're back," a familiar and terrifying voice calls behind me.

Whirling around, I'm surprised to see Kythrall's true form instead of the shimmer. Well, it's how I imagine Kythrall's soul to appear. No scars marr his face here. If I didn't know better, I would almost call him handsome.

"I wasn't aiming to come here," I reply.

He raises an eyebrow. "So you arrived on purpose this time?" A lopsided smirk pulls up one side of his mouth. "Does this mean you finally believe this is real and not just a dream?"

A laugh bubbles out of me. "I'm still debating, but I'm starting to come around to the idea. Then again, I may just be crazy."

He chuckles softly. "Fair enough." Stepping over to the side of the room, a sofa seems to materialize out of nowhere. With a simple wave of his hand, he indicates I should sit. "Where were you aiming to go, out of curiosity?"

I wait for the warmth to flood my cheeks, but then realize that not having a body does wonders for my constant blushing. "The castle."

The smirk widens. "To visit your boyfriend no doubt."

While Charaide and I have confessed our feelings for each other, I'm not exactly ready for it to be known to everyone, especially someone who has vowed to kill me. Instead of answering, I shift away from him and allow my eyes to trail around the room.

As before, it's rather empty and blindingly bright. The sofa is the only discernible piece of furniture, though I imagine Kythrall could manifest more items if he so desired.

"You could as well," he drawls, reading my mind.

The idea of creating something from nothing both exhilarates and terrifies me. I clear my throat. "I'm good with the couch, thanks."

He chuckles again. "You'll come around eventually."

I ignore his teasing and decide to take advantage of the situation. "Are you always here? Seems like any time I show up, you're around."

"Well, you mostly show up in the evenings or late at night. So, yes, I'm almost always here."

I cock my head. "Do you not sleep?"

A shadow crosses his face. "I wasn't created to sleep."

"But you must have some hu—" I catch myself. "I mean, fae weaknesses. While they don't sleep as much as humans, they do sleep."

He turns his head from me, presumably to hide his expression. It's several minutes before he speaks and I wonder if perhaps I pushed for too much too soon.

"I was designed to have all of the abilities of the mystical creatures from which my... parts were harvested." He says "parts" with a disgusted tone. It dawns on me that maybe he hates his existence as much as I do.

As if reading my mind—which he probably did—he suddenly turns to me, a ferocity in his eyes I've not seen before, not even on the battlefield.

"I not only hate it, I have actively tried to end it."

Of all the things I expect him to say, that is not one of them. My breath catches in my throat and I scoot back on the cushion to put some distance between us.

His expression softens. "My apologies, princess." He holds up his hands, and I marvel at how smooth they are compared to what I recall from our brief interactions in the fae realm. "Please don't be afraid. Nothing can harm you here." A bitter laugh. "Not even one such as me."

For reasons I can't explain, my heart goes out to him. A part of me believes that he didn't choose to be an assassin any more than he chose to be created into the monster he is. Without thinking, I reach out to touch his hand, expecting to meet with nothing but air. To my surprise, and his if the way his eyebrows shoot up his forehead is any indication, I touch warm skin and my fingers wrap firmly around his palm.

"How...?" He raises his eyes to meet mine and my heart begins to beat erratically.

"Is this not normal?" I ask, even though I know the answer. One look at his face confirms that nothing about my presence here is normal.

"No. The astral plane isn't like the physical realms." He shakes his head. "I mean, it's not exactly impossible *but it's rare." He searches my face. "There's something about you... I can't quite figure out what it is."*

I laugh awkwardly and pull my hand away. "I'm a halfblood who won the genetic lottery only in so far as who my family is. That's all."

"If that were true, there wouldn't be an army of men trying to hunt you down right now."

The harsh reality of his words causes me to flinch and I stand to put some distance between us. It reminds me of why I tried this failed experiment in the first place. My heart pangs at the thought of Charaide.

"I'm sorry," Kythrall says.

When I glance back at him, he's staring at the floor. I'm not sure whether he's apologizing for bringing up the army of rebels or if he read my mind to know it's not his company I seek.

"Both." He's looking at me now. "I don't know why you didn't end up where you wanted to, but I imagine it has a lot to do with the fact that you're just starting to recognize your powers. Astral projection often takes years of practice, but you managed to do it in your sleep." A soft smile pulls at his lips. "That alone should prove to you how truly special you are."

"Is that why you didn't kill me when you had the chance?" I ask before I can stop myself.

The smile falls, replaced by a frown. "No, I—" He seems at a loss for words. "I don't have an explanation for that. The first few times I was alone with you, I was thwarted by an outside force, whether the guards or your boyfriend." He stands suddenly and crosses the room to me.

"But I'll admit I was intrigued watching you learn your powers. And I guess a part of me felt it was a waste to cut you down when you were just starting to come into your full potential."

"What's stopping you now?"

He grins as if I'm missing the joke. "I can't travel to the human realm."

"So if I came back to the fae realm, you'd be there waiting to end me?"

His eyebrows pull together. "I've an obligation to fulfill."

"And if you didn't?" I challenge, not sure what answer I'm hoping for here. But as he draws nearer to me, my heart races again and I'm not sure if it's from fear or something else.

For a moment, we just stare at each other, the air around us seeming to slow with the tension building between us. Then he breaks eye contact and takes my hand. Lifting it to his lips, he brushes them over my knuckles and it's all I can do not to lean toward him.

When he raises his eyes to my face again, there's a fierceness there that scares and intrigues me. "If I didn't, I'd rip apart anyone who tried."

A Throne of Shadows and Spies will release in 2026. Preorder here.

FAERY WHISPER PRESS BOOKS

A Home for Christmas

The Love Birds Omnibus

When Cardinals Appear

When Swans Dance

When Doves Lament

Heartstrings and Hops Series

The Tides That Bind

The Halfling Princess Chronicles

A Crown of Secrets and Lies

A Throne of Shadows and Spies

ACKNOWLEDGMENTS

Normally, I begin my acknowledgments by thanking the first person who ever believed in my writing. But this time, I need to begin with my daughter. This story was born with her. It grew through the struggles of her first year: from sleepless nights, to bleary-eyed mornings, and those hard-won first smiles and first steps. Over the years, it stayed with me, shaped by every moment since. Eighteen years later, it's finally come to fruition, and I know I couldn't have reached this point without her.

To Denise, thank you for the privilege of being your mother, for choosing to be my best friend, and for beginning this next chapter with me — just the two of us, finding our way forward together.

While I worked on this book, I was learning what it meant to be seen and these next few people never looked away.

To Caroline, thank you for believing in me and my writing, and for gently nudging me to become a better version of myself.

To Dan, thank you for introducing me to *His Dark Materials*, and for quietly reminding me that kindness is its own form of magic.

To Kady, thank you for buying every book I've written so far (twice!), and for providing the kind of support I needed most, exactly when I needed it.

I will forever be grateful to my late mother for believing in me enough to insist I make a promise that I've spent a lifetime trying to keep. It is in her memory that I found the courage to pursue my dream.

Huge shoutout to my siblings for their support over the years. I know my path didn't always make a lot of sense to you, but I appreciate your patience as I found my way forward.

Thanks to my father and stepmother. I'm not sure either of you will read this book, but I expect Dad will faithfully deliver the signed copy at Christmas.

I would be remiss not to thank my editor, Angela McCrea at Red Adept Editing. She has a knack for taking the mess I send her and making it shine.

Many thanks to my cover designer, Henar Lopez, for the beautiful cover and for putting up with my many changes!

To family and friends, thank you for supporting me for the last five years on this writing journey. I know this book was my most anticipated and I hope it lives up to your expectations. They say it takes a village to raise a child and I believe it takes that and more to raise a writer.

About the Author

K.D. Eagan writes romance and women's fiction under a different pen name. She also writes a cozy fantasy serial, Elder Enchanted, which is available for free on Substack. When she's not writing creatively, she can be found drafting federal regulations, baking for friends and family, or spending time with her daughter.

www.ingramcontent.com/pod-product-compliance
Lightning Source LLC
Chambersburg PA
CBHW021038310726
48969CB00006B/1709